The Sensitivity Chip

Rhonda Washington Nelson

RIVERHOUSE
PUBLISHING

The Sensitivity Chip

RiverHouse Publishing, LLC
1509 Madison Avenue
Memphis, TN 38114

All **RiverHouse Publishing, LLC** Titles, Imprints and Distributed Lines are available at special quantity discounts for bulk purchases for sales promotions, premiums, fund-raising and educational or institutional use.

First RiverHouse, LLC Trade Paperback Printing: 07/15/2015

ISBN: 978-0-9962725-3-7

Printed in the United States of America

This book is printed on acid-free paper.

www.riverhousepublishingllc.com

As always, I thank my God for allowing me the privilege to love, honor and worship Him. Secondly, much love and kisses to my children and all the newest additions. Lastly, thanks to all who fervently pray for me….I do understand that's the key.

Ephesians 4: 31-32

"Let all bitterness, and wrath, and anger, and clamour, and evil speaking, be put away from you, with all malice: And be ye kind one to another, tenderhearted, forgiving one another, even as God for Christ's sake hath forgiven you."

Chapter 1

Holiday Times

Clara silently poked at the tiny green specks the chives made in her creamy white potatoes. Smoldering with chips of melted cheese, she stared at the starchy mountain until it made her nauseous. It was the gross silence in the room, however, that caused the lone nerve traveling along the back of her neck to tighten much like a tourniquet. She gazed up as she watched the thin, black second- hand sweep quietly across the clock's surface. She thought... "Time was certainly being cruel. It seemed to know she yearned for it to move along faster, but intentionally held on to each second a bit longer." While she hadn't realized until she loosened the grip on her fork how visibly the whites of her knuckles shone, there was one thing she was keenly aware of— she hated sitting at this table.

"Is everything okay?" Ellen asked softly. She knew she was pushing her luck saying anything to Clara. Ever since she arrived home, talking to her was off limits, but she still felt the need to try.

"Mother, I'm fine," Clara snapped, tossing her hair. "It couldn't be any better, so there, just finish your dinner."

Realizing it had been a mistake coming home for Thanksgiving dinner, Clara forged on. She hadn't eaten at the table in months and was kicking herself for deciding to do so today. "Should have followed my first instinct and just written the letter," she scolded herself. She methodically piled her potatoes into a heap of sorts onto one side of her plate. It reminded her of the paper mache she played with as a child when their father brought home gifts like that.

As she toyed with her food, her mind shifted to Eric. Those were the one and only thoughts that provided her any real sense of comfort and she held on tightly to them.

"It certainly feels good to finally have you home," Ellen said, screeching an end to her now, 'calm place'.

Clara stared hard at the plate. After all these years, her mother, the 'ex- Mrs. Ellen Andrews,' was still clueless. She had to know she wanted to be left alone, but was just so persistent. She sat there ignoring the comment as she managed to swallow only small bites of the turkey. She might as well have been chewing rubber.

The silence returned as the sounds of the forks scraping the plates filled the tiny dining area. Quietness now controlled the space—expanding with each mouthful they took.

"Can you believe the Bradley's are already putting up their Christmas decorations?" The words bounced off the walls like a mallet taken to glass, shattering the silence into a million pieces.

"They received enough complaints last year, you'd think they would learn," Gwen said, reaching in the basket for the last of the crescent shaped - homemade rolls. Everyone knew it was her feeble attempt at filling the void in the room. It was typical Gwen, however. She was two years younger than Clara and possessed all the characteristics of a middle child.

"They over do everything," her mother quickly chimed in. "If they add another trinket in that yard, the city will have every right to fine them for violating some type of ordinance.   Maybe, the Christmas lights code," she laughed.

"Yeah, why would anyone put those patriotic Fourth of July lights along their driveway like that at Christmas?" Gwen chuckled.

Clara gazed up slowly as she shifted her eyes between the two who dared to speak. She squinted, rolled them, and proceeded to stare back at her very full plate.

As the quietness crept back in, Gwen's patience fizzled along with it.   She'd had enough of Clara and her rudeness. "It was time for the foolishness to end," Gwen thought. She would not control her or continue to taunt her family this way anymore.

"Actually mother, I don't see anything wrong with the Bradley's creativity," Gwen said her eyes now narrow and piercing into Clara. "It's just their over indulgence that seems to bother the neighbors." She took no mercy on the poor candied yam she chopped down hard on.

Ellen flinched, now very much aware of Gwen's motives.

"We have grown up looking at our neighbor's unique style for years. I've kinda gotten used to it," Gwen continued as she all but whispered her last few words. Filling her mouth with another hefty bite of the moist turkey and dressing, she swallowed hard. Never taking her eyes off her sister, she pressed out a smile, "Tell me…. what do you think of their extravagance, Clara dear?" she asked softly.

Ellen breathed deeply, "It's about to get ugly," she thought. Vigorously shaking her head, she tried getting Gwen to back off but knew it was too late. The atmospheric condition inside the house was just too right for the brewing storm.

Gwen smiled, ignored her mother's gestures, calmly readjusted herself, and restated the question.

"So, what do you think about their taste, Clara?"

Eyes now fixed upon each other, neither gave an inch.

It seemed an eternity passed before Clara finally answered. "It's hideous, but I'm not too surprised you can't see that," she shot back.

Ellen tried to intervene as she reached for the multi-colored Pyrex dish containing the French styled beans. "Now, now, let's not bicker over something so trivial," she said. She knew the raging storm was about to turn deadly. The battle between these two was long overdue and their brawls were historic. The kind you witnessed on the National Geographic channel between lions and hyenas—they fought until blood was spilled or feelings left wounded beyond repair.

"Girls, let's have a peaceful Thanksgiving dinner together, please. It may be the last one we get to spend with each other for a while," Ellen said, as she fought back tears—well aware of her eroding family dynamics.

"Her mother had finally gotten something right," Clara thought. It was without question the very last holiday she'd ever spend with any of them. She couldn't wait to leave this part of her life behind and rid herself of a family she was never supposed to be a part of in the first place.

Gwen tightened the scrunchy that held her long, curly ponytail. "I was just trying to engage our big sister in a little family discussion," she said. Pouring herself another glass of the raspberry tea, she sat up tall. "After all, she hasn't said two complete sentences to us since she's been home. I thought maybe, just maybe, she would finally open up and at least pretend as if she is enjoying this Thanksgiving dinner for goodness sake."

Ellen watched as Clara's jaw line stiffened. "Here we go," she thought.

Slowly laying her fork down, Clara inhaled deeply and leaned into her middle sister. "You do know why this Thanksgiving meal isn't enjoyable for me, don't you, my dear Gwen?"

A smile slowly emerged. At this point, Gwen knew nothing was going to stop her from putting Clara's repugnant self into a place she knew she belonged. "Let me see…. you ate your Thanksgiving meal in that prison cell you call a room, and have been hiding it from us this whole time. Is that it?" she asked. "Yeah….that's probably what happened," she said, shaking her head.

"Hmm, since I fail to see your feeble attempt at humor—and so that you need not bother that genius brain of yours, let me tell you why," Clara said. "It's too hard to sit here and watch a member of our own family destroy themselves right before our eyes, that's all," she said, shrugging her shoulders.

Gwen instantly stopped chewing. She knew where this was going. She hadn't intended for her to start in on their baby sister but knew it was too late.

"I'm sure you haven't noticed that, *Miss I Know Everything*," Clara seethed. She also knew what it took to get back at Gwen. She'd learned through the years that taking shots at her did absolutely nothing to her ego. They were both pit bulls when it came to fighting each other and their disdain had only increased throughout the years. They'd become desensitized to any hurtful remarks they lobbed each other's way. However, it was the thrill of mistreating their baby sister that generated the kind of response she wanted, and like magic it was working right now.

Dancing the fork in Gwen's face, her voice matched her truculent mood. "Gwen darling, as usual, your attention is focused on all the wrong things. There is something else at this table you should be concerned about rather than me."

Eyes blazing, Gwen recognized her opponent was circling in for the kill, so she said nothing.

"Look at her," Clara said nodding her head Rose's way, never taking her eyes off Gwen. "She's stuffing her face right now with all those fattening carbs."

Clara finally turned and faced Rose, "What size are you now? Let me guess, an eighteen? No, probably more like a twenty, huh?"

As usual, Rose ignored her comments. Continuing to chew, she washed the remains of her mouthful down with a gulp of tea.

Clara continued the assault, "Mother, you know you're just as much at fault as Rose is. The girl has absolutely no will power whatsoever. Didn't you know she would eat a ton when you cooked like this," she said, waving at the food spread out on the table. "I believe eventually she would be a good mascot for… what's his name? Oh yeah, one of the main characters at Sea-World," she said, snickering underneath her breath.

Ellen knew it had gotten out of control and decided to step in. She lowered her voice, "Clara, I wish you wouldn't talk about your sister that way, honey. She's been dieting and only wanted to enjoy this one Thanksgiving meal."

Her attempt to temper the situation failed miserably. Barely allowing her to finish the sentence, Clara shouted out over her words, "There you go again, the perfect 'enabler'! That's what's wrong with her. If you can't see what you are doing to your precious baby girl, maybe this will help you. Rose you're in what…the 12th grade now? How many dates have you been on?"

The chair creaked as Rose shifted.

"Okay, if that question is too hard, try this one. Are you going to your senior dance this year?"

Still…silence.

"Oh, I see, too difficult? What about this? How many friends do you have? Have they ever invited you to go shopping or just hang out with them?"

"THAT'S ENOUGH," Gwen screamed. "Can't you for once leave her alone," she said, slamming her fist hard on the table. "Who are you to judge anyone you pretentious, fake replica of a wanna-be Stepford -wife."

Shoving her chair back, Clara shouted, "I can't do this anymore," the contents in her glass spilling. "Please excuse me ladies, but I must be going." She reached for the cloth napkin, dabbed her mouth, crumpled it, and threw it into the plate of uneaten food.

"Oh, there Miss- spoil-this-year's-Thanksgiving-dinner goes again," Gwen said, mopping up the spilled tea with her napkin. "She will forever be the black cloud that ruins any good day."

Clara came charging back, "Oh really, is that what I am. I thought I was merely making a point, much like yourself. This dinner has been a total waste of my time. In fact, the whole visit here has been," she said, exiting the room. She suddenly stopped and turned back to face them. "While all of you are here, I may as well deliver the rest of my news." She breathed in and exhaled quickly, "My wedding is only six months away and as I see it, neither of you are invited," she said, pointing at her sisters.

Dropping the napkin, Gwen grabbed her chest. "No way! I could have sworn we would be the first names on the guest list—even having the privilege of escorting the bride herself." She paused, "You do know I'm kidding. You did get my attempt at humor this time, right? Who in the world wants to come to your tired-plastic wedding anyway," she scoffed.

Rose stared ahead.

"Clara, you can't be serious," Ellen said, standing. "Please, let's rethink this."

"I could not be more serious, mother. I would never have someone Rose's size in my wedding. By the way, have you taken a good look at Gwen lately? This is her sophomore year at the University, and have you ever seen her in anything except one of the two pair of jeans she owns? Does she even have a set of curling irons or is her hair just permanently stuck in that ridiculous horse-tail? I will not have them embarrass me or my fiancé on one of the most important days of our lives." Clara stormed down the hallway, "Look at your girl's mother or is it too difficult for you," she yelled back at her. "You're the one responsible for it all."

Clara slammed the door to her bedroom and snapped the lock. Throwing herself onto the bed, she pressed the pillow hard against her face and screamed. She felt she had suffered long enough at the hands of this severely dysfunctional family of hers and desperately wanted out. She laid there until darkness seeped its way inside the room. She recalled the countless nights she had spent crying and wondering what God was thinking when He placed her into a family like this. She tried hard to disassociate herself from them and create her own exclusive world, but nothing seemed to work. She thought about her high school years when she tried to befriend the girls that came from the *'storybook families'*. It was a name she had affectionately given them. A world like that could easily take her away from the one she was so miserably trapped in. She pressed her face deeper into the pillow when she remembered the unforgettable moment she introduced herself to the *'storybook girls'*. They flat-out rejected her. From their condescending comments about her clothes and un-manicured nails, to the cruel jokes about her run-down shoes, they teased her mercilessly. She had become their personal human target, making sure she understood just how much she didn't fit in. The crazy part of it all, she was willing to accept their bullying as long as they agreed to let her hang around.

She was clearly more attractive than most of them but understood that didn't matter, it was her upbringing that did. Fate had placed her on the wrong side of the tracks and refused to let her go. With a family possessing a complicated and humiliating past, they were poor and the entire town knew it. She had no means of trying to keep up with these girls despite all of her efforts. How could she fit in when she wore bargain basement specials, rarely had money for extras...hair-do's, accessories—things like that? Cheap and poor may as well have been written across her forehead. It was okay for Gwen and Rose to look that way, shabby and all, but not her. That was not her lot. She recognized all families had their fair share of problems, she wasn't that naïve. Still, she'd made a point of studying the '*story-book girls*'. Difficulties seemed to evade them in their very small private worlds. First of all, they had hand-some fathers who could afford to let their moms stay home and take care of their families. The mothers on the other hand dressed in the latest fashion and so did their cheerleader-daughters. They had weekly hair appoint-ments, manicures, and pedicures to-boot. The girls got their beautiful, shiny cars at their outlandish 16th birthday parties which, by the way, they never invited her to. These girls hung out together and their parents were close friends. What was fair about any of that and why couldn't she be a part of it?

The '*storybook girls*' could uncover and touch feel-ings deep inside—ones she learned to hate. She knew in her soul they would never allow her to join their world and it was all because of her mother and sisters. Every now and then a cloud of guilt would wash over her when she wished her family were all somehow instantly done away with. Maybe, a tragic accident…she just wanted them out of her life.

Chapter 2

Planning Times

Clara's attempts to fit in with the girls she admired from afar had become such a miserable failure, she devised another plan. It was in the confines of her bedroom that she activated the masterful scheme. She was determined to take full advantage of both her brains and her beauty. Being left alone allowed her to work hard at school and her grades proved it. If she couldn't be a part of the '*storybook world*', then she would belong to the '*smart-girl group*', by default. She was in the top ten percent of her graduating class, sporting a GPA of 4.3.... mastering the ACT with a score of 34.

Inside her sanctuary, she would also dream and sometimes even act out the fine, classy woman she was destined to be. She would watch herself for hours in the mirror, as she dressed and practiced perfect diction followed by gestures that went along with speaking that way. She would take a long look at herself and talk to the real Clara.

Locking herself inside for days, she would not come out except for school, dinner, and bathroom breaks. It was understood no one was allowed in her room. They made that mistake once, barging in uninvited. After the tantrum she'd thrown, it left their mother crying for days. Since then, none of them ever dared venture inside her room again.

No one was surprised when she received scholarships to several major Universities. The only complication, the largest scholarship offered was in a city only one hundred miles away…not nearly far enough for her to shed the god-forsaken town of her past.

Nevertheless, she accepted it and worked extremely hard after school so she could be prepared when it came time to leave. Working all the overtime she could manage, she accumulated a nice nest egg for college.

Finally, high school graduation came and true to form it turned out to be one of the most horrific days of her life. The continuous parties and gatherings she let go by. They hadn't officially invited her anyway and she was tired of showing up and being ignored. If her mother hadn't pleaded for her to go to her own graduation, she would have spent that day in her room as well. She was just anxious to get on with life and suppress all the painful memories that had plagued her these many years. Her plan was to push forward and never look back.

Soon the University became her new sanctuary. It was a place where 'the plan' she devised to shake the town of her youth could finally be realized. She was one step closer to releasing the elitist princess that raged inside. With the money she worked so hard to save, she mastered the art of accessorizing. The hottest name brand scarves, hand bags, earrings, sunshades and a few stylish tops gave the illusion that all of her clothes were that way. When the affordable stores marked down a nice, classy outfit, she would grab it. Her nails were manicured to perfection and her hair was cut into one of the most flattering styles imaginable. When she finally walked onto the University's campus, she enjoyed the stares. A mere one hundred miles away and no one bothered about her family's history or where she had come from. All they saw was a smart, pretty, extraordinary girl.

The moment she opened the door to her dorm room, she was down-right speechless as her bubbly roommate came rushing up to her. How unbelievable was her luck when the young lady from the *'storybook world'* introduced herself. With a father as a neurosurgeon and a mother a lawyer, she knew Marty was the kind of girl she longed to hang out with. Unlike her high school days, and with a little help from Marty, the right crowd in college readily embraced her.

In a matter of days, her entire world changed. She didn't know much about sororities but just followed along when she joined the one all the females in Marty's family had been members of. Just like that, she entered a place where the girls of her newly acquired status lived. They rode her around in their sleek new cars and she ran among one of the most popular cliques on campus. She would have settled for that amount of phenomenal luck, but then the extraordinary happened. He was tall, dark, and good looking. His name was Eric. He came from a very well to do family and the attraction between them was immediate. After they met at a Greek gathering they became inseparable. For the three years they had been dating, she only allowed him a small glimpse into her very private world. On the other hand, she was completely absorbed in his. The moment he invited her home to meet his parents, she made every attempt after that to spend each holiday with them. Their estate was exquisite and the parties they hosted when she visited— well, she knew it was where she belonged.

She shuddered when she replayed the one day she felt it would all come crashing down around her.

Gwen.

As she and Eric turned the corner, there she stood, tall, her original nemesis, the thorn in both her sides. Now a freshman on campus, from out of nowhere she had somehow magically appeared. Dressed in her traditional uniform—jeans, tee shirt and a baseball cap, she remembered the instant embarrassment hugging her tightly.

"I've been looking everywhere for you," she recalled Gwen saying. "Got a couple of bucks, I'm starving. I was trying to get to the cafeteria before it closed."

Clara released a delicate gasp when the only words she could think of finally squeaked their way out. "What are you doing here?" she whispered.

"Hello-o-o, I go to school here or have you forgotten?" Gwen said.

She might have gotten it together a little faster but it was Eric's puzzled look that caused her words to come out much like a scratched CD. "No...no, no...I..I..didn't forget," Clara remembered stammering. She had not mentioned much about her sisters to him, let alone shared the news that one actually attended the University. Actually, she didn't see the need to. She had already made up her mind they would never get to know each other anyway.

Clara thrust deep into her purse, grabbed some cash, and shoved it into her sister's hands. "Here, take this," she said hoping she would just walk away.

Typical Gwen, however, she stood there.

At that point she knew she had no other choice but to introduce them. "Uh, Eric, Gwen. Gwen, Eric."

"Hi, Eric, I'm Clara's other sister. It is certainly nice meeting you."

She watched as Gwen wiped her hands on her jeans before shaking his.

She recognized the familiar trick, wiping her hand on her jeans like that. "She must have gotten that one from her," she thought. It was one of her old moves, a clear attempt at humiliating her.

Finally, she was able to steer Eric away as she slipped her arm into his. Clara looked back at Gwen and smiled. "We must be going. We'll talk later."

"Indeed she would call her later," she thought, as the smell of revenge all but carried her away. Her thoughts of pay back were short lived, however, when she was suddenly forced to deal with Eric's now obvious quietness. She knew exactly what was on his mind.

"You're not talking to me baby," she said. "Are you okay?"

He turned and faced her. "I cannot help but wonder Clara, are you happy? I mean... are you in love with me?" he whispered.

Her pulse quickened as tears welled in her eyes. "I can't believe you're asking me that. I love you so much—more than I have ever loved anyone. I can't imagine life—my existence without you." She forced the salty tears onto her cheeks.

"You never told me your sister attended school here. In fact, I haven't met anyone in your family before. I've introduced you to all my folks and they absolutely adore you. I guess I don't understand what's taking so long for me to meet yours."

"No, it's not that way at all." That was the only thing she could think to say which sounded half-way believable. "I simply forgot to mention Gwen being here. It really did slip my mind. Besides, I've told you my mother works these really weird hours, and I rarely get the opportunity to talk to her myself. Whenever we do, she always sends her love," she lied. "She can't wait to meet you, Eric." Clara dropped her head. "Maybe I should have introduced you by now," she said. "That was so insensitive of me."

He gently placed his finger under her chin, lifting it up until their eyes met, "Hey, I thought perhaps you were ashamed of me or something"

She remembered that silky smile of his as he pulled her into his arms. It was when they entered the shadows of the ivy archway that she looked up at him. She knew then she was going to spend the rest of her life with this man.

"You do forgive me, don't you?" she whispered.

He kissed her good night.

As she climbed the steps and slowly closed the door, she leaned her head onto it and listened as the lock clicked. She rested it there a moment, the blood rushing to her burning ears. Eyes narrowed, she marched towards the phone. "Listen to me very carefully and listen to me good," she seethed. "As long as the two of us are here, don't you ever speak to me. I hope you understand that. If you don't comply, I will take other measures to make you...nasty ones. Ones I'm sure even you Gwen Andrews won't like," she yelled.

Gwen had been waiting on that call. She'd finally met Eric. "Hmm, not bad," she thought, holding the phone away from her ear. She tried hard to keep from smirking but was finding it difficult not to. She reflected back on the incident and thought—"The cost of missing one good meal meant going to bed hungry. The cost of watching Clara squirm…priceless." The dial tone buzzed loudly. As she slowly pressed the button to silence the noise, she thought, "The girl really does have a sensitivity chip missing."

Chapter 3

Family Times
ROSE

Strange as it all seemed, Rose was glad their Thanksgiving dinner played out the way that it did. She was hoping it would finally put an end to the Clara saga and all of her strange antics. She absolutely hated being around her anymore. As long as she could remember Clara had been mean. No, take that back, she'd been downright cruel. She could not pass her without making a hurtful comment or insulting her in some kind of way. It was one remark, however, that seemed to seep its way deep into the fabric of her soul and remain there.

"What is that smell?" she'd ask anyone who would listen. She asked that question at least a hundred times. Finally, unexpectedly, she nuzzled up to her and sniffed. It was the closest she had been to her in years, but she will never forget the words that slithered out of her mouth next.

"Rose, as large as you are, dear, you should never go without bathing at least twice a day. The odor is quite offensive."

Afterwards, she had become so self-conscious about how she smelled that she made herself a special potion of scented spices she would spray all over her body. Still, matters went from bad to worse when Clara immediately broke out into a bright, red prickly rash from head to toe. The doctor figured it was her special fragrance that did it.

She remembered Clara scratching, crying, and complaining to him how her sister's special remedy was overpowering the house. Although she had to get rid of her homemade perfume, she couldn't help but gain great pleasure in watching Clara swell up like a giant blow fish as she scratched and smelled of the stinky medication she had to apply. When she finally felt better, Clara came back with such a vengeance, the teasing became unbearable. She harassed her incessantly about 'the smell' even gagging when she came around her. Finally, she decided she must be right and felt it was best to keep her distance from most people. Then, one day, miraculously the teasing suddenly stopped. The reprieve was short lived, however, and soon the ignoring began. That's when Clara began acting as if she didn't exist. She never said another word to her unless she absolutely had to.

Rose could never understand why it was so important for her to gain Clara's attention and affection—but it was. She knew her older sister hated her and it seemed so did the rest of the world. She blamed her enormous size mostly for the way people treated her. She didn't mind being as tall as she was, all of her sisters were. Still, it was beyond her wildest dreams why she had to be so large? She could not explain why she ate so much. She would give her right arm to stop. Was it always necessary for Clara to remind her of her size, though? "Have you dated? Do you have any friends," she mocked her in her thoughts.

The only date she had ever been on turned into a nightmare, and no, she didn't have any friends—and yes, she would love to hang out with some of the girls, but couldn't. She was too self-conscious about the way she looked and smelled.

The one thing she hated more than being so large was always being told… "You have such a pretty face." If one more person told her that, she was going to punch them in theirs. When she compared herself to her sisters, she knew Clara was the regal sophisticated one, emphasizing her beauty in a flashy, yet classy way. Gwen on the other hand was an extremely pretty girl but never flaunted it. She loved the out-doors, especially her baggy blue jeans and oversized shirts. No one would have ever known she had a knock out figure under there. Her long, extremely thick hair was always covered with that crazy baseball cap she insisted on wearing. Then of course, there she was the tall, fat, smelly one. While she was beginning to squeeze into size 20's, she appreciated Gwen for trying to suggest styles that helped flatter her hopeless figure. Her mother's tactic, however, was a completely different one. She tried desperately to help boost her self-esteem by playing up how intelligent her baby girl was. Whenever she introduced her, she would say, "This is my baby" and without fail end with, "She's the smart one." She guessed it was a mother's way of shifting the attention away from her numerous flaws and physical defects. It worked to some extent. She had started feeling half way decent about herself when one day she overheard someone describe her as the smart, fat kid in school. Her self-esteem plummeted. She realized then she would never be anything more than that.

Another dreg that pulled on the strings of her heart was the anguish…the hurt, seemingly always stamped on their mother's face. She knew it was the internal con-flicts each of her daughters faced that made her so sad. Ever since Clara went away to college, she never called and would prefer being the only student on campus rather than coming home for the holidays and being around them. Their mother never seemed to understand it wasn't her fault Clara hated them so. Then, there was Gwen, the possessive one. She believed it was their father's mistreatment of their mother that caused her to over-compensate and become so angry. Gwen couldn't see it, but that ill-temper of hers was slowly dragging her down a long, bumpy road of unforgiveness. Life was destined to be hard if she didn't get her attitude in check real soon. Lastly, it was her own hidden secret that complicated matters—one determined to trap her in a stealthy web of depression and never let her go. So, to cope with it all, she ate. Even when she wasn't hungry she devoured as much food as possible. For some reason, it helped calm the destructive demon raging inside.

If she was ever going to survive, she knew she had to get far away from the empty town of her childhood. She wanted to share with them the news her guidance counselor had given her right before the school break. A prestigious school in the northeast had offered her a full academic scholarship and she was ready to accept it. Soon she would know if moving away was the solution to all of her problems. If not, she had a plan for that too.

***

GWEN

Lacing her sneakers, Gwen tried hard to forget the Thanksgiving's day fiasco. She remembered hoping Clara wouldn't show up like she'd done in the past. Then they would be assured of having a nice, peaceful holiday dinner, just the three of them. It was only wishful thinking, however. As soon as Clara hit the door, like clockwork, their mother started defending her disgusting behavior. It infuriated her so much, she knew her mother taking up for Clara like that was the reason her stomach ached each time she came home. As far as she was concerned, there was just no excuse for any reasonable person to behave that way. There was nothing sane about Clara walking around the house, slamming doors, and giving everybody the silent treatment. It was just plain rude. Not only did it upset her, she was also finding it difficult to control the anger she felt towards her mother for allowing Clara to display such unreasonable behavior.

She tossed Ellen's classic line around, "I shouldn't have divorced your father." If she heard her mother say that one more time, she was going to scream and then go ahead and choke Clara. After all, it was what she had wanted to do for years.

Bundling up, Gwen stepped outside, her breath lingering in the brisk night air. Starting out with a light jog, she trotted along trying to clear her mind. Still, she couldn't rid herself of the menacing thoughts. She couldn't help but think back on the sacrifices their mother made throughout the years. She'd tried every way possible to appease Clara—even buying her the type of clothes she always demanded when she knew she couldn't afford to. She saw what that did to their mother and hated Clara for it.

Gwen took several quick puffs as she picked up speed. She'd tried for years to contain the rage she felt towards her oldest sister. Now that they were both attending the same University, she was finding it increasingly difficult to do so. She watched at a distance how she acted around her new friends, whom she grew to hate as well. "You would think the girl had been rich all of her life," she thought. All of her flashy dressing and artificial voice intonations disgusted Gwen, watching her live out such a lie.

As chance would have it, she and Clara ended up in the Student Center at the same time one day. It gave her the perfect opportunity to take a real good look inside her sister's head. Dressed in her usual attire, she pulled the baseball cap down lower, sat back and listened.

"Your hair is always so pretty Clara, did you get it all from your mother?" she heard one of her Sorority sisters ask.

Clara ran her fingers through her dark, wavy locks. "No, my father has hair to die for. I have hair just like his. Speaking of my father ladies, I have such good news. His side of the family lives in Bel Air and wants me to join them there as soon as I graduate."

"What about Eric?" one of them cried out in her girly-girl voice. "I just knew the two of you were so married once you got out of here!"

Gwen watched Clara sneer….that shifting of the left eyebrow and left lip all at the same time thingy that she did. "I never said I was going to move to California, now did I? Oh, but I do have the best of both worlds don't you think?" she boasted.

Gwen watched as she tossed her hair, adjusted the collar to her Michael Kors' suit, and led her entourage out of the building.

It made her ill.

Gwen burst into a full sprint as she dashed thru the narrow path careful to avoid the pot holes. Their father's family did live in Bel Air but they had not heard from them in years. If Clara had been foolish enough to contact them, she was sure they had probably out-right, rejected her.

Gwen had two more years left at the University and longed to pack up and leave the area for good. She knew that wouldn't happen though. It would be impossible for her to leave their mother behind. Clara was disappearing, planning never to return again, and she wasn't so sure what Rose was going to do. So, there she was, the only one left to care for their mother in a town that had so little to offer.

Like an arrow, she zipped thru the trail in a coordinated blur. The rushing wind did little to simmer the fury boiling inside.

***

ELLEN... "Mother"

Her ex-husband had insisted each of their girls call her, 'mother'. He was a successful engineer and gave them practically everything any little girl could want. While he was a strict disciplinarian, he always remained loving towards his precious daughters. It was quite the opposite with her. His anger seemed to mount each year and at some point she became fearful for her life. She promised herself if she survived the final choking he unexpectedly delivered one awful day, she would leave and never look back. With two black eyes and the prints of his fingers still on her neck, she left the following morning and filed for divorce. She knew once she made the decision to leave him, it would dramatically change their lives. They had to move to a side of town she never wanted her girls exposed to, but was the only place she could afford at the time. Slowly, he completely shut them out of his life. The part she did not see coming was how soon he remarried. He and his much younger wife immediately had another child and moved to California. "He had another life and it was just as well that he moved on," he told her when he finally phoned. The girls eventually adjusted to their new life-styles, all except Clara. A few years after he moved to the opposite end of the country, he was diagnosed with an inoperable brain tumor. Six months later he was dead. There was not much mourning from the three of them, although it seemed Clara would grieve forever.

They did, however, benefit monetarily from his death and it was the kind of help she desperately needed. The jobs she found around town paid lousy and somehow, he had successfully evaded paying child support.

While it seemed Clara would never recover from the divorce or his death, she noticed the impact it also had on Gwen and Rose. Gwen had become extremely over-protective of her. It was Gwen that plowed her father in the back of the head the night of the choking, causing him to momentarily loosen his grip and allowing her to escape. She will never forget the image of her little girl standing there with a poker iron threatening to kill her own father if he ever touched her mother again. Then, there was Rose. She simply went into a shell and never came out. Her struggles all seemed internal, manifested through her insatiable appetite. It was very difficult watching her baby girl, year after year, mushroom into an extremely obese young woman.

Clara's upcoming wedding was another source of unbelievable pressure. Her continuous excuses as to why she couldn't meet Eric had at some point become painful. To make matters worse, she overheard her making wedding plans with her friends and apparently Eric's mother. Was Clara that ashamed of them?

She knew the answer.

The thoughts depressed her. In fact, nothing in her life at the moment seemed to be going right. Two days ago her doctor had called and asked her to come in for a CAT scan. They found a suspicious spot on her lung. She hadn't shared the disturbing news with any-body….especially her girls.

Chapter 4

Part I - Wedding Times

"Clara, da-a-a-r-ling, this is Gloria."

"Gloria," she squealed. "I'm so glad to hear from you!"

Clara adored the way Eric's mother had mastered the art of speaking. She'd been grooming herself to talk that way for years.

"I do need to know whether or not your family intends on making the pre-wedding gala. We so desperately need an accurate head count," Gloria said in her thick northeastern accent.

Clara eased her own words out with clarity and precision. "Let me see." She paused, "No, Gloria, my sisters will not be able to attend, just include my mother."

"Will do, love. Oh, by the way, the day of the wedding according to the farmer's almanac should be absolutely gorgeous. I can't tell you what a brilliant move it was to have the ceremony here while the trees are in bloom. It is such a beautiful setting for an outdoors affair. Your mother is a doll for agreeing to such a splendid idea. Well, I've got to run. I will talk to you soon. Good bye, dear."

When Clara hung up, she knew it was time to have a long talk with her mother. She needed to coach her on how to behave around Eric, his parents and her new friends. It made matters somewhat bearable knowing she probably wouldn't have much to say when she met them.

It would, however, have been next to impossible to control those sisters of hers. Gwen would have insisted on that plain Jane look and as far as Rose was concerned, there was just no hope.

"The wedding couldn't come soon enough," she thought.

Despite the hectic pace, the months flew by and before she knew it the week of the wedding had finally come. Clara was glad fate had somehow intervened and all of her wedding plans had fallen into place. She personally picked out her mother's teal empire dress and made her an appointment with Juan, for a fresh new 'do'. She also rehearsed over and over what was appropriate to say and what was clearly off limits.

***

When it was time to head for the wedding festivities, it was Gwen and Rose that helped Ellen pack. They wanted to make sure she had everything she needed being that far away from them. As soon as Clara arrived home, she brought along with her the usual attitude. She stormed past them acting as if not inviting her sisters to the wedding was normal.

Gwen simply ignored her, but she couldn't help but notice Rose's behavior. She watched her fall deeper and deeper into a degree of isolation that caused her great concern. She knew how devastating it must have been enduring the constant ridicule from Clara all these years. The effect of it all had somehow crept into Rose's spirit and wreaked havoc in her mind. She tried protecting her, but couldn't be with her twenty-four-seven. She even made a point to be cheerful around Rose no matter how she felt in hopes it would somehow snap her out of that dark place. Still, nothing worked.

The thought of leaving their mother in the recalcitrant hands of 'the evil older sister,' caused Gwen angst as well. If that wasn't bad enough, not being invited to the wedding was actually starting to bother her. "Who does that?" she thought. "Not invite your own sisters to your wedding. It was okay not being a part of the bridal party, but not to be there at all, just didn't make any sense."

It was only when they left that Gwen was able to push the thoughts of Clara aside. Things began to settle back to normal as she and Rose sat alone in the den.

"Hey, are you hungry, kiddo? How about I make us our favorite?" Gwen said.

"Yeah, that sounds great." Rose picked up her book by Maya Angelou and began to pour over the pages.

When Gwen returned with a plate of tacos, she sat down beside her. "Do you think mother will have a good time?" she asked, biting into the crispy, toasty shell.

"No, I don't believe she will at all. She might have enjoyed herself a little more if we were there," Rose spoke softly.

"Well, that's not going to happen," Gwen said, wiping the taco sauce from off her mouth.

"I really would prefer not talking about Clara or her wedding if you don't mind. It depresses me to think about it," Rose said, with an unusual edginess to her voice.

"Just this once…I really need to talk about it if that's okay," Gwen said. She took in a deep breath, "I'm having difficulty processing all of this."

Gwen knew she was exposing her vulnerable side—something she was never comfortable doing. Sharing deep feelings like that often left her in an awful mood, but she pushed on anyway.

"While I'm angry with Clara, I'm just as ticked with mother for allowing her to treat us this way."

"What could mother have done?" Rose asked softly.

"Are you kidding me? She didn't have to stand there and let that…that….well, I can't call her what I want to, do this to us," Gwen said.

At a loss for words, Rose stared hard at Gwen, shocked at her reaction.

"I know…I know, quit looking at me that way," Gwen said. "That's why I really need to hear your thoughts this time. Do you think mother sort'a betrayed us?" she asked.

Rose sat quietly, tears filling her eyes. She was tired and just wanted all of the stress to somehow magically disappear. She eased the words out through the pain, "No, I do not. I don't think mother would ever betray us, Gwen."

"I have never felt that way either, and believe me it's not a good feeling," she said, fighting back her own tears. "It hurts, Rose. It makes me so angry." Gwen placed her taco back on the plate and slid it aside.

"Mother wants each of us happy and you know that. She will do anything to make sure that we are," Rose said. "It'll be okay." Those were the only comforting words she had for her. She picked up the book and began to read as she proceeded to eat all six of the tacos.

Chapter 5

Part II- Wedding Times

As they headed for the wedding rehearsal gala, Ellen took the nervousness out on her freshly manicured nails. When they pulled into the gated area, she tried hard to hide the sizeable chip she'd made on her pinky, but knew Clara had already seen it.

Her heart fluttered.

After the preliminary introductions she found a table in a corner and sat …fading deep into the background. From there she observed the entire scene. The servers in full regalia balanced trays of filet, salmon, and spring vegetables. With the east wind blowing across the Bradbury Lake, she felt slightly cool. It didn't seem to bother the other women though. Dressed in their pastel, neatly tailored-sleeveless dresses, some with matching hats, they laughed and occasionally whispered to each other.

She felt so out of place. Leaving Rose and Gwen behind had drastically affected her mood. In her heart, she was hoping Clara would change her mind and allow her sisters to attend the wedding, but it was mostly wishful thinking. So, when they arrived, just the two of them, scripted, and versed on what to and what not to say, she felt the anxiety close in. The shimmering reflection from the glistening waters somehow helped absorb her thoughts. Her attention now rested on the results of her CAT scan and biopsy. They weren't good. They wanted to operate right away. The surgery, however, would have interfered with the wedding so she decided to postpone it.

"Your mind seems to be a million miles away. Hi, I'm Eric's sister Miriam," she said, sitting next to her on the thick, peach cushioned chair. "You've barely said two words since you've been here. Are you enjoying yourself?" Miriam asked.

"I'm having a wonderful time. I was sitting here taking it all in," Ellen said. "It's an absolutely beautiful setting and I cannot thank your parents enough."

"I'm sure they know how grateful you are. Besides, nothing is ever too good for their baby boy," she said, laughing. "I'm glad you could come, Mrs. Andrews."

Miriam chatted a little longer so that the next question she asked wouldn't seem too out of place.

"Oh, before I leave, there was one thing I did want to ask. I'm told Clara has two younger sisters. Is that right?" Miriam paused, and then smiled. It was what she had been longing to inquire about the entire night.

"Yes, that's right. Actually, I was sitting here thinking of them, wishing they could be here to enjoy this wonderful afternoon." Ellen suddenly stopped, hoping she wasn't saying too much. She reached up and pressed against the area on her head that throbbed the most.

"Why aren't they attending the wedding, Mrs. Andrews?" Miriam asked.

"Oh, no, Ellen" thought, "Please let me get this right. Well, that's a long story," she said, taking in a long-cleansing breath.

"Why don't you give me the short version," Miriam said, patting her hand.

"Alright," her flitting thoughts scrambling to find the right answer. She briefly scanned the 'what not to say list' but finally just blurted out the truth. "One of Clara's sisters is a tad overweight and wouldn't be a good fit for the bride maid's gown and…."

Miriam gasped as she noticed the corner of Ellen's mouth quiver. "You mean Clara couldn't make adjustments for that? After all, they are her sisters. The two of them not coming to the wedding is really inexcusable."

Ellen knew she had blown it and tried her best to recover. "No, no," she said, taking a sip of water allowing the cool liquid to moisten her severely parched throat. She managed a half-smile. "It wasn't exactly that way, Miriam. Rose would have been just a little self-conscious to walk down the aisle because…"

"It's really too bad Clara couldn't make her feel any better about it," Miriam interrupted. She gently pushed back her chair, "Listen, I've got to run and it was certainly nice chatting with you. I'm sure my mom is looking for me by now. I hope you enjoy the rest of your evening, Mrs. Andrews. I'll see you at the wedding."

Ellen's nerves were now in shambles. It had all just gone horribly wrong. The urge to run tapped her on the shoulder, encouraging her to leave while she still had the chance. Instead, she sat there as if the lack of motion could somehow douse the flames that fueled the nervousness inside.

Fifteen minutes later when the crowd began to dwindle, it was only then that she entertained the idea she might have escaped not having said the wrong things.

"Here's a toast to the beautiful bride," someone shouted.

They all stood and lifted their crystal goblets trimmed in gold. Clara's face shone radiantly as the reflection of the moonlight fell softly upon it.

Suddenly, the whole scene turned into an out-of-body experience for Ellen as she watched Miriam take a sip from her glass. She noticed as she faced her mother and the following words eased out…"I wonder if it's too late to get Clara's other sisters here for the wedding. I'm told one may not be able to fit into her dress, but I know we could manage to fix that. What do you think momma?" her voice escalating just above the crowds'.

Ellen turned in time to see the color drain from her daughter's face. She watched as Clara gripped the arm of her chair and force out a tiny grin. It was a familiar smile—one she had grown accustomed to. The one she often displayed whenever she fought with Gwen.

***

The stretch-black limousine smelled of Lysol and liquor. The ride back to the hotel was long. Clara kept her head turned away from her the entire time.

Inside the hotel room they prepared for bed, careful to avoid each other.

The room was eerily quiet, when Clara finally whispered, "Mother, are you trying to ruin everything for me?"

"Honey…"

"No, please don't," Clara said. "Why did you have to discuss Gwen and Rose in the first place? Clearly, that subject was off limits," she said. "Was it too hard for you to abide by my wishes?"

Ellen debated whether or not to respond. She knew anything she said at this point wouldn't be acceptable, so, she listened.

"You're not going to talk to me, is that it? Why couldn't you have done that when you were around Eric and his family and just kept your mouth shut?" Clara said.

The lone tear inched its way down Ellen's face as she regretted every word she'd said to Miriam. She wanted so desperately to see her daughter grasp the happiness that always seemed to escape her. She closed her eyes and prayed.

Clara reached over and switched off the light. She adjusted herself and turned her back to her mother.

Neither spoke, as sleep eluded them.

Finally, Clara flipped over, "I know you are not speaking to me and I know you're not asleep, so please listen," she said. "Tomorrow is my wedding, the most important day of my life. I will not have it ruined or feel stressed because of something you may or may not say. So, I know you will understand exactly what I am about to tell you, mother. After all, you have always said you wanted nothing more than happiness for each of your girls. Well, guess what? It can happen for me, right here. Right now! I can be happy. The only thing that can ruin it quite frankly, is you being here. It makes me too nervous and I don't need to be the least bit upset on this special day. I know you wouldn't want that for me either." She hesitated, "I think it would be best for the both of us if you didn't attend the wedding ceremony on tomorrow. I'm not trying to hurt you. It's just that I need my space." Clara took in a deep breath, "I'm so thankful to have such an understanding mother like you," she said. "If I thought for one second you didn't under-stand how important this was for me, I'd just die."

Clara snuggled under the thick down comforter. There! She'd said what had been on her mind ever since they left home. She did not want to cause a scene and physically have her mother removed, but at this point, she knew she would if she insisted on coming. She scolded herself for even thinking it would work having her there in the first place.

The darkness of the room helped relax Clara's frayed nerves as she began to reminisce about when their father lived with them. It was the only time in her life she recalled being happy. His larger than life presence always seemed to illuminate their home. Yet, for some reason their mother appeared to be sad whenever he was around. She knew her dad yelled at her a lot but that should have been okay. Most parents sacrifice for their children and just deal with those sorts of minor inconveniences. After all, it was what she intended to do for her own kids someday. If the Andrews' girls were happy, that's all that should have mattered to their mother ....but no, she was selfish and inconsiderate. When she looked at it that way, it was easy to do exactly what she was doing right now. Ellen Andrews never considered her feelings, so why should she consider hers.

When she finally drifted off to sleep, she dreamed of her mother sitting alone in a chapel surrounded by rows and rows of empty pews. Across the aisle were crowds of other wedding guests. When Ellen got up to move to the other side and join them, Clara suddenly woke up.

The dream rubbed smartly against her conscious. She couldn't believe she was having second thoughts of allowing her mother to attend the wedding. Well, if she did, she would have to rehearse again what was expected, especially when she was around Miriam.

She turned over and stretched, "Mother, wake up. I've thought things over…." she said.

To her surprise, propped on the pillow of the neatly made bed was a note from Ellen. It read, "Clara, you are right, I just want you happy. I Love You, Mother."

Chapter 6

New Family Times
MIRIAM

Miriam knew next to her very own, her brother was having one of the prettiest weddings she'd ever seen. "She had been to tons of them and none could surpass the one being held for Dr. Eric Gordon," she thought. It seemed the entire town was in quite a stir about the over-the-top event.

A mixture of white lilies and roses made up the three larger arches and two smaller ones. Some of the special flowers accenting the platform had been shipped in from Brazil. The white chrysanthemums, sprinkled with shades of deep lilac and green primroses lined the long aisle—their fragrance penetrating the air. The floral arrangements draped neatly along the yard's perimeter outlined an area where the ten piece orchestra played. It all made for an extraordinary sight.

The setting and entire wedding was no doubt the envy of the women in the Bradbury community. Miriam knew once Clara moved the gala to their city it was going to be that way. "Nothing had ever been too good for their precious son Eric," she thought. He was their parent's pride and joy.

Miriam stood number five out of the twelve bridesmaids. The long flowing soft violet gown swished as she glided down the aisle. Embellished with silver jewels sprinkled throughout the bodice, the classic dress had been designed by Vera Wang. As she reached her designated spot, she thought... "She hated Eric was about to marry this woman."

Miriam had done her homework. She'd investigated Clara and found nothing about her to be real and neither were her friends. They were all pretentious, insecure, immature women who needed to be exposed and that was exactly what she intended on doing. How could her family, especially Eric not see through it all? Clara was poor and so was her family. She had been a waitress for goodness sake. When she finally confronted Clara about it one day, it was obvious she caught her off guard. It was delightful to watch her squirm and try desperately to explain.

"Oh that! It was the hottest gig in town," she'd giggled nervously. "The place is known for local and national celebrity sightings. Besides, they only selected the best and brightest students to waitress there. The tips were enormous."

Miriam wasn't buying any of it.

Then, there was the issue of her strange family. When she finally met Clara's mother, she understood exactly why she hadn't invited Eric home with her. It was something weird about how quiet she was. A top business woman like Clara described her to be just didn't behave that way.

Once she gathered enough information, she took it to her brother to let him in on the huge blunder he was about to make. That was the second biggest mistake she made. The fight between the two of them would easily go down as their largest.

"You have never liked any of my girlfriends," he yelled. "It doesn't matter this time, Miriam, I have always tried to respect your feelings, but now I am demanding that you respect mine. I love Clara and I'm going to marry her. Get over it!"

The night that he stormed away, she knew in her heart she'd lost.

She had to give it to the girl, she could spot the sport of manipulation miles away, and Clara was good at it. That was okay, she held the title to that game and hadn't met anyone yet she couldn't handle—she would just have to re-think her plans. Exposing her new sister-in-law and her artificial world was going to take some work but she was up to the challenge. The problem complicating matters most, however, were her parents. They were already as smitten with Clara as Eric was.   In the past, no one had ever been 'good enough' for their son, but it was different this time. She recalled the first Christmas Clara came to visit, dressing so elegantly, and attempting to impress everyone.   She gave her mother all the control she tried demanding from each of them for years. Clara followed her everywhere she went, agreed with whatever she said, and did whatever she told her to do. It was disgusting watching her follow-up behind her mother like a sick little puppy. It worked though, she had fallen hard, and now it was her daddy's turn. He was the easy one…always had been. She knew it wasn't going to be long before Clara had both parents wrapped around her little finger. Looking back, she was sorry she had given all of Eric's other girlfriends such a hard time. At least they were the real deal and seemed to truly love him.

Her brother was a great catch. He was handsome, rich and would one day make a fine doctor. Just about to enter his residency, he and his brand new wife would be moving only a few miles away from where they grew up. For a wedding gift, their father had already given him the deed to a refurbished condo.

As she gracefully stood in the bridesmaid's line, she glanced out over the hundreds of wedding guests. Miriam knew she had a lot of work to do getting this woman so obviously beneath them out of their lives.

***

MRS. Clara Gordon

The weather was perfect. The strong sun rays highlighted the end to a crisp, clear Saturday afternoon. Her bridesmaids were beautiful, each standing tall and regal in their rich, soft- violet strapless gowns. As the twenty plus bridal party posed for the photographer, Clara couldn't help but think how lucky she was to finally become a 'Gordon'. Only they could make her fairytale dreams come true. "It was such an amazing wedding," she thought. She knew this was merely the back-drop to her very own *'storybook world'*.

Eric whirled her around the mammoth, candle-lit tent that towered on the east side of the estate. Filled with over five hundred guests, the sparkles from the chandeliers fell like glitter upon them all. Clara didn't want the remarkable night to end as they danced 'til midnight. When they honeymooned in the South of France, again, it was magical. With Eric she felt safe.

As soon as they returned home, Eric immediately became immersed in his studies. She took a job as an elementary school teacher at the prestigious Carrington Academy. Gloria had insisted she work at the private school when they finally settled in. As a personal friend of the headmaster, she made special arrangements for her to become a primary grade teacher there. Needless to say, it disappointed many of those who had already been on the five year waiting list when she took the only coveted teaching spot.

Eric was doing well in medical school and talked nonstop of his interesting cases. His hectic schedule kept him away from her more than she liked—but she quickly learned to adjust to that. With Junior League, Racquet Club, and Country Club Wives, her social activities became the highlight of most of her days.

"Thanks Rosita, I'll see you next week," Clara called out to her housekeeper as she left for the day. She turned and walked towards the ringing phone.

She was surprised to hear Rose's voice. "It had to be an emergency," she thought.

"I was just about to leave for an important meeting," Clara said, even before the conversation began. Floods of unpleasant childhood memories flashed before her as she held the phone in silence.

"I'm sorry, I didn't mean to disturb you," Rose said quietly.

"Speak up, I can barely hear you," Clara said.

"How's Eric?"

"He's fine."

The silence was uncomfortable—for Rose.

"I hate to have to ask you, but, uh, I'm in a little bit of a financial situation and didn't know who else to turn to," Rose said. "I've been invited to take part in an internship program that's going to cost me five hundred dollars to register. It is a super competitive fellowship and I am lucky to have been considered at all. I, well… I was wondering if I could borrow that amount from my big sis," she tried joking. "I promise I will pay you back next week," she said. "I'm working overtime at the bookstore and I'll have the entire amount by then. The deadline for submission fell a week before my payday," she said, softly.

The long silent pause made its point.

"Are you there?" Rose mumbled.

"I truly am shocked to hear from you," Clara said. "Unfortunately, it's sad that the only time you do call is when you need a hand-out. Perhaps you're not aware, that my husband is in medical school. We are also preparing to open our own business and all of our money is tied up. So Rose, the answer is no. Sorry."

Clara knew they had in excess of five hundred thousand dollars in their savings account alone. She still didn't want any of her family thinking she would ever loan them one penny of their money. Besides, she hadn't seen Gwen or Rose in over two years and if their mother didn't call, she would never really think about any of them. She wanted to keep it that way.

Chapter 7

Times of Favor

As the years swiftly passed, Gwen was excited about graduation. Surprising even to herself, she was engaged to be married. She had fallen deeply in love with the only man she knew truly understood her. She often thought about the day they met.

Sitting on the campus lawn reading, she looked up and noticed a guy aiming a long lens camera her way. It annoyed her so much she turned quickly and moved away from the spot. The next day she felt a light touch on the shoulder.

"Hi, I'm Rick" he said, extending his hand.

"Hi." She gathered her books, ignoring it.

"Before you rush off, I want to show you something," Rick said, holding up a photograph.

As she turned, she glanced at the picture suddenly realizing it was a photo of herself. She remembered being so irritated it was a wonder he'd hung around at all after that.

"Where did you get that from?" she snapped.

"Let me apologize first of all for taking your picture without permission," he said.

"Yeah, well you shouldn't have," she charged back.

"The best way I can think of making up for my error is to give you this." Running to catch up, he tipped his hat, "I knew it would turn out to be a good shot but I was wrong."

She picked up the pace. "You bet you were wrong!" Turning sharply, she was hoping to lose him in the crowd.

"It turned out magnificent," he said.

She stopped abruptly almost sending him crashing into her. "Let me see that again," she said, snatching it from his hand. Holding it up to the light, she mumbled, "You got lucky, that's all."

"It would be the one day she decided not to wear her baseball cap," she thought. Tossing the picture back at him, she took even greater strides.

"You're a photographer's dream," he said, smiling.

"Now, I know you're crazy. No more pictures," she said.

"Hidden beauty when captured the right way can be extremely gratifying. Hey, please slow down a sec., I promise I'll leave you alone if you just hear me out."

Gwen kept walking.

"Let me put together a portfolio of you, mostly black and white and free of charge. I can show you better in pictures than trying to explain it all to you," he said. He tried to catch his breath. "Oh, come on, what do you have to lose?"

"Will you go away if I allow you to take pictures, right here? Right now," Gwen demanded, hoping it would run him away.

He dropped his bags, reached for his camera, adjusted the lens, and started snapping, "You're making it awfully difficult, but that's alright. I have something to prove," he said, aiming his camera closer to her face.

She allowed her eyes to burrow deep into the lens. "Okay, okay, that's enough." She gathered her books and scurried inside the classroom.

Several days later, Rick slid a flat package in between her books. "Tell me what you think," he said, walking away.

"You have a habit of sneaking up on people like that," she called out angrily. She thought about him the entire drive home. As she parked, she snatched the gear in place and slammed the car door shut. This guy was a nuisance and when she saw him again, she knew exactly what she was going to do to make the point it wasn't safe to bother her anymore. Well, that was the plan. Once she ripped open the package, she took one look and stared. The black and white pictures highlighted a woman's finest features capturing them in silhouettes of gray. The striking photos were pictures of her with catlike eyes, deep and penetrating. By the third time she picked up the card he had enclosed inside, she finally gave in and called.

"Is this Rick?" she asked.

"Yes, it is, and who might this be?"

"This is Gwen and I... 'em, think your pictures are amazing."

When he saw the unknown number, he felt it might be her. He answered it on the first ring. "Ah, my run away model. You know it would have been a tad easier if I had a little more cooperation from you," he laughed.

"I can't imagine how they would have turned out had I done that," she said.

"If I took my time, you would see my real work," Rick interjected quickly.

"Listen, I just wanted to compliment you, that's all."

"Let me photograph you," he said. "If it's not what you expect, all you have to do is walk away. I need to show you something."

When he first saw her on campus, he couldn't take his mind off the stunning girl. Not only was she a photographer's dream, she was alluringly beautiful. He remembered hesitating before taking her picture that day, but finally gave in. He couldn't believe she looked up at the exact moment he snapped it. Realizing it was too late, he continued his quest to photograph the young lady in the baseball cap that had captivated him for months. Now that he finally had her on the phone, he wasn't going to let her get away from him so easily.

"Let me show you what I know you are not aware of, Gwen."

"You're pushing your luck. I said no thanks."

"Come on, if you don't, the thought will always haunt you of what this strange guy had to prove."

"Do you always beg that way?" she pushed back.

When he actually laughed at her boorish comment, it took her off guard.   She remembered it being the moment that changed both their destinies. She agreed to let him photograph her.   The session was way beyond what she ever imagined. She had every intention of not cooperating again, but his team was so professional she felt compelled to comply.   The hairstyle, make up and outfits they chose for her, completely transformed her into someone even she barely recognized.   The back-drops and color coordination accented her face to perfec-tion. It was clear Rick was at the top of his game and proved it with each of the photos he took.

She had no idea how well known he was in the vast world of photography. His professors were in awe of his skills and encouraged him to pursue the many opportuni-ties being thrown his way.   After he presented her portfolio over dinner, the dinners never stopped. They were to be married in the spring of the year.

"Hey babe, I have some news that may be worth you checking out," Rick said, as he walked over to where she stood. "Turner Modeling Agency called and wants to meet with you."

"About what?" she asked, kissing him on the cheek.

"Several of their top execs approached me months ago about working for them. When I used your portfolio to showcase my talent, they were quite impressed with my work, but they were also very interested in the young lady that posed for the pictures," he said smiling. "I didn't hear anything further, so I never mentioned it, but today they phoned. They want to meet with you to discuss some modeling opportunities."

"Hey, get real. You know I'm no model."

"That's not what they seem to think. They are serious, Gwen. Turner is an extremely reputable company with a list of some pretty impressive clients. Who knows where this might lead you, or should I say, us. You could at least hear them out don't you think?"

"We'll see," she said, with serious doubts swirling through her mind.

They moved about the kitchen preparing a meal in the tiny duplex her mother helped her rent. Located only a block away from the university, it was sheer luck when she found the place. She knew she had absolutely no patience for roommates or dorm life, so she took out early one morning on the hunt for somewhere to live. As she drove around in her gas-guzzler—the car her father had given her mother years ago, she stumbled upon an elderly couple just as they were about to place a 'for rent' sign in the window. She never gave them the chance to. Along with her part-time job and the monthly allowance from her mother, the payments were affordable.

While Rick seasoned the fresh cut of salmon he brought over, she tossed the spinach salad, and neither brought up the potential modeling offer. That afternoon as they sat on the porch sipping tea from their favorite mugs, Gwen leaned her head onto his shoulder. She trusted his judgment more than anyone's and already knew what he wanted her to do.

"If you think I should go, then promise you will go with me," she finally said.

He smiled. "That's a promise." Rick prided himself in seeing through the hard shell that encased the love of his life. He knew inside was a sensitive, caring woman who had a gigantic heart. She just had a strange way of showing it sometimes.

The following week they found themselves sitting in the waiting area at Turner's Modeling Agency. Gwen's heart raced as she gently reached over and slid her hand into Rick's.

"Mr. Turner Jr. will see you now," the receptionist said. Leading them down the long hallway covered in deep green, plush carpet, they entered an over-sized boardroom that overlooked the bay. They both eased in behind the large rectangular mahogany table surrounded by tall leather-studded chairs.

John Turner entered the room and vigorously shook Rick's hand. "Hey, how are you man?"

"I'm great, John, it's good to see you. Thanks for inviting us over," Rick said. "We really appreciate the opportunity. This is Gwen Andrews," he beamed.

"It's nice meeting you, Gwen. My, my, you are just as lovely as your pictures," John said studying her over.

Gwen blushed as she coiled away from him. She wasn't use to all the attention and was now starting to regret she had come.

John Turner was an extremely bright young man who had taken control of the agency from his father five years ago. The company's success now bordered on the line of the miraculous rivaling all the top modeling agencies. Even though the competition was stiff, models from around the world were clamoring to sign with them.

Three women joined Mr. Turner at the long table as they took turns questioning Gwen about her interests and career aspirations. While they slowly perused her portfolio, she told them of her involvement in tutoring inner city kids in math and reading. She shared her ultimate desire of one day becoming a teacher, quietly emphasizing that modeling was nowhere in her plans. Later, Gwen posed for a few shots. As she and Rick were about to leave, the tall female executive told her they may eventually call her.

Gwen knew she wasn't the 'modelly' type and never expected that they would be interested in her. While they were friendly and all, they didn't seem to like the way she posed. The photographer seemed frustrated, "Give me more of this. No, no, no," he snapped. She could feel herself about to wipe off the thick make-up and storm right out of the shoot as things began to fizzle. It was all a disaster.

"Hey, babe, cheer up, don't let it get to you," Rick said, driving along.

She swept all of her massive curls into one giant po-nytail. "I don't know why I put myself through any of that," she said.

"What about grabbing something to eat at Forties, I'm starving," Rick said. He had already planned on them having dinner there anyway. This was the day he was going to ask her to be his wife.

Later, when the agency never phoned, it didn't seem to bother either of them.

Graduation and wedding plans now consumed their lives. However, there was one other thing that had Gwen concerned besides her hectic schedule—she had barely seen or heard from her mother in months. With Rose now on the east coast, she constantly worried about her being left home alone. Whenever she planned to visit, it never seemed to be the right time. Her mother made the excuse of having taken a job running the campaign for the congressman of their local district and was never home. She said she was finally doing some-thing she had an absolute passion for. The last time they had spoken, Ellen vowed she would phone today, and Gwen anxiously awaited her call. When her special ringtone finally chimed, she ran into the bedroom to retrieve it.

Reaching for her cell, Gwen made up her mind she was going to be a lot more persistent with her mother than before. She needed to see her and delaying it was no longer an option. When she walked back into the kitchen, she reached for the first chair to sit and eased her head onto the table.

"Whoa, what's wrong, babe? Is your mom alright?" Rick asked.

She shook her head and gave no response as she rested it there.

"Talk to me," he said, walking up to her. "Are you okay?"

"That was Turner Modeling Agency," she whispered. "They said the photos I took blew them away. They are offering me a full contract along with modeling classes and the works."

She looked at him, "They're talking a lot of money, Rick. What about being a teacher? What about our wedding? I don't know what to think about all this…that life-style…I…."

He reached for her, gently wrapping her in his arms. "Calm down," he said. He stared into the beautiful eyes he had grown familiar with. "It will all work out for you. I know you will make the right decision."

"They said I need to move to New York, right away." She rested in his arms with thoughts of her mother. She knew her advice was the only thing that could help calm her brittle nerves.

It wasn't long before they were on their way.

"Surprise," Gwen said, pushing open the heavy wrought iron door to her childhood home. Her smile slowly faded, replaced by a deep furrow in her brow as she noticed her mother's baggy, gray top matching the paleness in her skin. She was at least fifteen pounds thinner and now sported a short, curly wig. Gwen knew what was wrong without having to ask.

"Come here," Ellen said, reaching for her daughter and hugging her tightly. She wanted to shield Gwen from the obvious pain now clouding her eyes as she held on a few seconds longer. Rick finally managed to move them both inside.

"How bad is it?" Gwen sputtered.

"Let's sit down," Ellen said, leading her to the living room sofa. "I wanted to tell you a while ago," she said, looking down. "I had a portion of my lung removed about a month ago."

Gwen clutched her chest.

"They wanted to operate right away, but I wouldn't let them," Ellen said. "I did not want it to interfere with Clara's wedding. When I returned home earlier than expected, I went ahead and scheduled the surgery. I just didn't want to trouble you girls. Clara was getting married, you were taking final exams, and so was Rose."

Displaying a childlike innocence, her eyes deep and sunken, Ellen prayed it was a reasonable enough explanation to help settle Gwen's now fragile emotions. "Hopefully, they got it all," she added.

Gwen drew in several deep breaths. She tried hard to control the little mechanism that held back her tears, but it proved next to impossible. They spilled out everywhere.

Rick stood watching the two women for a moment at a complete loss for words. He had never seen Gwen that upset. "There's only one solution that can make all of this better," he blurted out. "My homemade soup, ummm-m-m, one taste of it and it will have you feeling better Ellen, uh… in no time."

The comment was so way out there, tears and all, Gwen burst into laughter. "That might not be such a bad idea," she said, drying her cheeks with the cuff of her blouse.

His special mixture of fresh vegetables and large hunks of beef tenderloin was what they all needed. He also made a pan of cornbread and a pitcher of lemonade to compliment his grandmother's recipe.   He was an excellent cook and they could actually see the color slowly returning to her mother's cheeks as they sat around the table laughing and reminiscing about Gwen as a child.

After the dishes were put away and her mother napping, Gwen and Rick walked along her familiar jogging trail.

"The modeling thing—well, that must not have been for me," she said. "I kinda' had a feeling this old town wouldn't let me go that easy." She turned and faced him, "I've got to take care of my mom, Rick."

"I understand," he said. He knew Ellen needed her daughter and no matter what, Gwen was going to be there for her.

"I could never leave her in the condition she's in. Even though graduation is only a month away, I almost feel the need to move back home, today," Gwen said.

He reached for her hand as they walked the trail. "Take care of your mother the best way you know how. Whatever you decide, I will be there for you."

Gwen wrapped her arm into his. "It's funny how life makes decisions for you," she said.   She kicked a rock, watching it skip along. "Who knows, maybe I'll be able to get a teaching job here at the high school."

They walked to the small neighborhood ice cream shop just around the corner where she ate scoops of black walnut and cookie dough mix. Sitting there, her mind drifted as the hypnotic 'open' sign blinked off and on in the parlor's window. She momentarily snapped out of it when she noticed how quiet Rick was—only paying attention to his large cup of ice cream.

"Are you tired, babe? All that 'on the spot cooking' got the best of you." She smiled. "You haven't said very much," she said, brushing his hand.

"Got a few things on my mind, that's all" he said.

"Can you let me in on a few of those things, Mr. Haley?"

"We'll talk about it later. Let's just enjoy the ice cream for now."

"Rick, come on, please talk to me. It's been a pretty rough day and I don't need to be concerned about you too. Are you okay?"

She squeezed his hand tightly.

He started slowly, "I hope you know I understand how important it is for you to take care of your mother. With that in mind, I do have something I would like to talk to you about. Turner also wants me in New York as soon as possible. They asked me to be the photographer assigned to your first project. Since you don't have the experience yet, they thought I could help coach you along. They liked my initial photographs of you so much they felt we would make a dynamic team," he said smiling. "So, I was thinking, maybe you would consider this in your list of options. What if we were to move to New York and take your mother with us? She would have both daughters to look after her there. With the money they are willing to pay us, we could afford to give her the best medical care for this stage of her disease. Plus, I really don't believe I can stand being away from you that long," he said, holding her hand.

He noticed the tears as soon as they began inching their way down, slowly outlining her cheeks.

"Please don't cry," he whispered. "It's okay. Let's just stick with your plans." He shook his head, "That's why I didn't want to bring it up."

"Sh-h-h, let me enjoy the moment," she said softly, gently running her finger alongside his face. "I'm looking at the most loving and kindest man in the entire world."

Chapter 8

Missing Times

"Slow down Gwen, I'm not following you, honey," Ellen said.

She started over from the beginning—Rick taking photos of her on campus, to the meeting they had with the Turner Modeling Agency executives.

"Mother can't you see, we've been given a once in a life time modeling and photography opportunity we can't turn down," Gwen said.

"You mean move all the way to New York, where Rose is?"

"Yes, ma'am and you will have both of your daughters together with you again and the best medical care New York has to offer." She was trying hard not to let her excitement outpace her hopes. She wanted to spare herself the disappointment just in case she refused the offer. "What do you think about the idea? Do you think it will work?" she asked.

"I don't know. That's so far away. Besides, I've finally found a job I truly enjoy. No, I don't want to be a burden," Ellen said.

"You could never be any bother to us. As for your job, you won't ever have to work again if I can help it. It'll be perfect, you'll see. Please say yes," Gwen said. The long pause caused her to beg, "Please mother," she said. "I can't leave you like this."

After they batted reasons for and against the move, hours later Ellen finally consented.

"Well….maybe I'll give it a try," she said.

Gwen grabbed her tightly and held on, "Thank you so much," she whispered.

Rick hesitated giving his opinion initially, but finally joined in as they talked about their move to New York. He knew both mother and daughter had to settle this one on their own and wanted to support whatever the outcome might be. Meanwhile, he proudly showcased his best photographs of Gwen.

"These are the ones she wouldn't cooperate," he said, pointing to her pouting mouth.

Ellen laughed, "It's hard to believe how beautiful she looks, pouty face and all." As they talked, she was starting to adjust to the idea of moving, as excitement about it slowly crept its way in.

A few hours later, Gwen noticed the subtle change in Ellen's mood as the gaiety in the room gradually subsided. She eased up beside her and reached for her hands, "You're not having second thoughts are you?" she asked.

It was Ellen's next comment that drew the life out of the room.

"Mother," Gwen exclaimed, "You haven't been in touch with Rose in over a week?"

"I've tried to talk to her, but she's not answering any of my calls and only a few of my texts," she replied.

"What about her roommate? Have you contacted her?" Gwen asked.

"The young lady had to move back home last month. Rose told me she was looking for a new one the last we talked."

"Exactly when was the last time you spoke with Rose?" Gwen asked, trying to suppress her mounting fears.

"It was Monday morning, two weeks ago."

"Two weeks ago! Mother, why didn't you tell me?"

"I didn't want to bother you any more than I already have Gwen. I really am sorry."

"What about the bookstore where she works? Have you tried there?"

"I did call them," Ellen said. "They told me she had a few vacation days and wasn't expected to be back until next week, and that calmed me down somewhat. Now, I'm just ready to hear her voice."

"Hey, you know your moody daughter," Gwen said. "She likes to be left alone sometimes. Maybe this is one of those infamous spells of hers. She'll call soon." It was her way of sounding upbeat while camouflaging her dwindling hopes.

"That's why I didn't want to tell you until now," Ellen said. "She has done me this way before, only to call right when I was about to go into that panicky mother mode. This time I must admit, I feel strange about it all. I can't explain why, but I really do need to speak with her. I hated to be a pest, but I called the school's administration several times," she confessed.   "In fact, I'm waiting on them to phone back to let me know if she's attending classes."

"It will be okay," Gwen said, pacing the floor.

Later that afternoon, the administrative assistant from Rose's school finally contacted them.

"Mrs. Andrews, I'm afraid I'm not going to be able to give you any more information than before," the assistant said. "Some of her professors have over ninety students in their classes and it's a little difficult for them to recall specific faces. The good news is, she did take her final exams. We're sending someone back to her apartment to see if we can't find her there," he said. "Listen, we have concerned parents calling all the time, Mrs. Andrews and we've always found our student."

She eased the phone back into its cradle and looked up at Gwen. "I'm going to New York," she said. "I need to find Rose."

Rick took charge of all the flight arrangements. "I'm sorry the plane is leaving so early," he said, handing her the itinerary. "It should get you there in plenty of time to search for her, though." He felt uncomfortable saying those words.

"Thanks, Rick," Ellen said, "but the earlier the better. I just need to know if she is okay."

They stayed overnight in order to drive her to the airport the next morning. While Rick bunked out on the den's couch, Gwen felt at home again in her old bedroom.

When Ellen awakened at four a.m., the old house creaked as if complaining about being prematurely disturbed. She placed her feet on the cool, hard-wood floor and immediately reached onto the night stand for her medication. She popped two of the anti-nausea pills in her mouth and downed them both with a gulp from her filtered water. After the warm shower, her stomach settled as she slipped into the printed dress she laid out for the trip. She listened as Gwen stirred around the kitchen, a sound she hadn't heard in quite some time. Soon, they were all headed for the airport.

Once on board, Ellen leaned back with her seatbelt fastened. She tried to relax, but the flight seemed endless. Her nausea had returned and was essentially nonstop by now. She attributed some of it to the news she'd received from the school's administration right before they left. They still weren't able to locate Rose. The manager was helpful and allowed the university's representatives to look around her apartment, but they didn't see anything unusual. She was glad the campus police were now involved.

Ellen closed her eyes until the announcement overhead aroused her. "Ladies and gentlemen, place your seat in its upright position and put your tray tables away," the stewardess crackled into the speaker.

After landing, Ellen followed the signs to the baggage claim. There she saw a tall, lanky kid holding a sign with her name on it.

She walked up to the young man, "Hi, I'm Ellen Andrews," she said.

"Hello, I'm Bill. I was sent by administration to pick you up."

She looked at him hopeful, "Do you know whether or not they've found Rose?" she asked.

"I'm sorry. I wish I could tell you they have. Don't worry, they will find her. Sometimes I go days without phoning home. When my parents finally get hold of me, my dad acts as if he wants to kill me."

"Can you take me to her apartment, Bill? Perhaps I'll find something that will lead me to where my daughter is."

Bill tried to make light conversation, but realized Ellen just wasn't in the mood. Most of the way they drove along in silence.

The manager opened the door to Rose's apartment and once inside, Ellen stood in the middle of the room taking it all in. Spotting the stereo she had given her for Christmas, she eased the CD into its pocket. Soon the melodious voice of Whitney Houston filled the air. The apartment was meticulous and extremely neat, almost as if someone had just tidied it up. A strong scent of bleach penetrated the air.

The ringing phone interrupted her thoughts. "No, I haven't found her Gwen. I promise to call the moment I get more information."

As soon as she hung up, she buried her face in her hands and wept. She wanted to be strong, but there were too many trials, too much pressure. "Oh God, where is my baby," she cried out to Him. She fell across the bed and laid there until sunset. It may have been her body or mind's way of protecting her, but she slept for hours. The voice on the answering machine caused her to stir. It was someone leaving Rose a message.

"Hey," the young lady said. "Call me as soon as you get this message. I didn't see you in class and got a little worried. Bye."

Ellen rubbed her pounding head. As she turned, placing both feet on the floor, she spotted an object sticking out between the nightstand and bed. She reached in and pulled it out. It was Rose's journal. She hated violating her daughter's privacy, but knew she had no other choice as she flipped page after page.

"It should be okay, but it seems as if my whole life is a joke," Rose wrote. "The only thing that seems to control the depression is William. He makes me happy. I really do love him, but I don't know if that's enough. I'll probably end up losing him too."

"William. Who was that? Rose never mentioned anything about a man in her life," Ellen thought. She picked up the phone and dialed the number on the card the apartment manager had given her. It was the officer assigned to the case. Once she explained to him what she'd found, she was suddenly no match for the overwhelming weakness that seized her body. She dialed 911.

Gwen was scheduled for the next flight out when the hospital phoned about her mother. As she gathered her things, she toyed with the thought of calling Clara. Each time she called her, she always vowed it would be the last. She was finding it extremely difficult to deal with the level of cruelty Clara now spewed out. This time, however, was different. She thought she deserved to know their sister was missing. Against her better judgment, she phoned.

The moment she heard the tone of her voice, she knew she'd made a mistake.

"Listen Clara, your sister is missing for heaven's sake," Gwen tried explaining. She did everything she could to maintain the little composure she had left.

"Listen Gwen," Clara yelled. "If Rose turns up dead, that would be alright by me. If that happened to you, I wouldn't mourn at all. Then all of you would be out of my life. Forever," she screamed.

Reminiscent of their college days, she held the phone listening only to the dial tone. Gwen knew at that moment, she would never speak or want to see her sister again.

If they didn't find Rose, the only real family she would end up with was her mother and Rick. The thought of it made her heart ache. She wasn't going to lose someone that meant the world to her—the one she could talk to about anything. Life was changing so fast and she had a lot to tell Rose. She recently met with the Turner Agency's execs and the contract they offered her was a lucrative one. Rick's contract was equally rewarding. After graduation they were going to live in New York where they intended to marry.

"Are you okay?" Rick asked. He knew that, 'I can handle it' look upon her face. "I know you will find Rose," he said.

"I know, but I still wish we knew where she was and what she's doing," she said. As she grabbed her purse, securing the airline ticket inside, she reached for the ringing phone.

"Hello."

"Is this Rose Andrews' sister?"

"Yes, it is."

"Are you coming to New York any time soon?"

"Who is this?" Gwen cried out.

"When you get there ask William if he knows where Rose is."

The phone went dead.

Chapter 9

Separation Times

Clara called the headmaster and told him she wouldn't be in again today. Her stomach virus wasn't getting any better. She thought it was best to make a doctor's appointment for later that afternoon.

As the doctor examined her, she stiffened when he asked about her last menstrual cycle. She couldn't believe she'd missed that. Her cycles were always irregular but thought it would be on its way. It wasn't. She was eight weeks pregnant.

Clara wouldn't let herself become too excited about the news until she spoke with Eric. They hadn't planned or discussed having a baby and she didn't know what his reaction would be. She called him the moment she got inside the car. When she took a deep breath in and told him the news, he shouted so loudly she almost dropped the phone. They were now both ecstatic about the pregnancy.

Months later the ultrasound confirmed they were having twin girls. She immediately began planning her daughters' futures—where they would attend school and who they would be friends with. The list went on and on. One major decision she stood firm on was that her daughters would not have any contact with her side of the family. Clara debated even telling her mother about being pregnant. She didn't want to give her any excuse to come and visit.

The last time they had spoken, she told her she was moving to New York with Gwen and her fiancé. It thrilled her. That would finally put the geographical distance between them she longed for. She had come to the conclusion this would be the year all ties and communication with her family would be severed. Rose had already been written off, but her mother was just so persistent. Then, there was Gwen. She'd called the other day about her marriage to some guy she had never heard of and had no intentions of meeting, and something about Rose being missing. Whatever she was talking about was of no concern to her. They were all beneath her and would never be around to spoil things for her ever again. Life as a Gordon was all that she ever wanted and needed.

The moment Eric found out about the pregnancy, he wouldn't allow her to do the simplest of household chores. Several months later, they decided it was best for her to go on an early maternity leave and focus on preparing for the birth of their children. They had also purchased their first home. All of this took the majority of the savings they had acquired, but Clara was okay with that. She knew her husband. He would easily replace it all.

The spring of the year was fast approaching and she felt the tremendous load of carrying two babies. One more month to go and nothing about this stage of her pregnancy was exciting. Eric had done everything in his power to cheer her up, but her expanding figure left her miserable.

"Mom just called," Eric said. "They want us over for dinner."

She wanted to stay home but dared not complain, es-pecially when it came to his parents. She had overheard Eric's dad discussing his will the other day and definitely didn't want to interfere with any of those decisions.

They were ready to leave within an hour.

"Here, let me help you," Eric said, swinging the door open to the Range Rover. Gripping her firmly under the elbow, she slowly and awkwardly inched her way out. Placing one hand on her back and the other on her stomach for support, she toddled along.

SURPRISE! It seemed the entire house shook, caus-ing her to throw her hand onto her chest.   There were helium-filled pink and white balloons floating every-where—making for a festive scene. The fresh pink and white flowers trimmed in tons of greenery, towered in tall crystal vases. They made beautiful centerpieces for each of the large decorative tables. The pastel pink table cloths with the patterned-embellished runners made the entire place come alive.

Clara was elated to see so many of her sorority sis-ters, but it was only when Marty jumped out that she screamed. Her old crew immediately broke into their signature song and dance while her co-workers stood in amazement as she attempted the little shuffle even with her very large stomach. The room was filled with laughter and gaiety, the atmosphere primed for a really good time.

Clara opened gift after gift and it soon became appar-ent that a silent competition had begun among her friends. They were always an aggressive group and it seemed as time passed, nothing had changed. It was obvious they were trying to outdo each other, and as a result of their generosity she received everything twin girls could imagine... even down to the tiny 14 carat gold spoon and plate sets.

When she sat back and scanned the room, a comforting feeling found its way into her heart. All that she had been working for was now in place, and the shower was just another example of how successful she had become. She knew her daughters would be exposed to only the best and she had single handedly made that happened.

One thing she couldn't help but notice, however, was her sister-in-law sitting in the back of the room very much disengaged from the rest of the crowd. It was the scowl on her face that caused Clara the most delight. She knew Miriam never accepted her even when she initially tried to befriend her. No matter how nice she had been, nothing seemed to work. When she accidentally discovered Miriam trying to find out about her family, she immediately went into action—drawing up a plan. It was a brilliant one...an idea she had to admit was the best she'd ever conceived. The scheme was to slowly and systematically begin excluding Miriam from her very own family. When she had dinner parties or birthday gatherings, she would conveniently leave her off the guest list. Using the excuse, "I thought you invited them, Eric." She would apologize profusely about it for the rest of the week. The last party she had, she purposefully held it on the date she knew Miriam and Ted were out of town. On the other hand, whenever they invited them over, she would always have some kind of 'pregnancy pain' that kept them from going. "Miriam didn't know who she was dealing with," she thought. "If she could take Gwen on, clearly, this sister-in-law of hers was no match." As their eyes met, Clara's smile widened.

***

Clara had no idea Miriam was nauseous for several reasons. She'd just discovered she was pregnant again and had absolutely no success in getting her new sister-in-law out of their lives. She found the thought of Clara having not only one child but two by her brother—repulsive.

Chapter 10

Expanding Times

Clara went into labor the day before her due date.

"I can't do it. I can't do it anymore. I'm too tired—Eric please help me," she cried. She grabbed the side rails tightly and pushed until her chin touched her chest.

Eric placed the cool towel on the back of her neck. The tiny, red spider veins in both eyes now evident, she only had a second before the urge to bear down swept over her again. He wiped away the sweat. "You can do this. It's almost over."

"No, I can't. Help me Eric, please."

"I'm right here, Clara. Come on, we will do it together. PU-U-U-SH."

"Ugghhhhhhh," she screamed. Two more pushes and out came another beautiful, healthy baby girl.

"Identical twin girls, Clara, you have made me the happiest man in the world." He watched as the nurses cleaned and swaddled the babies in the warm bassinet.

"They both have all of their fingers and toes mommy," Eric said, in his childlike voice, admiring his screaming babies.

"Did I hear you say twin girls," Eric's dad said, pushing through the door. To Clara's utter surprise, Miriam walked in with her parents glancing at the babies as she sat.

Despite all that she had gone through, Clara couldn't resist. "Dad," she said, taking in a deep breath, "What do you think about having the first set of twin, grand-daughters in the family? That must make them real special."

"Indeed it does," he said, gazing down lovingly at the girls. "Indeed it does."

***

Miriam could not believe her parent's reactions. Her mother was so busy preparing Eric's place for the arrival of the twins, she rarely acknowledged her pregnancy. Once the babies came home, they officially became the doting grandparents they longed to be. Her mother even stayed overnight as she claimed—"To make sure Clara got her rest and the twins were well cared for." She knew the frills that came along with having twins was exactly what she lived for. She just couldn't help it. Dainty girls seemed to mesmerize Gloria Jean Gordon. It was no secret her mother hadn't carried on like that over her son. For Miriam, the aggravating Clara situation had escalated to a new height.

Ted reached out to her as she paced back and forth on their bedroom floor, "Now, don't go getting upset again," he said.

"I don't understand my family anymore," she said, moving away from him. "That girl is trying to take over and no one seems to care!"

"Don't you think you're over reacting?" He sighed. "This melodrama surrounding Clara is going a little bit far, Miriam." In his opinion, which he had successfully hidden from her, the only reason she was this upset— someone else seemed to be getting a little more attention than she was for a change. He needed her to get over it.

"Can't you see what she's doing to our family or has she beguiled you too," Miriam said, waving her fingers at him.

"Take it easy, now. So, she didn't show up for a few of our outings. The girl was pregnant with twins for goodness sakes!"

"No, I will not take it easy! I don't like her and even more, I do not want her in this family!"

"I think that might be a little too late," Ted said. "After all, she is married to your brother and the last I recall, that does make her your sister-in-law."

"Don't be smart, I know who and what she is."

"Come on," he said, massaging her shoulders. "I'm just trying to get you to see it in a different light, that's all."

She reached up, held onto his hand, and leaned her head against him.

"Hey, what is this all about?" he asked. He searched her eyes and instantly knew it wasn't the usual brattish behavior he had grown accustomed to. Something else was bothering his wife. "What is it about Clara that has you this upset, Miriam?" he asked, softly.

"Nothing about her is real, Ted. Every time I'm around her I get this strange feeling. I can't explain it, but something about her makes me really nervous. It might be how Eric and my parents are responding I suppose that has me so concerned. I don't know… but what I do know is I have never seen them act this way before. She looked up at him… "It has nothing to do with me being jealous, either. I know that's what you're thinking. It's bigger than that."

She turned, dropped her head, and proceeded out of the room.

She sat in the cozy nook adjacent to their bedroom and curled up in her favorite glider. As she swayed back and forth, she thought of all the drama Clara had caused the short time she'd been married to Eric. She was making it virtually impossible for her to have any sort of relationship with her brother and if that wasn't bad enough, all her parents ever talked about anymore was Eric, his wife and the twins. Her heart nearly exploded the day her father casually waltzed in the room and announced... "I have talked it over with mom and we are going to change our wills." Something about making sure all the grandchildren were well cared for— especially for their education. It was the final straw and after that, she knew she had to move quickly. After weighing her options, she decided it was best to confide in her mother to get her take on it all.

"I can't believe you are saying that to me," was her mother's immediate response. It must have taken her completely off guard because she instantly burst into tears—something she had not seen her mother do in a very long time.

"How could you possibly think we are not showing Little Teddy enough attention?" she said. "Miriam Johnson, you have to snap out of whatever this is that's making you feel this way. Your sister-in-law has been nothing but a wonderful asset to our family. I think this pregnancy of yours has something to do with how emotional you've been lately, darling. I hope you'll start feeling better soon," she said, reaching out to hug her.

"Stop it momma, just stop it. I don't need your hugs or your well wishes. I need you to listen!" Miriam snapped.

"No, you stop it Miriam Elaine Johnson. I will not entertain another second of this silly conversation. You are my only daughter and Little Teddy is my only grandson. I love you both with all my heart, and I won't have you thinking anything less." She sniffed as she pulled out the tiny white handkerchief she always tucked neatly inside her top. She meticulously unfolded it and dabbed her eyes.

"Well, that didn't work," Miriam thought. Clara was slowly but surely taking over her family and it seemed there was nothing she could do about it. Clara and her parents were getting along better than ever and no, it was not her imagination—her father was smitten by those two beautiful granddaughters of his.

Chapter 11

Searching Times

"It will be just a little stick Mrs. Andrews," the nurse said, as the blood squirted into the narrow purple top tube. When she finished drawing her labs, increased the IV fluids, and hung a bolus of potassium, she hurried out of the room.

Ellen glanced up at the monitor watching the line displaying her heart beat methodically spike to the rhythm of a drum. The oxygen rested gently underneath her nostrils flowing at two liters—causing the pulse oximetry to register at ninety-nine percent. The nurse monitored her vital signs frequently. They had been treating her in the hospital's observation unit for over twelve hours.

"Your electrolytes are completely out of balance, Mrs. Andrews," Dr. Span said, approaching her bed. "We need to admit you for a couple of days or at least until your blood work stabilizes."

"I'm sorry, Dr. Span, that's impossible. I will stay until this IV finishes but not a minute longer. I need to find my daughter."

The doctor listened intently as she told her why she had come to New York in the first place.

"Do you have any other family that could help?" she asked. "At least until we get you feeling better."

"I do and they should be getting here momentarily."

"We'll repeat your labs once the IV finishes. Hopefully by then, your family will have arrived."

Several hours later, Gwen came rushing into the room. "Hey you... I'm beginning to think I can't leave you alone for one second anymore," she said.

"Oh my goodness, thank you Lord, perfect timing," Ellen said, motioning to Dr. Span. "This is my daughter."

Kissing her mom on the cheek, Gwen looked over at the doctor, "How's the patient doing? I hope she's not giving you too difficult a time," she said, snuggling close to her mother. "I got here as fast as I could."

"Honey, I've got to get out of this place and help find Rose," Ellen tried pleading.

Gwen closed her eyes long enough to collect her thoughts. "Listen mother, I can't afford to lose you too," she whispered. "I'm going to find Rose. The campus police think they have a few leads. All I need for you to do is exactly what the doctor says."

Dr. Span shook Gwen's hand, "I'm glad you're here," she said. "I will need to admit your mother and it looks as if you're the only person that can convince her to stay. I'm afraid if she leaves without the proper care, she will end up back here anyway."

"You hear that. That's it, you're staying," Gwen said.

After an hour and a half of negotiating, Ellen was finally checked-in as an inpatient.

Settling into a private room, Gwen knew time was working against her. She had to follow up on the only lead she had been given. William. She had no last name and she didn't know if he was even a student at NYU, but was determined to find him. She felt the best way to start her search was at the apartment complex Rose lived in.

Gwen ran down the long hospital corridor, tore through the revolving doors, and hailed a cab.

The campus was formidable and the grounds seemed endless. She was relieved Rose's apartment was in a pretty good part of town. She watched as a continuous stream of students walked by her building. "Any one of them could be William," she thought. She approached a few with backpacks as they hurried along and showed them Rose's picture. Never slowing down, they would either shake their heads or wave her away. She walked over to the manager's office in the apartment complex and introduced herself. While they were nice and extremely cooperative, they still didn't have any more information.

She wandered around and was just about to call it a day when she noticed a young woman walk up to the apartment next to Rose's. Before she could unlock the door, she quickly approached her, "Excuse me," she said. "Would you happen to know the young lady that lives in this apartment?"

"Yeah, I've seen her a couple of times," she said, turning the key and releasing the door. Just about to step inside, Gwen propped her arm up against it. "Wait, can you please help me?" An unexpected tiredness washed over her. She ignored the unwelcomed guest and pushed forward. "My sister lives here and I need to find her," she said, holding up Rose's picture.

The young girl glanced at it, "Like I said, I've seen her a few times but I don't know if I can be of any help. We were both pretty busy." She stepped inside the apartment and faced Gwen. "Sorry."

"When was the last time you saw her may I ask? Please try and remember."

"It's been a while."

"You live next door and you can't give me any more information than, 'it's been a while'?" Gwen knew it was becoming next to impossible to tame that razor sharp tongue of hers threatening to shred this poor girl into pieces.

"I don't want to get involved," the young lady said. "I saw the police and …no….it's none of my business," she said, slowly easing the door closed.

Gwen placed her foot inside and with one hand pushed the door back open. She leaned closer and found the eyes that wanted to avoid her. "If you can't seem to tell me any more than that, maybe I'll get the police involved to ask you these questions. They are experts at getting the kind of information I need."

"Wait a minute, Gwen now don't go getting all upset. I'm sure you will find Rose. She will probably show up any day now."

Gwen froze. "How do you know my name? I never told you my name."

It was that 'deer in the headlight look' from the girl next door that told the rest of the story.

"I truly didn't want to get mixed up in any of this," the young woman said. "I was just trying to be neighborly, that's all."

Gwen knew she recognized her voice. It was the one she heard right before leaving for the airport.

"I'm trying to find my sister," Gwen said, lifting her head to keep the tears in place. "Will you please help me?"

The young lady chewed on the corner of her lip and quickly glanced over Gwen's shoulder. She breathed in deeply, "Okay, why don't we start all over?" she said, as she slowly reached out her hand. "I'm Whitney."

"Hi Whitney, I'm Gwen," she said grasping her hand. She shook it and held on for a brief moment. "I need your help."

"Come on in, I think I may have a little more information for you."

Please promise me you will keep me out of this as much as possible. I just want to graduate," she said, handing Gwen a cup of the herbal tea she made. She sat down in the chair facing her. "You see, I try and stay as far away from cops as possible. I got off to a rough start my teenage years, and had horrible run-ins with 'em. My record isn't the best, but….when I was given a second chance to get things straight, I vowed I would never find myself on their bad side again."

Those words caused Gwen to stiffen.

Whitney paused a moment and then continued, "I got used to seeing Rose and William at the Jazzspel club on Wednesday nights. We all kind of started hanging out there and every now and then would go to the corner grill for sandwiches. We all knew William was very protective of Rose, sometimes, a little too protective if you know what I mean? The last time I saw them, I waved as she and William were going inside her apartment. It just wasn't her typical greeting. A kind of half wave, if that makes sense. The next moment I heard a lot of commotion going on over there. I couldn't make out all that was being said, but I know I clearly heard Rose scream." She paused and looked at Gwen, "She yelled, 'no William, please stop.' Anyway, a few days later she was nowhere to be found and the cops were at her door."

Whitney walked over to the window, looking out she continued, "When I saw the cops I just didn't want any trouble. I noticed the lady that came and was later taken away by ambulance. I assumed it was Rose's mother. I thought perhaps she had received some horrible news so I figured I had to help in some other kind of way. I gave the clerk in the manager's office a few bucks for any contact information on Rose's family. He gave me your name and number—and—well, you know the rest."

"Whitney."

"Yes."

"Do you know where I can find this William?"

"Yes I do."

***

Even as they discussed him, William bit his thumb nail until it bled. How could he have gotten himself mixed up in something like this? He was a good kid, an excellent student and had never been in trouble a day in his life. Growing up, they had labeled him the shy, nerdy-church boy. By the time he got to college he actually liked being called that. His time at NYU had been unremarkable until he met Rose. She was smart, pretty and very much the type of girl he would like to date. There was just one problem—dating. It was such unfamiliar territory he almost believed he'd never go on one again. He had only dated two girls in his whole life. Well, actually, one. The other date's friends had actually bet her she wouldn't go out with him, but she did it to prove them wrong. After that, she dared him to ever call her again.

Then there was Debra whom they'd labeled the shy, nerdy-church girl. They spent a lot of time together, but never even held hands. When both of them received scholarships to college, she went one way and he the other. They tweeted and sometimes kept up with each other on Facebook, but he had not heard from her in quite some time.

It was as if heaven was on his side when Rose entered his life. He noticed her the moment she walked into his Bio-Chemistry class. He wanted to say something to her, but never mustered up the nerve. Then one day he knew God had given him a sign that it was okay to approach her.

They took a very difficult exam and all the students complained about not doing well. When the professor wrote down the number of A's, there were only two. There were a few B's, quite a number of C's, D's and even F's. He watched closely when the professor handed Rose her test. She tried to cover it up, but he'd seen the *A*.

He knew he had the other.

After class, he garnered every ounce of courage he could to say something to her.

"Hi, I'm William."

"Hi," she said.

"Uh, that test was pretty hard, huh?" he said.

"Yeah."

That was the extent of their first conversation. He planned to never say anything else to her. By now he was sure she thought him to be some kind of creepy, nerdy-weirdo. Then it happened, he could have sworn she glanced at him. Thinking it too good to be true, he dismissed the notion. Then, there was no denying it.

While it was only a glance by god, she had, she looked at him, and he knew that was his second sign.

So, he tried it again—saying something a little more meaningful than before. He pushed aside the shyness that had crippled him throughout the years.

"Hey, uh, what do you think Dr. Brown will test us on next week?" He couldn't believe it. If there was a hole in the floor, he would have eased right through it. He'd never be able to explain why his brain conjured up such a lame line.

To his surprise, however, Rose opened her book and showed him the material she thought would be on the exam.

"If he tests me on antiholomorphic functions, I'm toast," she said. "I don't have a clue on how to properly compare holomorphic to antiholmorphic domains."

All William heard was, *wah...wah...wah...wah....* His mind was still on the fact that she was actually talking to him.

"Perhaps you could help me with that. Would you like to meet at the library to study before the next exam?" she asked shyly.

It blew him away so, much so, he stumbled to press out the next few words. "Yeah, that, uh, might work."

"Was he ever going to think of anything more original to say," he chastised himself?

When it finally came time for them to meet he remembered being so nervous, he was nauseous most of the day.

Walking up to the large library table, he was greeted with a pleasant yet much needed surprise. Rose's demeanor was not only inviting and kind, her warm smile essentially bottled up his years of shyness and floated them all away. She was engaging and it helped him to just be himself. In fact, they talked about everything other than what originally brought them to the library. With only one hour left before the library closed, they reviewed the material for the examination. He didn't have to spend a lot of time explaining, she readily grasped the concepts.

"How did you do," he asked her the following day.

"No, you first," she said, smiling.

"Okay, okay. I got an *A*."

"Me, too!" she exclaimed.

It was the beginning of a great friendship and they studied together from that point on. William knew he was falling in love with Rose but resolved they would only be friends. The shyness that handicapped him for years kept him from taking it any further.

Then one day the miraculous happened again. They agreed to meet at the movies after their evening class. During the scene when the camera suddenly brought the killer into view right behind the victim, ready to attack, Rose jumped and buried her head into his shoulder. With that one move, he held her throughout the rest of the film.

William knew he had never met anyone with a heart as good as Rose's. As their friendship grew, so did the sharing of intimate details about their lives. Apparently, she had a sister that impacted her life deeply. He was no psychologist, but the level of abuse and disrespect she received at her hands left Rose permanently scarred. Her sister's attacks seemed vicious from Rose's account and he wondered if people like that didn't have some underlying mental problem. "How could your own flesh and blood treat you that way?" he thought.

As they spent more time together, he could tell something else was bothering his friend. He tried to dismiss it, hoping it would eventually go away. The one day he showed up at her apartment, he could not avoid the noticeable changes inside. The two-bed room flat, had dishes piled up, books strewn about and clothes scattered all over the place. While chaos was all around, Rose was oblivious to it all. When he found himself studying alongside her most of the day, void of their usual hearty conversation, he got up to leave. She looked up at him and with a deep sadness in her eyes, waved good-bye.

He researched her symptoms in the library until he'd pieced together a diagnosis. Rose was depressed and possibly suicidal. She had gone into a downward spiral right before his eyes. The changes started immediately after her sister called—something about cutting off all ties and some other extremely hurtful remarks.

He tried everything to get her to snap out of it but nothing seemed to work. "Don't worry about what your sister said, your life is wonderful and will continue to be, even if she's no longer a part of it."

It infuriated him to think she would do that to someone as kind as Rose.

The following day when Rose didn't show up for class, he was so worried he couldn't concentrate on what his professor taught. Trying not to panic, as soon as his class was over, he dashed out of the building. Peddling his bike harder than he could remember, he arrived at her door in record time. The sweat on his hand made handling the key next to impossible. Drying it on his pant leg, he placed the slippery metal inside the lock. As soon as he opened the door, he spotted her slumped over the table with an empty pill bottle on its side.

His slow-motion movements seemed to encase him inside an invisible pool of quicksand. It caused him to struggle to get to her as fast as he wanted to.

"NO! ROSE," he cried. It was too late as she slid like gel into his arms. He shook her violently and began CPR.

***

Gwen stood outside William's apartment, hesitant to go up to it. She knew this was a crucial moment and didn't want her fragile emotions to override common sense. She watched the door—the one she knew could easily harbor a predator or an innocent man inside. No one came out or entered as she stood there. She listened to her intuition and decided talking with William would have to wait. Her nerves were too tenuous and besides, it was past time to check on her mother. She wanted to make sure she wasn't trying to leave like before. She tore herself away and took a taxi back to N.Y. General. She arrived just in time too. Dr. Span was at her mother's bedside explaining how she couldn't promise she would only be there one more night.

Gwen interrupted, "Mother, let's take it one day at a time, please," she begged.

"No, Gwen, I need to go and find Rose."

"I know the person she was last seen with. I'm supposed to meet him tomorrow," Gwen said, hopeful that would convince her.

"Gwen, I can't—I won't."

"Yes, you can mother…one more day."

"Okay, okay, but first thing in the morning, I want out of here," Ellen said.

"No promises but we'll do our best," the doctor said, walking away.

Gwen slept on the narrow pull out bed in her mother's hospital room. The sun's orange, tangerine hue barely peeked over the horizon as she quietly eased through the door the following morning. She headed for William's apartment.

She didn't go up to the dark apartment right away. Fifteen minutes later, when a light came on, she knocked. She was about to bang on it a second time when he opened the door.

"Hi, I'm Gwen Andrews and I was wondering if I could speak with you for a moment. I'm looking for my sister Rose Andrews.   May I come in?"

William hesitated, "Uh, sure." He was surprised to see her. He knew Rose's mother was here, but had no idea her sister had come as well.

Stepping inside, she quickly scanned the room.

"Let me get right to the point, William." She turned facing him, "My sister is missing, and I'm here to find her."

"I heard about that, her missing and all. I wish I could help but I haven't seen Rose lately."

As Gwen paced back and forth, she pressed hard against her temper. He was her only lead and she didn't want to frighten him away.

"When did you see her last?" she asked, having forced herself into a much calmer state.

"It's been a couple of weeks and she looked fine. I'm sure you will find her. Now, if you don't mind, I need to get dressed. I have a class to get to."

"Wrong response," she thought.   She had to stall him, to look around and see if there was anything there that could connect him to Rose.

She couldn't. She knew then it was a job for the police.

"Let me know if you run into her, please. Here's my number," she said, jotting it down. Walking away, she turned back, "Call me with anything you may hear. Anything." At that moment, she stared into his eyes. She knew then he was hiding something.

The cab ride back to the hospital was short, even with the traffic. She wasn't prepared to face her mother. She had spoken to her only lead and there was still no Rose.

As soon as she stepped out of the taxi, she froze. A book of poems by Maya Angelou flashed before her. Resting on the corner of the counter in William's apartment—was that the book? A piece of literature Rose was never without, said it brought her great peace. Had it all been her imagination or was her mind playing tricks out of desperation to find her sister? Gwen knew if she saw the book again, she would be able to recognize it. A piece of the cover's corner was missing.

"Quick, take me back," she told the driver. "Go back to the place we just left. Hurry." As they sped off, she thought, "By the time William would have showered and dressed, she should have just enough time to get there."

They arrived in record time as she skirted up the walk and knocked on the door. No answer. She stood there and waited. Punching anger back in its face, she knocked harder, pounding over and over against it.

William opened the door, swinging his backpack onto his shoulder, glaring. "Did you forget something?" he asked. She could tell he was annoyed, but it didn't bother her. She had one goal and one goal only, and that was to find her sister.

"No, I thought of something I needed to …" She coughed… "ask you.   Do you remember…" she coughed again. "Do you…" cough… "Excuse me, but may I get some water?" she asked, clearing her throat.

William sighed as he ambled over to the sink.

She followed him close behind quickly skimming the small room. It took all of thirty seconds, but there was no book.

"Okay, now what did you want?" William asked, handing her the plastic glass filled with tap water.

Holding up her finger, she downed it all. "Whew, that really helped," she said, giving him back the empty cup. "I know you are in a hurry, but I wanted to ask if you took any classes with Rose. Administration has made plans for me to speak with a few of her professors and I thought perhaps you would know the best ones to talk to."

"Not really, I don't know many of Rose's teachers," he answered quickly.

"Well, it was a shot, I thought maybe you did." She knew she couldn't leave until she searched everywhere in that apartment. "May I use your bathroom? The water and all…I've been traveling quite a bit you know," she said, squirming.

He sighed hard.

She ignored it.

Reluctantly, he led her to the bathroom.

Locking the door, she leaned against it. 'Think', she challenged herself. She drew in two long, cleansing breaths. She knew full well satisfaction would elude her if she didn't search everywhere for the book. Flushing the toilet, pretending to have used it, she slowly cracked open the door. Great…he hadn't heard as he stood gazing out the window. She eased through the small opening like a flitting dragon fly and darted into the bedroom. She immediately spotted a paperback book turned on its face, resting on the corner of the dresser. In a flash, she scooped it up. It was the book of poems by Maya Angelou and it had a corner piece of the cover missing.

"What are you doing?" William asked.

She jumped, her eyes large and wide—heart beating like a ticking bomb. She hadn't seen him come in.

"NO, the question is, what are you doing?" She opened the cover and there it was in bold letters, ROSE ANDREWS. "This is Rose's book, William," she said.

"I know whose it is. She let me borrow it, okay? Now, you need to leave!"

"No, sir!" She'd lost control again and this time she didn't try reeling in her volatile emotions. "Rose wouldn't let anyone borrow this book. It has never been out of her possession."

"How do you know what Rose would do?" he pushed back.

"I would know because I am her sister. Listen mister, when was the last time you've seen her?" she yelled.

"Please leave," William said, adjusting his backpack. He seemed even taller than his 6'2" thin frame, as he hovered over her.

She didn't care, and with the bite from her own 5'9" frame, she challenged him back. "I will leave William, but I'm only going to wait outside your apartment until the police arrive. You'd better start talking man."

William desperately tried to hide the tremor that caused his hands to shake. It was true he was nervous in part because she was seriously invading his space—but this was the sister that caused Rose to end up in the shelter for abused women in the first place. Rose told him in great detail the harsh treatment wielded at the ruthless hands of this heartless sister of hers. Even when she called for a little bit of financial assistance, she flat-out rejected her. He wasn't about to let her in on anything. He knew Rose's mother was in town and that was the only person he was willing to talk to. Not only was he going to tell her mother about Rose's plight, he was also going to share with her why she was struggling so—this lady standing before him was at the heart of most of it. The problem was, her mother seemed to have disappeared. He stopped by Rose's apartment to share with her what happened but she wasn't there.

Now the campus police were involved, and that made him nervous. Today, he knew he would need to tell Rose's mother where she was or else go ahead and alert the cops.

"I'm waiting," Gwen said. "I need an answer. When was the last time you saw my sister, William?"

"I told you and I will tell the police, Rose and I are friends and that's it. I know you're upset, but it's not going to do any good accusing me of knowing where she is."

Gwen stood holding the book tightly to her chest, tears flooding her eyes. She whispered, "I will not lose another sister. Tell me what you know."

William eyes penetrated through her. He didn't believe a word coming out of her mouth. "I've already told you all that I'm going to, so please, I have to go."

She stomped towards the door, "I'm sorry if I bothered you," she said, her cheeks now flushed. "I need to find Rose. My mother and I have come a long way and we won't go back without her."

"Good luck," he said, closing the door.

At her lowest point, Rose had confided in him that she never wanted to see or talk to this girl again and he was going to make sure that happened. "Why was she acting so concerned now? Boy, did she pour on the theatrics," he thought. "She did not want to lose another sister. Well, she should have taken better care of the one she had when she was blessed with the opportunity." He knew it was time to find Rose's mother and planned on stopping by the apartment again after his first class ended.

He tried giving Gwen ample time to leave before opening the door. He cracked it slightly and looked up and down the walk. Now, nowhere in sight, he glanced at his watch. He had exactly ten minutes before his class began. Dashing outside, he grabbed the lock on his bike when suddenly he replayed the words—another sister. He stopped fumbling with the chain and thought to himself, "She did say that!" Why had he assumed this was the sister that had abused her? Something inside began to scream, "Those were real tears." He rushed back into his apartment and headed straight for the trash. Grabbing the crumpled paper he'd tossed inside, he smoothed it out and punched in the number she'd written down.

"Hello, uh, Gwen, this is William. I know we left on a bad note just a minute ago, but I need to ask you a question if that's okay." He didn't give her time to answer. "Is your other sister here too?"

"No, she won't be joining us. Now, what is this all about William?"

So, she did have another sister. His pulse quickened as he pressed further.

"One more question, please…I must know. Was Rose close to that sister or did she prefer not being around her?"

"No, she wasn't close to her and yes we would all rather eat soap than to be near her. Now, why all the questions! Do you know where Rose is?"

He ran his hands over his head several times, "Can you hurry back?" he pleaded, now very much regretting all that he had assumed. "I think we need to talk."

In less than twenty minutes, William held the door open as Gwen raced up the walk.

"I didn't know," he said, as she rushed in. "I didn't know Rose had two sisters—or I must have forgotten. I don't know why I thought…"

"Hey, calm down," Gwen said. She could care less what William was fumbling on about. Right now, all she wanted to know was Rose's whereabouts. "Please tell me what you know. Where is my sister?"

"Here, let's sit down. This may take a while."

When he finished, Gwen sat stunned. She slowly shook her head as guilt clung to her like a wet garment. She knew she had ignored the obvious signs of depression Rose had been struggling with for years.

"Take me to her William, please. She needs me and I need to see her," she whispered.

"Okay, but let me call her first." He reached into his back pocket and pulled out his cell.

"Hi, Rose," he said.

***

"William, I've been waiting on your call."

Chapter 12

Another Plan Times

Clara knew she wasn't capable of plotting a more masterful plan than the one that had just fallen into her lap. While the attention Eric's parents showered them with was overpowering, like the adoring daughter-in-law that she was, she withstood the outpouring of love. Her in-laws made unexpected visits at least two to three times a week and even more phone calls. "I just can't get enough of these cutie pies," Gloria would squeal each time she held one of the twins. She barged in time after time with arm loads of pink frilly outfits and all the matching accessories. Some of the over-the-top-girly-girl ones she disliked but didn't dare complain.

As Clara neatly packed the clothes in the tall vintage chest, she glanced over at the proud grandmother.

"Mom, do you think you could spend a couple of days with us while Eric is away at the hospital? Rosita had a family emergency and I will be left alone."

"I couldn't think of anything I'd enjoy more," Gloria beamed.

Clara knew she wouldn't refuse the offer. She had been hinting at it all week long.

The next day, however, she was shocked and very much annoyed when she brought Little Teddy along with her. She instantly knew it was her motherly way of trying to appease Miriam. "You never spend any time with your grandson," she always whined.

That was okay. She had another plan for that too.

While Gloria changed the diaper on one of the twins, Clara had time alone with Miriam's 'little brat'. He was looking for his grandmother and started to whimper when he couldn't find her. She pulled him to her, tightening her grip. He opened his mouth, letting out a long-silent scream that came deep from inside. After holding his breath, which seemed an eternity, she braced herself for one of the loudest shrills ever. Never loosening her grip she said, "Stop crying. Stop it, right now."

Gloria came rushing in cuddling the baby in her arms only to be met by a very flushed cheeked little Teddy.

By then, Clara was rocking the other twin and petting Little Teddy on his back as he screamed.

"I couldn't pick him up," Clara said. "He wanted me to pick him up and I couldn't."

Gloria reached for him, "Oh, come here sweetheart," she said, as she laid the sleeping twin down. She rubbed and kissed him until he finally calmed down.

Clara thought to herself, "By the time he leaves, he'll never want to come over here again." Actually, she would be glad when they all were out of her home. Her thoughts were of Eric, and she needed time alone with just him and the girls. She noticed how tense he had become lately and wondered what was causing it all.

***

Eric was indeed stressed even as he sat alone at the corner table in the hospital's cafeteria. He treasured his time away from them now. With the birth of his twins and the attention Clara demanded, he was having a hard time juggling his studies and hospital rotations.

"Definitely too many distractions," he thought.

Despite dealing with all of that, he knew it was the news his father shared a while back that troubled him the most. When his dad showed up unexpectedly at his home with an undeniable look of concern, he eventually got to the bottom of what brought him there.

"You seem worried. Is everything okay?" Eric asked.

"If you have the time, I would like to discuss a few business matters with you," he said, his comforting fatherly smile now lighting his face. "First, you must promise me you'll take that worried look away or I won't be able to talk to you the way I need to."

Eric understood trying to hide his feelings from his dad never worked. He knew him better than anyone else in the world.

"Sorry, you know how worried I get," Eric said.

Randy stood and strolled over to the large window gazing out as he spoke. "The company's in financial trouble and I'm thinking of selling the majority of my stocks."

"Dad, when did all of this happen?" Eric whispered. He rushed over to where he stood. He didn't want to take the chance on Clara over-hearing any of their conversation.

"I've been trying to keep my head above water for the past two years son, and I believe it's getting the best of me."

Eric listened as he watched his dad try hard to explain. He hadn't noticed until that moment how frail he had become, the deep facial lines accented by his snow white hair. He'd seen his dad struggle to make the company a thriving one. To lose everything now would be an awful blow.

"Can you get a loan until we figure this out?" Eric asked.

"I tried, and it appears in this economy my credit isn't quite what it used to be." He attempted to laugh as he watched Eric pace back and forth. "I wanted you to know that you and Miriam are still very well taken care of. I refused to take any risks with your stocks," he said, his voice tender.

"How can you think about that in a time like this, dad?" Eric whispered. "You should cash in everything you have to save the company. We're grown now, and we can take care of ourselves."

"Absolutely not, Eric, that's why I didn't want to tell you until now. I knew you would react this way." He placed his hands on his son's shoulder. "Listen, I vowed my children would never have to struggle like I did. I made myself that promise a long time ago and I'm going to keep it. I have protected your assets and I'm selling my rights to the company to protect mine. Your mother and I should be able to live comfortably after the sale, so don't you go worrying about us, you hear!"

Randy could tell by his son's expression he hadn't quite convinced him.

"Eric, you've got to take my word on this. We are going to be just fine."

Ever since that conversation, he was having difficulty focusing. He made a few phone calls of his own to see how he could help, but quickly discovered his father was indeed in serious financial trouble. To make matters worse, he hadn't shared the news with his mother yet. He made him promise he wouldn't let Clara or Miriam in on what was happening until they had at least gotten the paperwork squared away.

Eric thought about his sister. Miriam was a stay at home mom and her husband worked for their father. If he sold the company Ted would be unemployed. To complicate matters, she was now seven months pregnant with his second nephew. Even if their dad protected her stock, it wasn't enough to continue the life-style she had grown accustomed to. Miriam was the baby and she didn't know anything other than this privileged life.

He carved out as much time as possible to meet with his dad and help him go over the books. As he combed the pages of the financial report, he paused momentarily—his thoughts drifting. Now, he regretted moving into the new house with all the amenities Clara had insisted on. It caused them to have to spend most of their savings. "That five hundred thousand dollars certainly would have been a welcomed cushion," he thought. It was going to take that and at least eight hundred thousand more to pay off both the house and all the bills he accumulated from medical school. Plus, he'd just signed off on the complex he was about to open his medical practice in. If that wasn't bad enough, he was now part owner of the company—something his father had insisted on making him even when he told him about medical school. He felt guilty not being able to offer him the kind of financial support he needed right now. Still he wished his dad would wait it out another year. Somehow he was sure he could turn the business around if given more time—but his father was a stubborn old man. When he made up his mind like that, there was nothing anybody could do about it. This time Eric knew he couldn't fault him for going ahead with the deal. He saw it in his eyes, his father was tired.

The next challenge was telling his mother. If anyone thought Miriam had lived a privileged life, their mom was royalty in disguise. Her typical behavior was depicted when she walked in the room one day where he and his father stood.

"Honey, I have something I need for you to do," she said, nestling up to him.

"I'm listening dear," Randy said.

"Eric and Clara must have a pool identical to the one we put in for Miriam and Ted. The girls couldn't possibly grow up without that special kind. I'll call the people tomorrow that did the job," she said, turning and trotting out the room.

Eric stared at his father.

"That's a good idea honey," Randy said, calling after her. "That's a good idea."

Chapter 13

Wind of Change Times

When Eric kissed her goodbye and headed for the hospital, Clara's concerns grew. She knew his demeanor had changed. He had never snapped at her like he did the other night. He was much quieter than usual, even going to bed right after dinner lately. Something had to be troubling him and she was determined to find out what it was. She pushed the button to her ringing cell.

"Is Eric there, he's not answering," Gloria, said, her usual chipper tone now absent.

"No, he's not here, mom. Is everything okay?"

"Miriam was admitted into the hospital for premature labor. She's hysterical and I'm afraid she will deliver early. She wants to speak with her brother."

"How many months is she?" Clara asked, calmly.

"Seven, dear. They have given her medication and it's stopped her contractions for now. She's terribly upset though, and I'm afraid if she doesn't calm down, the pains will begin again. I think seeing him will help some."

"I was just about to call Eric. Don't worry, I'll tell him to get over to the hospital right away. What room is she in?" Clara asked.

"Room 204. You're a doll," Gloria said. "I need to go and check on Little Teddy. We'll talk later."

"Tell Miriam I said to take it easy and relax," Clara said. As she hung up the phone, a smile slowly emerged.

Walking over to the large window, she watched the men operating the crane's claw dig deep into the fresh moist soil. The new amenities to her swimming pool were coming along nicely. As she sat down to watch them work, she took a sip from the cup of cappuccino she'd just made.

She knew she had absolutely no intentions of calling Eric.

**

Miriam drew in another slow, deep breath. It had been over four hours and she realized Eric wasn't going to call. With school and now the twins, she never saw her brother anymore. Clara made sure of that. Whenever she tried phoning him, she would always tell her he wasn't home, asleep or just plain unavailable. Her heart ached and longed for his company. She was losing the battle for her brother's affection and the very thought generated a pain that was foreign to her. Eric, her best friend, was slowly being removed from her life. She tried everything in her power to warn them that it was happening, but no one would listen. She licked the salty tears as she clenched her teeth. Another contraction was on the way.

Six hours later, her doctor had finally succeeded in stopping the pain. He placed her on strict bed rest for the rest of her pregnancy. "Bathroom privileges only," he warned her. She felt that was the only reason her mother stayed close by. She knew she would rather be at Clara and Eric's doting over those identical twin girls of theirs. This time, however, she kept her thoughts to herself.

The bed rest helped, but even at that, the baby came three weeks early.

"Momma, thanks for helping me out" she said, when they finally brought her baby boy home. "He's so tiny and different from Little Teddy, I'm afraid to hold him."

"He'll fatten up soon enough," Gloria said, rocking the tiny bundle in the wicker rocker she once used for her own kids.

Miriam watched her mother as she gazed gingerly at her grandson. She noticed the glare the tears made in her eyes from where she sat.

"Momma, are you okay?" she asked. "What's wrong?"

Gloria bit down hard on her bottom lip maneuvering the wires to the monitor they sent the baby home on.

Miriam reached out and gently stroked her arm. "Talk to me, tell me what's going on."

"You must promise you will not let your father in on any of what I am about to tell you."

"Okay, okay, I promise. What is it, you're making me nervous."

"We're in serious financial trouble, honey. The company has been in the red for the last two years and it's getting worse. Your dad has tried everything possible to turn it around, but nothing seems to be working. A larger chain is interested in buying us out and your dad is considering the deal."

"Are you serious? When was anyone going to tell me?" Miriam asked.

"We were going to tell you today. In fact, in the morning, Randy, Eric, and I are going to meet the potential buyers tomorrow. When your father talks to you Miriam, please don't let on that you know."

Miriam handed the baby to the nanny, came back, and sat on the long sofa next to her mother. "I hate to bring this up, but what about Ted? He won't have a job if you sell the company. Has anyone thought of that?"

"You need not worry, dear. It'll be a part of the deal your daddy will make."

"Come on," Miriam asserted. "That's no guarantee. You know as well as I do when we relinquish ownership they have every right to do whatever they please. They're not obligated to take care of Ted."

"Honey, please calm down. Your father is doing all he can to take care of you and Eric. I'm told Ted will transfer over as Senior Vice President. We will make certain that's in the contract."

Miriam's tone suddenly shifted—the sadness on her mother's face sobering. "What about you and daddy, momma? Will you be okay?"

"Selling the company will give us enough money to pay off our debt. We can live pretty comfortably after that," Gloria said. "We'll have to scale back some, but we will be okay."

Miriam reached over and hugged her. Resting her head on her mother's shoulder a little longer, they both sighed.

It was difficult acting as if she didn't know anything when her father arrived, and it certainly complicated matters when Eric walked in with him. It was the first time they had seen each other since her baby was born. How could she forgive him for never coming to check on her when she needed him most? Besides that, he still hadn't come to see his nephew since she brought him home. All of it grieved her greatly, but she knew it wasn't the time or place to hash out complicated family matters. So, she avoided the subject all together.

Several cups of coffee later, she could tell the discussion was taking its toll on her parents. They all finally said their goodbyes and prepared to meet in the morning.

Putting on his jacket, she could hear her father pleading with her mother to stay at home instead of traveling with them.

"Gloria, Miriam needs you," he said. "I'll be fine."

"Are you still having chest pains?" she asked.

He didn't respond, his quietness affirming the answer.

"That's why I must go. I would never let you go without me. I promise not to get in the way this time," she said. "I'll only be there to take care of you."

"Yes, dear," Randy said. "Of course."

They were ready to leave before dawn the following morning. When Eric pulled her to him and hugged her goodbye, she saw in the gesture a glimmer of hope. "He might actually be missing me too," she thought. It was the spark she needed. She decided as soon as they returned, she would once again reach out to her brother so they could get back to loving each other the way they used to.

She faced her mother, and with tears in her eyes, she said, "You're the strongest woman I know. Take care of daddy and by the way, take care of yourself." She smiled and kissed her on the cheek. "Everything is going to be just fine."

It was her daddy's turn as she looked up at him. "I love you," she said. They rubbed noses like they did when she was a little girl.

She waved goodbye to Eric.

As they drove away, Ted wrapped his arm around her. She knew he was trying his best to comfort her.

"He was always so miserable at that," she thought.

She decided to take a relaxing bath while the boys slept and it proved to be exactly what she needed. No longer on the brink of tears, she prayed the deal would actually work out to their advantage.

Later, Miriam moved around the kitchen trying to busy herself. She hadn't seen her neighbors since the arrival of their newest addition and accepted the invitation from a few of her favorite ones to join them for lunch. While she occasionally wondered how things were going with the business deal, the distraction did help as she sipped on the tomato basil soup. They caught her up on all the drama going on at the country club, especially with the councilman's second wife. The governor's cousin showed up for lunch also. She was on the revitalization board with the councilman and talked non-stop about his marital woes.

Occasionally Miriam would glance down at her watch, expecting her cell to ring. When another hour passed, she cut the lunch date short. Driving along, she slowed when she turned the corner and noticed the black and yellow sheriff's car parked outside her home. An alarm set off and by the time she parked and reached the door, she was in a full sprint. Ted and the two officers turned to face her.

"What's wrong?" she asked, panting, her face ashen.

"Ma'am, I'm Officer Bailey and this is Officer Carter…"

"What's wrong, Ted? Is it my dad?" She searched for any kind of reassurance in his face. She reached out to him for support—her strength now waning. "Is he okay?" she asked, her voice trembling.

The uniformed officer tried explaining. "There was a car accident involving a drunk driver. They ran into the car with your brother and parents."

"Are they in the hospital? Are they hurt?" she panted out.

"That's why we're here Mrs. Johnson," the officer said. He hesitated.

"There were no survivors," Ted said as he grabbed her tightly in his arms.

"TEDD-D-D!" Miriam screamed gasping for air. *"No-o-o-o-…No-o-o, please God…No-o-o-o. Please, tell me it's not true. Please God, it's not true,"* she cried. She crumbled in his arms as he scooped her up.

The car had fallen down a ravine and burst into flames.

Clara let the phone ring when Miriam's number flashed. She hadn't been in a good mood ever since Eric finally told her about the business deal. They had been up all night discussing the matter and she was tired. He hadn't called and she couldn't help but wonder maybe the deal hadn't gone through. Perhaps Miriam had heard something, so, she picked up the phone.

"Hello," Clara said.

"Clara, this is Ted."

"Yes," she snapped. "Have you heard from Eric?"

"Not exactly," he said pausing. He wrapped each menacing word with as much gentleness as possible. "There has been an accident, Clara, and I'm sending my brother over to bring you here," he said.

"Why would I need to come over to your home? Is Eric alright?" she asked, her heart rate increasing.

Ted stammered… "I think you…may need to…come over."

"Is he okay? Answer me Ted."

"No, I'm afraid not Clara."

He didn't have to say anything else—she already knew.

"My brother is on the way to your home. There was a drunk driver involving the car Eric was in," Ted said.

Clara's screams could be heard clear through the other end.

He quickly dialed on his office cell. "Hurry Dan and get to Clara's, now!"

Dan found her rocking back and forth on the floor. The babies were crying as he picked up the one screaming the loudest. "Come on and go with me Clara. It's going to be okay."

"NO! None of this is true," she said, jerking her arm away from him. "I'm going to sit here and wait for Eric to call."

He tried a different approach, "Why don't we go over to Ted, and Miriam's to see what's really going on?"

She sat rocking—a hollow, vacant look in her eyes.

He continued coaxing and at last convinced her to go. He reached for the babies, buckled them into their carriers, and sped away. Ted's personal physician met them in the drive.

One look at Clara and he knew she was in shock. "Mrs. Gordon," he said. "I know you're not okay right now. I need to give you something to help you relax."

It was at that moment Clara understood life as she knew it was over. Eric was dead. In fact, the family she had made her own was gone. She laid her head back on the seat and screamed. She continued screaming until the doctor eased the sharp-beveled needle deep into her arm.

The next few days were a blur as they braced themselves for an occasion none of them were prepared to handle. Large, towering white roses, sprinkled with white lilies faced them as they sat on the first pew of the church. There were three life-size pictures—one each of Eric and his parents, surrounded by three decorative urns housing their ashes. Friends, governmental officials and heads of companies spoke well of their deceased family while their hearts were breaking. Each sat stoically, completely absorbed in their own grief.

After the two hour memorial service, every room in Miriam's home was filled with men and women dressed in variations of black. As they offered their condolences, she never managed a smile. Even though many of the relatives she hadn't seen in years had come, she still wished they would all go away.

Ted searched the house looking for his wife and finally found her sitting alone in the alcove to their bedroom. "Can I get you anything, honey?" Ted whispered.

She leaned her head onto him for a moment. "Not right now, I'll just be glad when this part is over," she whispered.

"It will all be over soon," he said, massaging away the tenseness.

He closed the door to their bedroom and held her tightly as she wept again. When the last guest finally departed, he fixed her favorite tea.

"Here, drink this," he said, handing her the cup.

She had to admit, he had certainly stepped up to the plate this time. When he wrapped his arms around her in bed that night, she cried again softly. In just one day, her life had changed forever.

Miriam aroused to the smell of coffee as she stretched and rolled over, the time on the digital clock displaying 9:52 a.m. She felt a slight sense of relief because she didn't have to deal with the boys. Ted's sister had agreed to keep them for the remainder of the week.

She knew the pain in her heart wouldn't go away any time soon. The gloomy, cloudy days followed her wherever she went. It was hard not to be able to pick up the phone and call her mom. They talked at least three to four times a day. There was no room in her imagination living without her. Yet, everyone in town called her a daddy's girl. He was the real reason 'rotten' was added to the word 'spoiled' when they described her.

Eric….. Eric….. Eric, what was she going to do without her dear brother? It was the thought of him that made her heart ache the most. They hadn't gotten things right between the two of them, and now it was too late. Carrying the burden of Eric not knowing how much she loved him—how much she yearned for their rich relationship, was unbearable. Over-and-over, she buried her head in the pillow and cried. It was the extra-large bed that she spent most of her days wallowing in grief. She wasn't getting out of it today no matter how much Ted encouraged her to. She reached for the medication her doctor had prescribed and added an extra dose. Sleep came in great quantities, and she gladly opened her arms to embrace it.

"Miriam," she could hear Ted calling her name. "No, not now…please go away," she thought.

"Come on and eat something," Ted said, sitting down next to her with the silver tray.

Opening her droopy, swollen eyes, she pushed it away. "No, I'm not hungry," I'll try to eat something later," she said, her voice hoarse from all the sobbing.

"You haven't eaten in days. Here, take a little of the soup. It's homemade potato broccoli, your favorite kind."

She took two spoonfuls and immediately laid her head back down on the pillow, and again, the sleep was welcomed.

"Okay, that's it, no more medication," Ted said, hours later as he peeled back the curtains securing them with the large tasseled ropes. Rays of sunlight burst inside instantly overpowering the darkened room.

"It has been almost two weeks since you've eaten a full meal or gotten out of bed. The boys haven't seen their mother in days. They need you Miriam and I need my wife. I know it's painful, but we have to get a handle on this. I can't afford to lose you too."

Miriam faced him as the sunlight now shone upon an unfamiliar and unexpected sight—tears clouded his eyes. His words gently brushed against her heart. "Come, here," she said, patting the bed. "Stay with me for a while." She had only seen him cry once—when his mother died. She gathered his chin in her hand and said, "I love you. Where are my boys? I want to see them."

He had given her the temporary jolt she needed.

It was quite the opposite with Clara, however. No one believed when she returned to school right after the memorial service.

"It helps when I stay busy," she told her colleagues.

The teachers all marveled at her strength as she boasted about not needing the medication the doctor had freely offered to assist her through all the trauma.

"She didn't need anything clouding her thinking," she told them. She was determined to start working on another plan right away. The insurance policies along with her share of Eric's assets would be more than enough to maintain the lifestyle she'd grown accustomed to. "After all, her girls deserved nothing less," she thought. They were never going to grow up the way their mother had forced them to after she kicked their father out. As soon as she got her hands on the money, it would be enough to pay off the house and open the school of her dreams. The academy was going to officially put her on the map and give this town something to really talk about. Skill and intelligence were her most formidable assets and she would use them to make it happen again, even if she had to do it all by herself— without Eric. Life had indeed delivered her a blow, but she was determined to press forward and not look back.

Clara tried contacting Miriam a few times, but Ted finally confided that she wasn't doing well. She always knew that girl was a first class wimp. It was becoming extremely aggravating, though. Her weak behavior was prolonging the settlement of the estate and it was past time for her to start getting it together. The bills were beginning to roll in and she needed her share of that money. One more day, and that was all she was willing to give her. After that, she was going to call Miriam and become a lot more assertive. Her inability to grieve normally wasn't going to be the obstacle that blocked her from moving on with her life.

Clara headed for the teacher's lounge.

"I hope you got the invitation to Shannon's party," Karen squealed as she walked through the door. "It's going to be simply fabulous."

Karen had become the one friend Clara knew she could count on. Her coworker had been a great support during the tragedy and they talked every day. Even when she first came to town, it was Karen that made her feel welcomed at the Bradbury country club and had become her favorite shopping partner.

"I found this wonderful boutique in Narlton," Karen said. "It's to die for. You have to go and check it out with me. I know you'll probably find something wonderful to wear to the party. You are coming aren't you?"

"Yeah, I hope so. I was planning to meet Miriam on that day to take care of a few business matters. If she is still 'grieving', and won't be able to see me, then I'm sure I'll be there."

"You really don't know what the settlement is going to be, do you?" Karen whispered. "Everybody's talking about it. For goodness sake, what's taking her so long? It's been six weeks, already! That should be more than enough time to grieve. Although, I do hear she's not doing well at all—stays in bed most of the day. Her housekeeper and mine are the best of friends and she tells me everything."

"I never have been able to understand that girl," Clara said. "She has had ample time to get it together. She wasn't that close to her parents anyway. We all know she and Eric hated each other and hadn't spoken in months."

"Well, I'm not one to pry into your personal affairs," Karen said. She moved in closer. "I heard she's mostly distraught over her parent's business matters. The word is they were in serious financial trouble. In fact," she said, lowering her voice further, "There is this horrible rumor swirling around, they were considering bankruptcy. As usual, Eric was said to be the knight-in-shining-armor and did whatever he had to do to rescue them."

Clara nodded her head, "Please don't mention it to anyone, but it's all true. Eric and his dad spent countless hours going over the books with their attorney, Brad. They were being forced to sell the business."

Karen gasped, "Are you serious? Maybe that's what has Miriam so devastated."

"Perhaps it is, but I wish Eric would have told me what he planned on doing. He wanted to wait until after they returned from Memphis and negotiated the sale to talk to me about it. Although, he did seem confident all of us would walk away financially as winners," Clara said. "I'm still in the dark about it all. That's why I need to speak with Miriam. Since they never got to sell the business, I don't know where any of this stands. My patience is almost non-existence with that girl right about now."

"I do understand," Karen said shaking her head. "Hopefully, she will get it together soon."

***

Just a few blocks over, however, Miriam was still grieving, quite hard in fact.

"You're thin as a rail, Ms. Miriam, you must eat something that will put meat back on your bones," Maria said, in her thick Spanish dialect.

"I'll gain the weight, Maria. I think my appetite is slowly coming back this way," she said, moving the uneaten eggs to the opposite side of the plate.

"Well……good morning," Ted said, sitting down at the table. He was happy to finally see his wife up and out of their bedroom for a change. "What time are we going to see Brad?" he asked.

"Nine," she yawned. "I wonder what's so urgent that he has to see us today."

"I'm not sure, but he felt you would want to know whatever this very important matter is," he said, perusing the Wall Street Journal. Maria placed his breakfast—two eggs, toast and two slices of turkey bacon in front of him.

"Let me throw something on so we can get this over with," Miriam said. She knew she wasn't ready for the reading of the will. She had just been able to pull herself out of bed and still had no control over her tears. A particular song, a thought, even her mom's favorite TV show caused her to bawl uncontrollably. Despite how she felt, she knew Brad was still waiting on her.

Brad had been their family's attorney for as long as she could remember. An astute and savvy lawyer, her father trusted him as much as he did Eric. If he said it was something that she really needed to know, it had to be important. That was the only reason she was going outside today.

When they arrived at the office a little ahead of schedule, he greeted them at the door. "Brad was always a stickler for time," she thought.

"It has taken a lot of effort to sort this matter out, but I have finally put all the pieces together," Brad said, as they sat. "I had my partner take a look at it also. It was just that complicated."

He handed them each a copy of the documents. Sliding his glasses up on his nose, he looked up at them and asked if they would follow the winding trail he was about to take them on.

"Needless to say, your parents were in financial trouble as a result of several years of loss profits from the company. Along with your brother's help, they tried everything to keep from selling the family's business. It finally came down to giving the company up and that meant selling the majority of the stocks. You know how your dad felt about touching yours and Eric's portion of the shares," he said. "However, Eric convinced your dad that he should sign all of his stocks and his part ownership completely over to him. Ultimately, that decision increased the amount of equity within the company and I must say was a very smart move. It made the business extremely marketable. The only way your father agreed to do that, Miriam, was after the sale of the company he would repay Eric with interest. Now, this is the complex part. Eric had much more debt than you did due to medical school expenses and preparing for the startup of his practice. Disassociating himself as part owner really helped the books. Essentially, when he removed himself completely from the company's proprietorship and turned it all over to your dad, it dramatically improved the bottom line. Pay close attention to what I'm about to say next. Eric terminated his insurance coverage, temporarily, until after the sale of the company. It was his way of providing the necessary cash flow the company desperately needed to ensure payroll was met each week. They had never planned, however, not selling the company and clearly not being here to put things back in order. Anyway, as a result of what Eric and your parents did, this is where you stand, Miriam. You are the official executor of the will. Secondly, you are entitled to one-hundred percent of all the company assets. Due to your parent's deaths, you alone have the right to the insurance money not only for the company, but on all parties as well. The sudden-death-clause tripled the amount of the insurance reward. It will be more than enough to balance the company's bottom line and hopefully make it thrive again. That's if you choose to. You may still want to sell it. Either way, Miriam, you are a very wealthy woman. Now, here's the situation with Clara. We know the intentions of your parents for Eric, but those plans were never officially written in the will or finalized. That means you have full control of the stocks, the company and the insurance money. It's essentially your call, whatever you want to do. If you wish to carve out Eric's portion that your mom and dad would have given him, just let me know. That move would also make Clara a wealthy woman, but right now, she is not legally entitled to anything. Your brother was a man of integrity with a whole lot of heart. He risked all that he had to help your parents. I was proud… to call him my friend." Brad cleared his throat, quickly pushing back on the unexpected emotions.

Miriam never took her eyes off him while he spoke.

He stared up at her as he placed his glasses on top of the document. "Do you know what you would like to do?" Brad asked.

"Yes I do," Miriam said. "I know exactly what I want to do," finally speaking with renewed strength. "Selling the company is not an option. I would like to try my hand at running the business for a while to see if I can make it as profitable as it used to be."

"Alright," Brad said, jotting the information down. He looked up at her knowing full well there was something else she had on her mind.

"Secondly, please sign all the assets over to me, stocks and insurance included, Brad." She stood ready to leave.

Ted glared hard at his wife. He wasn't the least bit surprised by her decision. He knew her well, and understood she would make sure Clara never received one penny of the money he knew she rightfully deserved.

"I will make this all official immediately," Brad said.

When they left, Brad took the deep breath his lungs had longed for. He had a feeling things would turn out this way. He'd really been pulling for Clara. The day Eric transferred all rights to the money over to his dad, he remembered initially trying to talk him out of it. While he had to admit, it was only a half-hearted attempt, as his lawyer, he knew he still had to try. He understood how risky a move that was. He never trusted fate. She was way too cruel for him. He witnessed the countless times that steel grip of hers crushed the hopes and dreams of anyone foolish enough to get in her way. This time it was Clara. Eric left her penniless. While the plan he put together seemed fool-proof at the time, the unexpected really did happen. They had not been there to put things back together again. Fate delivered her ultimate blow.

He pushed back in his chair, stood and walked over to the large, picturesque window. It was the sole reason he'd chosen this office, the view was magnificent and somehow had a calming effect on him. As he stared down at the large skyscrapers, he thought about the phone call he would soon have to make. Miriam had gone and done it again. He was tired of always having to clean up her mess. He'd known Miriam since she was a child. He knew her to be an insensitive, selfish, spoiled-rotten kid, who turned out to be an insensitive, selfish, spoiled-rotten adult.

Later, as he drove around the lake, he hoped the soothing waters would somehow calm the dark feeling he had looming inside. It did little to settle him as he reached for his cell.

"Hello, Clara, Brad here…may I come and visit for a while? I'd like to discuss some family business with you if that's okay." He could tell this was the call she'd been waiting for.

When he arrived, she greeted him with a look of anticipation and excitement. She had no idea what was about to hit her. He felt like one of those sicko's with a pipe bomb disguised in a neatly wrapped package ready to deliver. He decided to tuck the news away as long as possible.

She invited him into the comfortable sunroom adjacent to the spacious family area. It offered a perfect view of the lake and the crystal blue swimming pool. Their home was always one of his favorites. It ranked right up there with his other *A* list clients and in his opinion, surpassed most of them. As they sat, he watched her twist the long single lock of hair until it curled tightly around her finger. He knew she was nervous and so was he. To start off the conversation, he felt the easiest approach would be to have a mini discussion about the company's history. Finally, he gave in to the fact that there was just no easy way of breaking this kind of heart-wrenching news. When he shared the information that brought him there, the ill-fated words poured out like hot-searing acid.   He watched them snatch the color right out of her.

"So you're telling me he cancelled his insurance policy. You mean Eric left me with nothing?" she yelled.

"I'm afraid so Clara. I thought surely since both insurance policies made Miriam an extremely wealthy woman, she would have at least given you Eric's share of the stocks. Unfortunately, she didn't see it that way."

When it all settled in, Brad had never witnessed such raw emotions. It was a mixture of hysteria, desperation and disbelief all blended together… forming an explosive set of feelings oozing out of Clara.

"How am I supposed to live Brad, can you tell me that?" She stood suddenly, gasping for air. She ran her fingers through her hair as she paced the floor. "You mean I have no money? No, this is not happening," she said. "All I have worked for is gone. It can't be true. Tell me it's all a big mistake. Please, Brad." she pleaded, her voice now strained and very much over the top.

"Listen Clara, let's try and remain calm. Let me reason with Miriam one more time. In the meantime, why don't you give her a call and see if you can't talk some sense into her yourself. No one could possibly be that greedy."

He tried explaining it over again to make sure she understood, but no matter how he told the story, it still ended up with her not being left a dime. "I have another client to see, but please don't hesitate to call me. We will work this out," he said. He looked into the haunting eyes he knew would cause him a few more sleepless nights.

Closing the door, Clara leaned against it and slid to the floor. She listened as her heart spoke, and this time she paid close attention to the counsel it rendered. This chapter of her *'storybook world'* had officially ended. Miriam was going to make certain she never received one penny of Eric's money. A whirlwind of life changing thoughts whipped through her mind as she sat on the cold marble tile. Their savings had been wiped out to purchase the home of their dreams, to prepare for the birth of their twins as well as the start-up of Eric's medical practice. All the upscale furniture she insisted on purchasing for each room and the expensive interior decorating consultation had added an additional strain on their budget. She thought about the plan she and Eric had developed just a few weeks before his untimely death. Within five years, their strategy would have made them debt free. The masterful plan was one that was supposed to place them in a position to rule the Bradbury community. It would have allowed Gloria and Randy to gracefully move aside as she and Eric replaced them as the new reigning power couple of their generation. Years later, she would pass it on to her girls. If that was the plan, then why was she sitting here in the middle of this nightmare? She quit listening to her thoughts and began pounding her fists into her head as she sat there for hours.

Early the next morning she went to another lawyer to see if there was anything else she could do about forcing Miriam to give her their portion of the money. Unfortunately, everything Brad told her was true. She had no right to any of it.

Soon the nightmare that chased her, finally caught up. The bill collectors were calling and she had few answers. Clara knew she had no other choice but to make the phone call she dreaded the most.

"Hello, Miriam," she said. "I was wondering if I could come over and discuss a few business matters with you. I guess, uh… I really need to speak with you." As odd as the phone call felt, she'd made up her mind she was not going to beg. She did, however, acknowledge the strange sense of humility that had suddenly washed over her.

***

On the other end, what she couldn't see was Miriam smiling, thinking, "Come on over, I've waited a long time for this."

When the day finally came, Clara's opponent paced the floor like a caged cheetah—not sure of the source of her nervousness. After all, she wasn't the one coming over groveling to her very own arch-enemy. Miriam's nanny told her about the dilemma her decisions were now having on Clara. It was still beyond irritating when she phoned the other day trying to masquerade behind that upbeat tone of hers. The only reason she agreed to meet was so that she could actually witness 'the look' when she told her she wasn't giving her one penny of Eric's money. "Payback is rough," she thought, smiling. As far as she was concerned, it was all a closed matter, never to be discussed again. The paperwork was complete, the will finalized and the money was now officially hers. All of it.

The doorbell rang causing her to jump.   The unfolding excitement had her on edge.

"Mrs. Gordon is here," the maid announced through the intercom. Miriam stood slowly. "I'll be right down."

"Let her wait," Miriam thought, as she admired herself in the mirror.

Twenty minutes later, Miriam walked into the room wearing her special olive green Chanel suit accented with a large ruby pendant, matching earrings, ring and brace-lets. The accessories alone gave a touch of class to the already elegant outfit. Her attire along with the maids scurrying about, she knew spoke volumes to her success. It was no denying she and her family were living ex-tremely well. It was the exact message she wanted sent Clara's way as she would soon leave their home empty-handed.

"Good morning, Clara. What a lovely suit you have on," Miriam said. She had to admit, she did look pretty.

"Thanks, Miriam, you look very nice also."

"Thank you," she said, softly, nodding in agreement. "A compliment from her, hmm…now this was going to be good," Miriam thought.

As she sat facing Clara, she was mesmerized at the sheer nerve of her former sister-in-law showing up at her home in the first place. She remembered the countless times she extended invitations for them to come over and was met with a million reasons why they couldn't. She suddenly became extremely annoyed at her presence.

"So that I won't waste your time or mine, exactly what brings you here today?" Miriam asked.

Clara sighed and spoke calmly, "Miriam, you know Eric's death left me virtually penniless. The girls and I are going to have to move if I don't do something about paying the mortgage soon. Brad told me about the poor decision my husband made trying to help your parents out of their financial dilemma. He never would have done that had he thought for one second it would leave us in the predicament we are in." Clara searched her sister-in-law's eyes for any hint of sympathy as she spoke. When she found none, she continued, "So, I'm coming to you as family to see if you won't allow the kids and me access to Eric's money. Even if you don't want to give me all of it, a small portion would really help us out right now."

The contempt that came so naturally at that moment flowed freely from her as she unleashed years of hostility. "So, you're coming to me as family, is that it?" Miriam asked.

Clara nodded much like a scolded child.

"That's very interesting," she said, tapping the side of her face displaying the large ruby ring. "I'd like to ask you a few questions, Clara, if that's okay?"

"Go ahead, Miriam," she said, softly.

"Do you think real family would have driven a wedge between me and my only brother?"

Clara's face paled further.

"Do you think real family, would never invite my kids over for birthday parties and gatherings? So, you think my brother made a poor decision trying to take care of his elderly parents," Miriam said. "That's so typical of you. Unlike you Clara, he really did love them and would have given it all up to make sure they were well cared for. The way I see it is this, you never were real family and guess what, you never will be. At this point, I don't care what happens to you or those twins of yours. If I never see any of you again, that would be fine by me. Now, please excuse me. Maria," Miriam called out for her as she stood, "Will you show Miss Andrews to the door?"

Racing out, Clara's hands were trembling so hard she could barely start the ignition. She took a deep breath and tried again.

"Miss Andrews.... she called me Miss Andrews," she kept repeating to herself! Cranking the car, she swirled quickly out of the driveway, leaving a nice set of tire tracks as she sped away.

Even though she felt the urge to cry, she knew crying wasn't an option. "It just wasn't time to get all emotional," she thought. "There had to be a simple solution to it all, she would just have to figure it out and quickly put a plan together." The next most logical move finally came flowing in. She would reach out to her friends. "That's the answer," she thought. "They were owners of banks and real estate companies and without a doubt come to her rescue."

"Karen, if you aren't busy, I would like to drop by," Clara said, phoning her from the car.

"Sure, come on over."

They met outside on Karen's large patio overlooking the pool filled with kids. While the blue water glimmered, all the yelling and noise the children made caused the tenseness she felt to intensify.

"You are my best friend and I'm so thankful to have you to turn to. Karen, I'm in serious financial trouble and I'm going to need a loan. Do you think you could talk to Tom about it for me? As president of the bank I thought he would be able to offer me some assistance and help me out of this horrible situation."

"Wow, so it is true," she said, as they walked over to the grill. I couldn't believe Miriam would be so devious. They said Brad tried to talk to her until he was blue in the face....and... and....kids, the hot-dogs will be ready shortly," she yelled, right in the middle of her sentence. "Yay!" they screamed. "We're starving," the young man shouted as he did a cannonball in front of them, sending

the water splashing their way. "Now, where were we—
oh yeah, you know Miriam has an iron-will and everybody knows it. Not even that hen-pecked husband of
hers can make her change her mind when she has it made
up. I'm so sorry this has happened to you. How much
money are you talking about?"

"My accountant says it will take at least three hundred thousand dollars to put me back on my feet and to
keep me from filing bankruptcy," Clara said, wiping
away the splashes of water.

Karen fanned herself hard. "That's a lot of money,"
she gasped. "I'll talk with Tom, but I know my husband.
He's very strict about matters like this. What about your
mom? Surely, she could help you out."

"Finally, she had her complete attention," Clara
thought. "That's not an option, Karen. I would rather
not get her involved. I really need your help."

"Kids, get out of the pool now," she yelled. "The
food is ready." She looked over at Clara, "I'll call you
later and let you know what he says."

As Clara drove home she tried hard to keep from
thinking the unimaginable. What if she couldn't get her
hands on the money? She pushed the ominous thoughts
aside as she drove into the spiral drive. "That's not
going to happen," she said, trying hard to convince
herself. As she pulled in slowly, she parked next to
Eric's Range Rover. She thought of how comforting it
used to be to see his car when she drove in. It meant he
was home from the hospital and could finally spend time
with her. Now, the car represented something so incom-
prehensible she hated opening the garage. She laid her
head on the steering wheel, and this time her thoughts

fought back—determined to make her face reality. She was penniless.

"I really need you Eric. Why did you have to leave me? Why? Do you know what's happening to me and your babies?" She pounded her fist hard against the steering-wheel. "I don't know what to do." Still she refused to cry.

As soon as she walked through the door and saw Rosita, the cold truth hit her firmly in the face. It was going to be her last day as their maid and nanny. She had no money to pay her and dreaded telling her so.

"It's okay, Miss Clara, I love you and the girls," she said, reaching out to her. "Besides, my husband just got a raise and we will be fine until I find something else."

"I'm sorry. I really am, Rosita."

"No worry, between my mom and mother-in-law, they pitch in seeing that the kids have everything they need."

Clara stared at her. "That's unbelievable," she thought, "Someone of her status trying to be so kind."

The phone rang. "Si. It is Miss Shannon for you," Rosita said.

"Clara, are you okay," she screamed. "Karen told me all that Miriam did to you." She chattered on and on about the benefits of bankruptcy.

Clara couldn't believe Karen had told Shannon something so personal about her. Those were confidential matters and she had expected her to keep them that way. Who else had she told she wondered?

She soon found out. After Jan, Adrian and Beverly each phoned offering their condolences, she was sure the whole town knew by now.

Finally, Karen called. "Hi Clara, uh… Tom would like to speak with you."

"Clara, Tom here. Listen, it is never a good idea to go through a second party to try and obtain a loan. The professional way would have been to make an appointment and sit down with me at the office."

"I'm sorry, I was only trying to….," she tried explaining.

"Let me finish," Tom interrupted. "The chances of you paying back a five hundred thousand dollar loan are slim to none. So, it's out of the question. Here's Karen."

"Now, Clara, don't let that upset you. Bankruptcy may not be such a bad idea. I know a lawyer that I can refer you to."

"Karen, you made a mistake. You weren't listening. I only told you to ask for three hundred thousand dollars," she finally whispered.

"I know but I thought the few extra hundred-thousand would help. Either way, he wasn't going to approve it."

"Are you trying to help or hurt me, Karen?" she asked.

"I can't believe you are talking to me like that," she snapped. "I am your only true friend. While everyone else is saying you married Eric for his money, I never believed that."

"What money," she wanted to scream? Instead, she simply said, "Good night, Karen."

When she looked up, she stared at Rosita as she stood holding one of the twins. "If you have time," Clara said, massaging her temples, "Would you mind telling me all about your family?"

Chapter 14

Better Times

"Mrs. Andrews your blood count is extremely low, and we'll need to give you two units of packed cells right away," Dr. Span said. "That's why you're feeling so weak right now."

Ellen's concerns had only grown since she'd been admitted into the hospital. She felt too much time had been wasted not looking for Rose. To make matters worse, she knew she should have heard from Gwen hours ago. Now, she was worried about both her girls.

"I'm sorry Dr. Span, I'm going to have to refuse and check myself out of here."

Dr. Span sat next to her on the bed. "I don't want to frighten you, but if you leave you may die. You're a sick woman and we need to treat you. The problem is you're not handling your chemotherapy very well. Your blood count is so low it could actually damage your heart. If you were to leave the hospital it would definitely be against my advice."

Ellen had already made up her mind. She was not going to listen to another word the doctor had to say.

"You cannot hold me against my will. I know my rights and I have the power to check myself out of this hospital if I choose to. I understand your concern and I appreciate that, but you have to understand mine. I have a daughter that's missing and I will give my own life for

hers right now. Tell me what I need to do to get out of
here so that I can go and find my girls."

"Very well then, you'll need to sign yourself out
against medical advice, Mrs. Andrews. I hate to see you
do that, however."

"Thank you for all you've done for me," Ellen said,
swinging her legs over the side of the bed.

"Please try and take care of yourself," Dr. Span said,
walking away.

Ellen held onto the edge of the counter while she
dressed. Her head was spinning, but she attributed that
to lying in bed all day. She figured her blood count was
a little low and had probably been that way when she
arrived to New York. "Once she found Rose she would
come back and let the nice young doctor treat her again,"
she thought. "Right now, it was time to check out of this
place."

That was the last thing she remembered.

When she finally awakened, she couldn't talk anymore. An irritating tube had been placed down her
throat.

"No, Mrs. Andrews, please don't touch the tube. It's
helping you to breathe right now."

She opened her eyes to a young lady that gently held
her hand dressed in a printed scrub top. "We are moni-
toring your heart and blood pressure. That's what most
of these tubes are for," she heard the nurse say.

As it all suddenly began to fade, a glimpse of Rose's
face appeared. She gently reached out to touch it.

                              ***

Rose sat in a small private garden area at the Crisis
Intervention Center. The serene spot had become her
favorite where she often thought of William. She

couldn't believe that someone actually cared for her as much as he did. It was such a strange, yet surreal feeling. William was the only reason she was alive. Apparently he'd found her right after her ill-fated suicide attempt. He had revived her and made her breathe again.

She remembered thinking he was going to kill her since the pills hadn't—forcing his two fingers down her throat like that. After he did that a number of times, she mustered all the strength she could to yank his hand down. She vomited until her back ached. He then put her in a cold shower… clothes and all….the water feeling like electrical volts against her skin. She tried with all her might to get away from the freezing water, but he was too strong for her. She finally screamed at him to stop, but it did no good. After that, he forced her to drink strong, black, bitter, coffee. It made her vomit again and she remembered him saying, GOOD! After he poured the luke- warm coffee down her throat over and over, the true torture began. He took her outside in only a tee shirt, pants, and a thin jacket and made her walk by the lake. It was so cold all she wanted to do was just curl up and sleep. They walked nonstop until finally she was able to stand on her own. It was then and only then that he allowed her back into the apartment. The more awake she felt, the more embarrassed she became. Why had he saved her? What did she really have to live for?

Neither of them said a word until he suddenly jumped up and raced to the phone. In just a tee shirt and jeans, they left the apartment.

"Where are you taking me?" she asked.

"I'm trying to get you help, Rose," he said.

"I'll be okay, William. Take me back to my apartment so I can get some rest. When I wake up in the morning, I promise I'll go anywhere you want me to."

"No, Rose, let's get help now. Going back to your apartment is out of the question. If I take you to the hospital and tell them what you did, they will lock you up in some psychiatric ward. I would never let that happen to you and I know you don't want that either."

Rose knew he was right, so she sat back as they drove along. That's how she ended up in the Life's Defining Moment Crisis Intervention Center.

As soon as Gwen and William drove up to the center they immediately spotted Rose in the large day room conversing with another young woman.

"That's it, from now on don't you ever go a day without calling your sister," she said, walking up to her.

"GWEN!"

They stood hugging each other for a very long time.

"I mean it," Gwen said, pulling back cradling Rose's face in her hands.

"Gwen, I didn't know what else to do. I'm sorry…"

"Sh-h-h, I know, I know," she said, rocking her baby sister as if she was her own child. She gently brushed the tears from her cheeks. "It's okay. Now that I've found you, everything is going to be fine."

"Rose has been doing extremely well in the short time she's been with us. Hi, I'm her counselor, Adrianne" she said, extending her hand.

"It's nice meeting you. How can I get her out of here?" Gwen asked shaking hands. "I need to take her to see our mother."

"Let's sit down for a moment and chat," she said, leading her to a private area. "I feel Rose still needs therapy, but it could definitely continue on an outpatient basis. She's made great strides towards a full recovery and I'm extremely proud of her. She has been following a strict exercise and diet regime and based on all of her smiles, her self-esteem is soaring.   If she chooses to leave the facility, please make sure she continues with her counseling."

"Believe me we will take care of that. Her family is in the city now, and that will make all the difference in the world," Gwen said.

"That sounds wonderful. Now all we need to do is to fill out her discharge papers, go over a few other details about her release requirements and she can be out of here today."

For the first time in a long time, Gwen relaxed.

***

As Gwen spoke with the counselor, Rose and William walked along the winding walkway.

"I want you to know I told your sister everything," he said. "She was so worried I had to."

"It's fine, William. Gwen is not only my sister, she's my best friend." She turned and faced him. "I never talked about my family to you, well, because I didn't think you would be around long enough to get to know any of them. I guess it was my strange way of protecting myself from the pain of not having you with me."

William stared into her eyes, "I'm not going anywhere," he said.

They stood, taking in the quiet, peaceful atmosphere—enjoying the warmth of the sunlight.

"There you are," Gwen said, walking up. "You are free to go Rose but first, your counselor needs to speak with you."

Rose sat in the same chair she did when she first arrived. She knew it was different this time—she could feel it. Here sat a more confident, empowered and secure woman.

"You've been through quite a bit," the counselor said. "What a remarkable comeback you've made, Rose. Usually people in your condition stay with us a little longer, however, two weeks of intense therapy I do believe has made the difference in your case."

"I can't begin to tell you how grateful I am," Rose said. "I have been given another opportunity to get it together and I promise to take full advantage of it."

After all the paperwork had been completed, she stood, shook hands with the counselor as they said their goodbyes. At last she was out of there and on her way to see her mother.

The cool breeze blowing through her hair was the most exhilarating feeling Rose had experienced in a very long time. Everything felt different and new. At that very moment, it was an overwhelming sense of gratitude that caused her mind and spirit to revive. Her mother and sister were moving to New York and life was good again.

While the transformation inside had been a tremendous one, it was the outside that told a greater story as well. Rose had lost at least eighty pounds.

"Look at how much weight you've lost," Gwen exclaimed.

"I had actually shed a few pounds before I left for college. My clothes were super baggy during our last Thanksgiving meal together with Clara. You probably couldn't tell with all the commotion going on. I must say, that day was one of the most difficult times of my life, especially when no one seemed to notice my weight loss," she said. "Compounded with Clara's teasing, the depression really kicked in hard, and I guess I didn't have much of a fight left after that. For some reason, however, that feeling of gorging myself like I used to went away and the weight began really pouring off."

"I think she looks fantastic," William said.

"I'm pretty sure you do," Gwen said, laughing. She did not want to spoil the mood, but knew she had to.

"Rose, I need to talk to you about mother."

"What is it?" she asked, looking over at her.

"She's had some health challenges recently. Mother had a portion of her lung removed and hasn't been handling her treatments well," Gwen said.

Rose reached and lightly touched her arm.

"When she arrived in New York, she fainted," Gwen continued. "They had to rush her to the emergency department to find out why. The doctor wanted to admit her and needless to say, she fought that all the way. She wasn't going to be cooped up in any hospital and not out there looking for her baby," she said smiling. "I must say, she put up a pretty good fight too, but we finally convinced her to stay overnight. When I left this morning she was feeling a little better. I think when she sets her eyes on you, this whole health situation will do a one-eighty."

"Let's hurry and get there. I feel it's all my fault. She needs to know I'm okay," Rose said.

When they opened the door to room B408, the sight of the clean white sheets tightly gripping the empty bed, startled Gwen. "Where's my mother, Ellen Andrews?" she said, racing up to the nurse's station.

"Are you Mrs. Andrews' daughter?" the nurse asked. "We've been trying to contact you."

"Yes, we are," Gwen said, pointing also to Rose. Gwen glanced at her cell. She still had it silenced showing three missed calls.

"Dr. Span needs to speak with you. Have a seat in the conference room over there while I get her."

Gwen knew she had to remain strong at least for Rose's sake. Her face already told the story of fear and anxiousness as her color slowly began to fade.

"What's happening with her?" she asked, softly.

"I don't know, let's just wait on the doctor," Gwen said, reaching for her hand.

William put his arm around them both. "It's going to be okay," he whispered.

"Hi," Dr. Span said, entering the room. Adjusting the stethoscope around her neck, she wasted no time. "Please have a seat. Your mother is very ill. Her blood count is extremely low and it has endangered her heart. She stopped breathing and we had to resuscitate her. She's in the intensive care unit and her vital signs are not improving like we had hoped. We have her on medication that should help stabilize her blood pressure, but we won't know how well she's going to respond to it all for a couple of hours. I'm sorry this has happened to her," Dr. Span said.

Gwen sat with her hands covering her mouth. A funnel cloud filled with worry tore through her mind. "May we see her?" she asked, her voice shaking.

"Yes, but I must warn you she's going to look a whole lot different than when you saw her last. We have a number of machines attached to her so that we can monitor her closely. She won't be able to talk to you right now."

William glanced at Rose, aware of the tight grip she had on his arm. "Are you okay?" he asked. "Why don't we go outside and get some fresh air first."

"No, I'll be alright. I just want to see my mother."

They all walked quietly towards the unit. The presence of strange wires, tubing and machines overpowered the room as Ellen lay in the midst of it all.

Gwen inched closer to the bed holding her breath with each step. Bending down, she gently held her mother's hand and whispered softly into her ear. "I'm here now and I am not going anywhere until you get better," she said wiping away her tears. "Open your eyes if you can hear me, I have a wonderful surprise for you." She listened to the swooshing sound the ventilator made as it helped her breathe. "I really need you to open your eyes mommy." She leaned her head onto hers. "I found Rose," she said. "Please don't leave me. ... I found Rose," she whispered. When she glanced up through the tears, she noticed Rose had never moved away from the door.

"Come on and talk to her," Gwen said, reaching out for her hand. "It's going to be alright." She forced out those words.

By the time Rose crept almost to where her mother lay, Gwen assisted her the rest of the way. Switching places, she was relieved when Rose finally began talking.

"That's it Rose, keep doing that. She hears you," Gwen said.

"How do you know?" she whispered.

"She just squeezed my hand."

Gwen and Rose slept on the narrow cots in the critical care waiting room later that night. They went to see their mother at each of the scheduled visiting times.

"Good news, her vital signs are improving and she is very much awake," her nurse said. "She wants that tube out and I'm calling the doctor now to see what her plans are for making her a little more comfortable."

When Ellen saw Rose, she gestured with her hand to come closer. Placing several fingers up, she gently touched her daughter's face. Rose turned and kissed her hand.

At the next visiting hours a surprise awaited them when they walked into the room. There Ellen sat in the large bedside chair without the breathing tube.

"How-are-my-girls?" she asked, in a shaky, almost inaudible voice.

They ran to her bedside. Careful not to disturb the wires, Rose laid her head ever so lightly on her chest. "Mother, I thought I would never get the chance to….."

"Sh-h-h, I know, I know. I –came- all -the -way -to New York -just -to –see-you," she said, taking breaths between each word.

"Try not to talk too much," Gwen said, gently smoothing out the tangles in her hair. "Don't worry, we'll get you strong again."

The doctors were amazed at the progress she made. In less than a week Ellen was well enough to be moved from the ICU into a regular room.

Rose walked over to the window and gazed out from room 524. "Do you think we should call Clara and let her know how mother is doing?"

"Absolutely not," Gwen whispered. She looked over at their mother sleeping soundly. "She doesn't care and we must respect her wishes," she continued. "Plus, I don't ever want to talk to her again. Her love has escaped us these many years and I've learned to accept that and move on. You should too."

"No, Gwen, we've got to help her learn how to love her family," Rose, whispered.

"Let's not fight over this. You know how I feel," Gwen said.

"I know, but she's our sister," her voice now slightly elevated.

"That's right Rose," Ellen said softly.

They both looked over at their mother now fully awake.

"Sorry, we didn't mean to disturb you," Gwen said.

"That's okay, I'm glad you girls brought up the subject of your sister. I was thinking we should call her too," Ellen said.

Gwen curled her feet in the chair, "It's okay if the two of you decide to, but I won't be talking to her," she said, as she pulled out her novel and began reading.

Rose thought back on the many fights she witnessed between her older sisters. Even though they fought like two heavy weight champs she had never seen Gwen quite that defiant. She wondered what Clara had done this time?

She knew how far to push her sister and decided it was best to change the subject. "You'll never believe how William and I met," Rose said, smoothing the spread on her mother's bed.

It was a good move, because in just five minutes they were all laughing and talking again.

As the months swiftly passed, and their mother's health improved, Gwen and Rick were in the middle of their move to New York.

"Now…that looks great," Gwen said, arranging the pillows on the couch.

"It sure does, and I'm not moving another piece of furniture," Rick said. "William and I are going on strike. No more heavy lifting. Besides, I need to get ready for tonight. After all, this is one of my last nights as a bachelor."

"No way are you leaving me to finish all this. That's just not happening, sir," Gwen said, easing her arm around him.

Rose descended the steps balancing a decorative pillow on her head and a comforter draped around her shoulders. "This is how you should walk down the aisle, Gwen."

They all laughed at her uncoordinated imitation of a bridal march, the pillow threatening to fall with each step. The 3,000 square feet condominium overflowed with fun and laughter.

"Pizza time," Ellen yelled.

"At last," Rick said, marching towards the kitchen knocking the pillow off Rose's head. "I'm starving."

Gwen felt a sense of euphoria, reminiscent of her earlier childhood days. She was happy. In a few days she was going to be Mrs. Rick Haley, and for her, the day couldn't come soon enough. "What a magnificent spin on a seemingly plain life," she thought. She was slowly but surely transforming into a high fashion model and had absolutely no idea how it all happened. One day she was the cutie in the baseball cap and the next one she was walking the runways in Paris, London, L.A. and

New York. The best news came, however, when her mother was given a thumbs-up at her last doctor's visit. The X-rays and tests showed her lungs were almost functioning at full capacity. Her appetite had come back and so had the color in her cheeks. Rose was fitted for her bridesmaid's dress. A size eight! Was it all too good to be true?

While they ate, William pulled Rose aside and whispered, "My family is coming to New York this weekend. They are dying to meet you."

"What if you invited them to the wedding? I would love for them to come."

"I thought about it but I didn't know if Gwen would mind. You know she really wants a small wedding."

"Gw-w-wen," Rose yelled. Rose told her about William's parents coming to town the week of the wedding.

"Hey, it's going to be a great party. Do you think they would come?" Gwen shouted back.

"Sure, my folks love a party."

"That's it, they're invited!"

The day before the wedding, things were moving so fast Gwen was afraid she would forget something important. The thought of misplacing Rick's ring, the marriage license or anything that was absolutely essential for the day to go well, gnawed at her mind. She carefully scanned her 'to do' list as she raced upstairs. They were scheduled to pick up friends from the airport, swing by and get one of the bridesmaid's dresses and accessories for herself on the other side of town. Everyone was set to meet at Gables for dinner at six. It was already four-fifteen.

"Their plane will land in twenty minutes," Rick said. "Please hurry."

Grabbing her bag, she rushed out behind him. When they finally picked up their guests and completed the rest of the errands, they arrived at the restaurant around six-thirty.

All of their friends had gathered for the pre-wedding festivities. The paparazzi were out of control, but she was determined not to let them become a major distraction. The reason she had chosen the upscale restaurant in the first place was for its scenic view, but most of all the privacy it offered them. The secluded spot helped to keep her unwanted guests at bay once they were inside.

"Yay...Congratulations," her friends all yelled when they walked inside.

"You finally made it," Rose said, guiding them to the guest of honor's table.

William's parents were there and were surprisingly very outgoing.

As Gwen slowly began to unwind, she remembered why she got along so well with her college buddies. They always had a blast whenever they were together. It was no different today.

Gwen stopped chatting briefly when she spotted her mother standing alone—leaning against the railing, gazing out over the harbor. She eased away from her friends as she walked up to her.

"Hey there," she said, rubbing her shoulders. "Are you okay? Can I get you anything?"

"No, sweetheart, I'm fine." She leaned over and kissed her cheek. "This is such a beautiful place. It reminds me of where Clara's rehearsal dinner was held."

"Come on now, let's think happy thoughts," Gwen said, turning her slowly around. "Rose and I are here."

"I know and believe me, I'm happy about that," Ellen said. She was indeed delighted and glad to be able to enjoy the time with her daughters, but she missed Clara so much.

"Come on," Gwen said, leading her mother to the festivities. "We have a wedding to enjoy."

The wedding started on time—that was the only request the bride had in the midst of her hectic day and it was Rose that made it happen.

Rose was so busy giving last minute instructions, she didn't notice when Gwen entered the room. Looking up, it was Gwen's captivating beauty that caused her to gasp. The strapless, white wedding gown was painted on every inch of her thin five-foot-nine—one hundred-twenty-five pound frame. The diamond beading sparkling on the embellished band outlining her tiny waist, accented the dress to perfection. Her makeup artist had the unique gift of applying the right combination and hint of colors. Today, he used his talent brilliantly. Her face shone radiantly—her make-up flawless. Rose finally understood why most in the entertainment industry were so enamored with her. There was no denying it, Gwen was truly a strikingly beautiful girl with a uniqueness all her own. Rick was going to be proud.

The chimes bellowed as the old historic church overflowed with family and friends. Her wedding guests turned and whispered as Gwen slowly, gracefully walked the aisle.

The actual wedding ceremony moved along swiftly just as planned.

"You may now kiss the bride," the priest said.

"Hello there, Mrs. Haley," Rick said, kissing her.

"Hi there, Mr. Haley," she said, smiling widely.

They danced all night. It was their guests who reminded them they had a honeymoon to enjoy as they eased out the back door of the banquet suite.

One of Gwen and Rick's surprise guests was the managing editor of the largest magazine in the country. Visiting his New York office, his daughter had insisted he accompany her to the wedding and he was glad that she did. The moment he saw Gwen, he knew he had to sign her for his cover. She was exactly what he had been looking for...someone youthful, fresh, and definitely high fashion.

"Hello, I'm told you are the bride's sister," he said, approaching Rose.

"Yes, I am and thanks for coming." At this point, Rose was giving her canned 'thank you's' to everybody.

"I've been through one of these before with my oldest daughter. I know how much work it calls for and how tired you must be," he said.

"Exhausted is a better word, but it has been a whole lot of fun," she said, swinging her shoes in her hands.

He handed her his card, "Would you please give this to your sister for me? She can call me any time. Thanks, and try and get yourself some rest," he said, walking away.

"Nice meeting you too." When she read the card she realized exactly who the mystery man was.

"Look at this," she said, rushing up to William. "Can you believe Mr. Glen Brooks himself has actually been at the wedding reception this whole time?"

"Okay, now who is Mr. Glen Brooks again?" he asked, snuggling up to her.

"Only the biggest magazine editor in the country—maybe the world."

"That's pretty cool, I guess?" William said.

Rose guided him to the dance floor having received a sudden burst of energy. "It's better than cool William…it's all absolutely wonderful."

At the end of the fun-filled night, Rose changed her mind a hundred times about calling Gwen to let her in on the surprise she had waiting for her at home. She decided it was best to leave them alone and let the newlyweds enjoy their time away. Seven days later, however, as soon as they returned to the states, she insisted on seeing her.

"Rose, it was incredible," Gwen said, flopping down on the bed. "Our villa was surrounded by the bluest set of waters I have ever seen." She sat up. "We had our own personal chef for every meal. It was so romantic… Rick and I danced under the stars," she beamed.

Rose decided to wait until she had completely finished describing their honeymoon before handing her the card.

"Who gave you this?" she asked, flipping the card over and over.

"Glen Brooks in the flesh!"

"No way," she sat holding the card. "My friend Allison introduced Rick and me to him at the wedding, but that was the extent of our conversation. I guess I was so caught up in the evening I didn't think anything else about it."

"Can you imagine how hard this has been for me not to call you on your honeymoon? He wants you to contact him as soon as possible."

Gwen dialed Rick's number at his office.

"What are you doing on the phone with me then? Call him, babe," he said.

She quickly hung up and punched in the numbers as his assistant answered. "Hold one moment please, Mrs. Haley, he's been expecting your call."

Gwen mumbled to herself, "I will not allow myself to believe any of this is real until I actually speak to Mr. Brooks."

"I'm transferring you to his cell now," the assistant said.

"Hello and welcome back to the states," Glen shouted into the phone.

Her mouth stretched open wide.

"I'm glad you called, Gwen. I would like to get together next week and chat. I have a great opportunity I think you may want to consider. Call my office and tell Lauren to give you some time on my calendar to discuss the matter. By the way, how was the honeymoon?"

"It was great," she said, her voice now several octaves lighter.

"Well, congratulations again. Listen, 'gotta run. It was good speaking with you
and we will talk next week."

"Yes, sir."

Gwen stared into the receiver, the dial tone buzzing.

She screamed in Rick's ear when she phoned him. "I spoke with Mr. Brooks! It was really him! Can you believe it?"

Rick understood when she got that excited to expect just about anything from her. He was especially glad that she had called right then. Talking to her took his mind off the former call he'd received. His sister had phoned and was in trouble again.

"I can't wait 'til I get home so you can tell me all about it," Rick said, leaning back in his chair. He took a moment to relax, massaging the tenseness that had already found its way into his shoulders.

When he hung up, his mind quickly shifted back to his sister. Boy, how Jessica's life had changed. She had gone from this funny, vibrant kid, to someone he barely knew.

He noticed the dramatic change in her life the day their mother walked out of theirs. She left them at their grandmother's home and just never came back. Matters quickly went from bad to worse when their nana became ill. Jessica had been the perfect caregiver all the way up to her death. After that, she seemed to channel her emotions into some pretty self-destructive behaviors. It didn't take long for him to figure out what was keeping her out every night. She was a hard core addict—cocaine being her drug of choice. He did all he could to get her the help she needed, but she would always flat-out refuse him. He couldn't count the nights he ended up searching for her when she went missing for days. Soon, he shifted over to tough love when he'd almost gotten beaten up one night for going into the wrong crack house. He vowed he would never put his own life at risk like that again. Now, their worlds were miles apart. He would call occasionally, mainly to make sure she was still alive. It was Gwen, however, that always encouraged him to try and find her—to see if she was ready to get the help she desperately needed. Even when he spoke to her today, he knew drugs were yet a major part of her life.

He replayed their conversation. "What's up bro," she said. "I'm in a tad bit of trouble and I need yo' help man."

"I'm listening."

"They kickin' us out the hospital tomorrow."

That took him by surprise. "Are you okay?" he asked.

"Yeah, we ah' ight," she said.

"We? Who's the "we", Jessica? Did you and someone else get hurt or something?"

She didn't reply immediately.

"Jessica, what's going on?"

"It's a beautiful baby girl, man! You got yo 'self a niece. We gotta leave here and I ain't got no where's to go. I can make it on the streets by myself, but it ain't no place for no baby."

"Whoa, wait a minute. What am I supposed to do about that Jessica?" Rick asked, vigorously rubbing his chin. "The social workers at the hospital can help you find some temporary shelter can't they?"

"Yeah, but I thought I'd give you the first pass at her—seeing how she's 'yo flesh 'n blood 'n all. She's so pretty, Rick, I know ya'll ah wanna once you see her."

"Wait a second, Jessica! Slow down a minute."

"You take her, man. You can have her. She'll be safe with you."

"I don't think you need to give your baby away to anyone." He felt the hardened wall he'd built up for years began to crumble. "Listen sis, this may be a good time for you to come here so I can help you get on your feet again. Then you can take care of your own baby."

"Man, that sounds straight and all, but I've kinda gotten myself into something I can't get out of. It's all a mess man. Ricky, they offering me some dough for the baby, and maybe I should accept it."

He could tell she was crying. He also knew when she called him Ricky, she was extremely vulnerable.

"You and I both know if I take that money it'll be gone in a New Yawk minute," she said. "Then I won't have her or the money no 'mo. Man, this is so messed up. What am I gonna do?"

"Jessica, calm down. Let's talk about it more tomorrow. In the meantime, I'm going to see to it that you have somewhere to stay until we can figure this all out. We don't want to make the wrong move because we didn't take the time to think things through." He promised he would call her in the morning after he'd spoken to the hospital administrator.

Following Gwen's great news, he just didn't have the heart to share his.

Later that night, he sat quietly as he listened to Gwen's third rendition of her conversation with Mr. Brooks. He had an awful headache thinking about Jessica, but refused to let that dampen her happy mood. She was at an all-time high as she rattled on and on about the day.

"It's completely amazing," she said. "Doors that can open as a result of being associated with him are usually incredible, babe."

He watched her as she took in mouthfuls of salad. "What a remarkable woman she was," he thought. She always found time for the two of them to be alone, even with her very busy schedule. She had already seen to it that her mother's living arrangements were extremely comfortable.   Rose was now able to afford medical school and didn't have to worry about student loans, mainly because of her. She was the most generous and loving person he knew and he understood how blessed he was to have married her.

"You're quiet honey, anything wrong?" she asked, later that night.

"Nah, I'm okay. Just a little tired," Rick said, yawning.

He tossed and turned in bed, finally getting up to pop a couple of Ibuprofen in his mouth. When he returned, Gwen gently wrapped her arms around him.

"What's wrong?" she asked.

He turned to face her and elaborate about his conversation with Jessica.

Gwen sat up and turned on the bedside light. "That's your niece, Rick. Plus, your sister needs you now."

"A baby, Gwen, how can I ask you to do something like that? That's just not fair."

"Life's not always fair, but please make me this one promise….we will always take care of our families," she said, tears forming in her eyes.

"So, you really think you would be fine with us taking the baby until Jessica gets herself together," Rick said.

"Yes, but tell Jessica this for me. We will come and get our niece—and take very good care of her. We will also give her exactly one year to get her life together. If she is not back here at that time and completely drug free, let Jessica know we will begin proceedings to adopt her baby, and give her the type of home she rightfully deserves."

Rick kissed her softly. "You are an amazing woman Gwen Haley."

Two days later, Gwen and Rick stood in the hotel's lobby waiting for Jessica to arrive. She was already an hour and a half late. They had flown hundreds of miles to see her and had no idea how she ended up in Charlotte, North Carolina.

Finally, she came barging through the door swinging the baby carrier rather loosely. When he saw her, he tried hard to hide the shock that was probably apparent on his face. Her beautiful hair was now stringy and matted, and all of her side teeth were missing. She was thin except for the baby pouch, and looked much older than when he'd last seen her.

"Yo, yo, yo, say what's up to yo' Uncle Rick, Elizabeth," Jessica said handing him the baby. "I named her after the queen herself. One day she'll thank me for it. Hey, you must be Gwen. What's up, 'sista in law?" she said hugging her tightly.

"Oh, Jessica she's absolutely beautiful," Gwen said, reaching for the baby.

"I told ya. She's the prettiest baby I seen in a long time."

"Hi, I'm your auntie," Gwen gushed as she gently stroked her tiny pink shirt. Her heart was already melting.

"Why don't we get out of here and grab something to eat," Rick said. "We all need to talk."

While they ate at a nearby restaurant he explained in full detail their plans for the baby.

"So, it mean ya'll 'givin me a year to git her back?" Jessica asked. The baby started to cry, but she ignored her as she took huge bites of her hamburger, much of its garnishments sliding out the bun.

Gwen reached over to soothe the baby placing the pacifier in her mouth.

"Listen, Jessica, I am giving you exactly one year to clean up your act, get off drugs and be a good mother," Rick said. "We are willing to help you do that. If you go back with us to New York, there is a rehab facility all set up for you there. They have a great reputation of getting clients clean and keeping them that way," he said.

Jessica sat for a moment and then a giant, toothless smile emerged. "It's a deal," she said.

Rick gathered his sister's hands in his and kissed them. Those three words took away the many years of hurt and worry he experienced while she was out on the streets. He knew his sister and was familiar with her capricious behavior. She would never agree to that kind of assistance if she wasn't truly ready to rid herself of her demons she faced each day. He thanked God for his niece as he looked down into her tiny, angelic face. He was convinced she was the sole reason he was going to get his sister back before it was too late. Jessica loved hard and Elizabeth was the catalyst she needed to help turn her life around.

"Yahoo," Jessica yelled, "I'm going to New Yawk Cit-tay." She held her finger up as she stuffed the last of the hamburger into her mouth, swallowing hard. "Ya'll watch Lizzy while I go and grab a few of our thangs. The hospital loaded us up with diapers and milk. I'll meet 'cha back here at the hotel in a 'coupla hours. Then I'll straight be going with ya'll all the way to the Big Apple," she said, wiping her mouth.

"Don't worry about whatever it is you have to get, Jessica, it can all be replaced. Why don't we go shopping and get you and the baby everything you need for the trip?" Gwen said, smiling. "Come on back to the hotel with us, besides, the baby is really cranky right now."

"I'm telling you, I will only be 'gawn a 'coupla hours." She looked over at the crying baby and continued, "I have some personal stuff to git." She hesitated for a moment and then looked at Rick, "I gotta go git nana's Bible. That's the only thing I have left of her," she said, a hint of sadness in her eyes.

Rick kissed his sister and said goodbye. That was the last time he would see her alive. When she hadn't shown up in three days, the police finally came to the hotel and told him she had been found in a crack house stabbed multiple times.

Jessica's funeral was simple. She was cremated. Rick had also been successful in finding his own mother. He was surprised when she showed up for her daughter's funeral and cried the entire time. She promised him she would keep in touch. He finally acknowledged the fact that it was her mental challenges that kept them apart these many years.

Rick was beginning to appreciate the new chapters unfolding in his life…getting to know his mother and now officially adopting Lizzy as their daughter.

The baby added a splash of happiness each one of them needed. She had become a wonderful source of comfort for Rick after the murder of his sister. He blamed himself for not insisting that she stay at the hotel that day.

Gwen loved becoming an instant mom and Ellen absolutely adored being called, grandmother.

"Gwen, she is so beautiful," Ellen said quietly. "I'm glad you guys are allowing me to keep her instead of hiring a nanny. Between shopping excursions and trips to the park, we are having tons of fun." She watched as Gwen gently rocked Lizzy to sleep. "She is so much company for me and such a happy baby. My problem is when Rose comes home from medical school. That's when the real war begins," Ellen chuckled softly.

"She and William will make up any excuse to keep her with them all the time," Gwen said, settling Lizzy into the crib. "There's just not enough of you to go around, is there," Gwen whispered to the sleeping baby.

They retreated to the day room as Gwen stretched out on the sofa. Ellen noticed her constant yawning and the tiny circles beginning to form under both eyes. While she was glad she and Rick had somehow managed to juggle their schedules to ensure one of them was home with Lizzy, she could tell her daughter was exhausted. She'd just flown in from London walking the runway in a major fashion show there. Before that, she had been in L.A. where she attended the premiere of a blockbuster film she played a small role in. "It was the jet lag that was probably catching up with her," she thought.

"Hey, you're looking awfully tired," Ellen said.

"Our schedules are crazy right now. Rick and I are being pulled in so many directions. We have some of the finest agents and managers and they are getting us some pretty incredible assignments—it's hard to say no to the offers."

"To say the least," Ellen said. "You, on the Art Letterman show. Now, that was unbelievable. You looked so beautiful sitting there."

"It was such an awesome experience," Gwen said.

Ellen loved all of her girls, but knew there was a special place in her heart for Gwen. She was the daughter whom she shared her most intimate secrets with—the one that had a special way of brightening her day. It was a given she could get just about anything from her, especially when she heard her say, 'mother, you're my best friend.' So, if she seemed overly concerned it was because she cared so deeply and knew her so well.

"Is all of this still fun for you?" Ellen asked in that distinctive nurturing voice of hers.

"You can't imagine how much fun I'm having, mother. Every day, I feel like pinching myself to see if I'm dreaming. The best part of it all is we have Lizzy in our lives," she said, "but I do need your opinion about something. My agent phoned yesterday and told me a major Hollywood producer wants me to audition for a part in his movie. He saw me on the Letterman show and also liked the part I played in my last film. He thought I would be perfect for the supporting character role. What do you think?"

Ellen knew what was at the heart of her question. Gwen loved being a wife and more than anything she loved being Lizzy's mother. She was thrown into the heart of stardom and was determined to excel at all three of her now demanding roles.

"Is that something you want to do?" she asked.

"I love modeling but I am also fascinated with acting. Sometimes I feel as if I'm turning my back on the profession that gave me my break, especially if I decide to accept the role. I'm already finding it difficult to take on as many modeling assignments as before. Then there's Rick and Lizzy and you....whew!" she said, smiling at her mother. "I just want to make the best decision."

Ellen smiled. She knew exactly what she wanted to tell her at that very moment. There may not be future opportunities to give motherly advice like this. She was well aware of that.

She gazed lovingly at her daughter. "Modeling gave you the opportunity for the world to be introduced to someone very special. Acting is now giving you an even wider range of exposure," she said. "It's all coming together quite nicely, but it all comes with choices and sacrifices. When you choose wisely, life has a way of confirming it all for you. When Rick is satisfied and Lizzy feels your love, it will be obvious you are making some pretty wise decisions. You may have to take risks from time to time, but always choose those things that God places in your heart. Those are the choices that yield the greatest results and lend you the greatest peace—despite the circumstances. He won't lead you wrong, baby."

Gwen recognized good advice. She relished the insight... hiding it all deep inside.

After she was placed on the cover of one of the most popular magazines in the world, the acting opportunities came pouring in. It had to be true, everything Glen Brook touched turned gold. Virtually every top designer in the world wanted to work with her. At this point Gwen knew she had the freedom to select whom she wanted to work for and when.

Besides the offers she had just accepted, there was one she found hard to refuse. She was asked to audition for a role she knew was reserved for only the experienced and most popular stars. Skip Jetter was 'the' producer to work for in Hollywood and known for catapulting actor's careers into the stratosphere of stardom. When it came time for her audition, she remained calm and confident. The more she read, the more her confidence grew as she nailed line after line. She even wondered herself where the inspiration came from.

Skip kept using words like, 'amazing, and very impressed' over and over again. She knew in her heart the role was hers. Two weeks later she received the phone call she had been waiting on.

"I could not see this film without you," the high-powered, Italian director said with his thick accent.
Playing one of the leading roles in a film that was sure to be a number one hit pushed her life into the express lane. Up early and sometimes leaving the set at the break of dawn, she now understood how grueling acting could be.

As predicted, the movie had become a huge box office smash and it didn't take long for the additional offers to follow. She was glad the next movie was being filmed in New York, allowing her to spend more time with Rick and Lizzy.
She decided to leave the set early and arrived home just in time for dinner. As she walked in from the garage, she headed for the family area.

"What in the world?" she said. Newspaper articles were spread all over the table and draped over the chairs. Inching closer to the first black and white, it read, "The new breakout star of the year has to be Gwen Haley."

Every article she picked up gave rave reviews for the part she played in her most recent film. She took in a deep breath as her eyes grew large. It was one line that gave her a rush like none others—"There is already buzz in the Hollywood circles that she is the front runner for Best Supporting Actress at the Golden Globes."

Rick and Ellen were both watching, secretly enjoying Gwen's reactions. She turned when she heard Lizzy squeal, reaching out for her.

"Are you kidding me? This is too much! Am I dreaming?" she said, picking up the baby.

"Congratulations," they both yelled as Lizzy clapped her hands.

It was all true, exactly one month later she was nominated.

"Did I hear you say something about BEING NOMINATED FOR A GOLDEN GLOBE," she yelled in the phone.

"I'm not fooling around, kiddo," her agent yelled back.

She blew kisses through the receiver, barely hanging it up as she raced upstairs.

"R-i-i-ck, RICK, R-i-i-ck, where are you?" She grabbed his hands and twirled him around—finally giving him a kiss. "I am so glad I have you, Lizzy and my mother here to enjoy this moment," she said.

Chapter 15

Hard Times

"That's the last of the furniture Mrs. Gordon." The lead mover took the large faded handkerchief from his back pocket and wiped his brow.

Clara reached into her wallet and pulled out most of the cash.

"That should do it," he said, handing her the receipt.

She'd sold practically everything and still it made only a small dent in all that she owed. It was when she handed the keys over to Eric's Range Rover that reality truly set in. Selling his car gave her the immediate cash she needed, but she was determined to pay off as many bills as possible. Having done so took her bank account back down to virtually zero. Even at that, most of the money left was already promised to others.

Clara walked around the empty rooms they had once called home. Forcing herself to leave the premises, she bundled the twins and sat them in their carriers. Backing out of the garage and heading towards her new apartment on the other side of town, she had just enough gas to make it there and to get to work in the morning.

Early the next day, Clara dropped the girls off at the day care attached to the apartment building. That was her sole purpose for moving there. It would help save on gas and the fees were affordable.

This was her new routine for now and she was forced to embrace it until things got better. She wasn't worried.

She had done it before—made herself a success. She was more than confident she could do it again. In the meantime, she also knew what it took to maintain her dignity. She thought, "accessorize"! Purchasing inexpensive clothes and designer accessories like she did years ago was the only way to go.

Even at that, Karen stopped speaking to her and so did most of the other teachers.

"Mrs. Gordon, may I see you in my office," the headmaster said.

She walked into the large decorative room with her head held high. She sat gingerly in the antique chair facing his desk.

"I need to make you aware of a very important matter," he said. "The Board of Directors asked me to make cuts to our budget this month. This is a first for Carrington Academy I might add, and unfortunately it will affect several of our teachers." He looked away briefly and then back at her. Wiping the glistening bald spot in the top of his head, he said, "I'm sorry to inform you, but this will be your last week here."

Clara wasn't surprised. Ginny, the only teacher that did speak to her warned her it was coming. Mr. Tremble was the other teacher they let go. Everyone knew it was personal between him and the headmaster. They just never got along. She also understood why she was being asked to leave. She no longer fit in. Between Karen and Miriam, they both had done a great job of exposing her story to the entire town. Her mother was not the well to do business woman she reported her to be. In fact, they were raised dirt poor. That was the cliff note version of the story. By the time those two had finished, she was essentially a gold digger that caused total chaos in the Gordon family.

She knew that group and understood how well they operated. It was an effective network and once activated could crumble the reputation and life of anybody that got in their way. Now, instead of being a part of the clique and enjoying the thrill of being one of the main instigators, she had become the intended target. To make matters worse, she couldn't find anyone who would hire her in the local area as a teacher.

Clara drove along I-40 to her apartment. Realizing it was too late to swing the car around as she parked... the last person she wanted to see stood before her.

"Mrs. Gordon, your rent is due the first of every month," the apartment manager said walking up to her. "I understand you are having a hard time right now, but I need my money." His voice remained flat.

"I had to pay the day care, but I'll have your money by the end of the week," Clara said. She jumped out of the car racing to get her girls. Looking over her shoulder, she yelled, "I promise, Mack."

She knew he would come looking for her. He always did.

"You better," he shouted back.

Waitressing was the only job she could find until she secured another teaching position. It put fast cash in her pocket and kept the lights on. She worked the late shift at an upscale restaurant in the suburbs. Her ultimate goal was to save enough money so she could move as far away from the Bradbury gang as possible. "She wanted to find a place where no one knew her and it couldn't happen soon enough," she thought. She stuffed her tips into the pocket of her pencil skirt and headed for table eight.

"I'll be right back with your drinks," she told the couple. When she looked up, she stared directly into the faces of Karen and Shannon as they strolled through the door.

"Sure," she heard the young hostess say as she motioned for her. "Right this way," she said to them. "Clara, they have requested your table."

"My, my, isn't this a coincidence," Karen said, sliding into her seat.

"What may I get you ladies to drink?" Clara asked.

"I'll have a rusty nail," Karen said. "Make that two," Shannon added.

"Right away."

"I told you we would find her here," she heard Karen whisper, their heads almost glued together when she left.

Clara thought about walking through the double doors of the restaurant and never looking back. Then she remembered Mack and her rent that was already two months behind. She endured the humiliating evening until her two unwanted guests were plastered and all but asked to leave by the manager.

When she arrived home and put the girls to bed, she fell onto hers having only removed her shoes. They had been extremely busy which helped take her mind off her loud, obnoxious visitors.

As she slept, she dreamed of Eric and the girls swimming in their brand new pool. The girls were yelling and splashing water everywhere. "Daddy, catch me! Catch me!" they shouted. The screaming became so loud that eventually she sat straight up in bed.

It was one of the twins crying as she ran to her. "Oh my, you are burning up," she said reaching for her baby. She ran to get the thermometer gently sliding it into her ear. It immediately climbed to 104. Grabbing her keys and the other twin, she raced to the emergency room.

"Both ears are infected and we are going to have to start an IV," the emergency room physician said. "We will give her IV antibiotics and see how well she responds. In the meanwhile, the medication the nurse has already given her will bring down the temp. Don't look so worried, mommy," the doctor said. "She's going to be fine."

It was the first time Clara felt like bawling, but it didn't take her long to quickly pull it together. She rested her head against her baby's. Closing her eyes, she thought... "Her life was definitely spiraling out of control." She found herself wondering if this was her fate—was she ever going to pull it together again. No! She dismissed every thought that was bold enough to suggest she would never live out her dreams. She defiantly replaced them with the fact that she had pulled herself from the depths of nothing before, and would do whatever it took to do it again.

It was four a.m. and she was scheduled to open the restaurant for the eight a.m. crowd. She needed to be there by six—in just two hours. Her employer was a strict, quiet man, extremely short in stature. It was the first time he had ever asked her to come in early.

She glanced at her phone and was immediately concerned about the possibility of a poor reception when she phoned him. The last thing she needed was to hang up on her boss. She walked to the nurse's station and asked to use the phone. "Mr. Mascarina? Hi, this is Clara

Gordon. I'm at the hospital with my very sick child. I don't think I'll be out of the emergency room in time to get there to open up."

"Okay. I understand," she whispered into the phone.

She was running out of options. She had just been fired.

Clara watched as the last of the IV antibiotic infused into the tiny tubing connected to her baby's arm. Shutting her eyes briefly, she wiped her own runny nose. She wasn't feeling the best as she leaned her head over and dozed. There was nowhere else she needed to be.

Twenty minutes later she stirred when the nurse unwrapped the gauze that held the baby's IV in place, slowly removing the needle.

"Her temp has come down considerably," the nurse whispered. "Keep giving her the medicine as prescribed and she will get to feeling better in no time." She repeated the instructions to her.

"Thanks," Clara said, rubbing her eyes. Gathering both babies, she stopped by the pharmacy to get the prescription for the oral antibiotics. She dipped into her grocery money to purchase the medication.

When she arrived home, she welcomed the long hot shower. As she dried her hair, she thought of the interview she had next week. It was the only bright spot in her life. The teaching assignment didn't pay as much as she was used to, but along with the social security checks she would somehow manage. The job was almost fifty miles from the city, a perfect opportunity to move away from the cruel hands of her tormentors.

She was glad the rest of her day was uneventful. Later that night, she wrapped her arms around both girls as they climbed in bed. She allowed them to sleep with her so she could check the sick one's temp often. When they were all comfortable, she reached for the remote and tuned in to Art Letterman. She always found him amusing. Her eyes were heavy as she buried her head into the soft satin pillow. The satin sheet sets were her favorite and she simply refused to sell them along with a few other personal items after her financial debacle.

Just as she was about to doze off, she heard Letterman announce—"Now ladies and gentlemen, please welcome Mrs. Gwen Haley." Through eyes half shut, she watched as the pretty, tall thin girl smiled and hugged Letterman before she sat down. She heard the model say something about her sister Rose. Her sister Rose, how weird was that? "Both women had her sisters' names," she thought, right before slipping quietly into a deep-peaceful much needed sleep.

The following week, she had plenty of time to spend with her girls. They took long walks in the park, always careful to avoid the manager's office. Even though she had no money she still didn't panic. She guessed it was the interview scheduled for tomorrow that helped her keep it together.

The next day the twins were clingy and followed her everywhere she went. She wanted to look nice for the interview, but found it difficult trying to dress and deal with both girls.

Running a little behind, she raced next door. Her neighbor had agreed to watch the twins for a couple of hours until she returned.

When Clara moved in, Pat was already living in the apartment next to hers. She was an extremely quiet young lady, but nice. Even though she had three kids of her own, she never refused whenever she asked her to watch her babies. Clara promised she would be home in plenty of time for her to get to the appointment she also had scheduled.

Finally on her way, the speedometer gradually inched its way pass eighty. She knew she would have to push it if there was any chance of her getting to the interview on time. She hated speeding, but being late wasn't an option to the only job prospect she had in months.

Suddenly, all the cars ahead of her braked, eventually slowing to a complete stop. Peeking out the window, Clara saw a line of cars in front of her. The sun was bearing down hard but she dared not turn on the air conditioner. The last time she tried to cool the car it took her forever to get it started again.

She struck the steering wheel, pushed back hard in her seat and sat.

Finally, she passed the last of the orange cones. Quickly swerving into another lane, she glanced at the clock. She had exactly fifteen minutes to make it there on time.

She parked in the first empty space in the school's parking lot and ran into the building. The heat from the car made her damp shirt cling to her back and the running did little to help. She looked for a bathroom to freshen up, but there was no time. Taking in a deep breath, smoothing her hair and then her skirt, she walked slowly through the door that read, Administration.

She had exactly two minutes to spare. Clara smiled brightly as she shook hands with the principal.

"The interview is going well," she thought. The administrator knew the headmaster at Carrington Academy and that was her only tense moment. It was when he talked about not 'fitting in with that kind of crowd either', that she relaxed again.

"Maybe, just maybe, "Clara thought, "she would get the job." It would certainly mean the world if she did.

"We look forward to working with you, Mrs. Gordon," he said, extending his hand and the job offer.

She walked swiftly to the car and once safely inside threw her hands in the air. She was now beginning to understand what gratefulness felt like.

"At last," Clara thought to herself. "Life was about to get back on track again." As soon as she got home she planned on searching the ads for a better place to live.

Glancing at her watch, she knew she would have to hurry if she was going to make it back by four.

The traffic around the construction site was even more congested on her side of the highway.

"Ugh," Clara said when she came to a complete stop. Pat was meeting her real estate agent about a possible foreclosure in less than an hour. She knew how badly she wanted to get out of those apartments and find a nice home for herself and the three kids—almost as bad as she did.

If she could just see her way around the two cars ahead, she would be able to maneuver past the last of the construction and be free of all the congestion. Cutting it ever so close, she inched past the first car and then cleared the second.

She floored the accelerator.

Out of nowhere the yellow Buick pulled in front of her and suddenly braked. Swerving to keep from rear ending it, Clara could feel the car begin to skid. In a split second she'd lost control. Snatching the steering wheel in the same direction to stop the car from spinning all but made the concrete medium unavoidable. The impact of it forced her into the opposite lane. A truck turned sharply to keep from hitting her. When she saw the large SUV screeching, heading directly towards her, she braced herself for the inevitable. The blow flipped her car onto its side, sliding it several feet until it eventually landed on the roof, tires spinning in the air.

When she slowly opened her eyes, Clara couldn't believe she had been through four hours of surgery and was now recovering in the intensive care unit. She had ruptured her spleen, fractured her left ankle, and had a severe concussion. The chest tube was in place for a collapsed left lung and a large bandage on her head protected the deep gash along her hairline. Cuts and bruises covered every inch of her body.

For several days she lay alone in the hospital determined to fight the excruciating pain. She was glad for any progress, especially when they removed the chest tube and later transferred her into a regular room. It was her shattered ankle that caused her the greatest amount of discomfort and kept her in bed most of the day. They were scheduled to operate on it again in two more days.

By the fifth day in the hospital, she was depressed. She tried talking herself out of it, reasoning…it was just a spurt of bad luck. Things would soon turn around again. This time, however, her mind wasn't buying any of it.

She looked up one afternoon and to her surprise Pat walked through the door. "Finally, someone had come to see her," she thought. She was actually glad to see her neighbor.

"I really appreciate you seeing after the girls and I know how inconvenient it must be. It's my stupid ankle and concussion that's keeping me from coming home. If I could, believe you me, I would walk right out of here."

Pat sat in the chair close by. She really did understand Clara's plight, but she also had one of her own. How could she expect her to watch after two additional kids this long? She noticed her neighbor's dramatic weight loss, the fight in her eyes obviously snuffed out and she didn't have the heart to confront her.

"All I need for you to do is get better and come home as soon as you can," Pat finally said. "Here, I brought your mail. I saw a letter from the school you had the interview with. Do you want me to open it?"

Clara nodded.

"Dear Mrs. Gordon," she read softly. "I regret to inform you that the position I offered you is no longer available. Since I haven't been able to contact you, I assumed you no longer desired the job offer..."

Clara held her hand up, "Please stop."

Pat did not want to deliver the rest of the news, but knew she had no other choice. "Clara, I know this probably isn't a good time to tell you, but there is something else I need to share with you."

Clara stared at the ceiling and shook her head. "Go ahead," she whispered.

"Mack came by yesterday and told me to let you know he has done all he could, but he's getting pressure from the big boss. Unless you pay your rent today he will have no other choice but to kick you out. That's mainly why I came by to see you. He asked me what he should do with all of your things just in case. I gave him some money to put most of it in storage. Clara, I used my car payment to pay him."

Clara stared at Pat as she watched the tears in her neighbor's eyes sparkle. Now is not the time to shed tears my friend. Please suck it up and let's think this thing through. That's what she wanted to say, but swallowed hard and kept it all inside.

"I hate to bring this up. I really do," Pat said spilling the rest of her news. "I'm moving to the other side of town. I didn't get the house I wanted, but I did get approval for a larger apartment. When we move, my kids won't be going to the daycare with your girls anymore. In fact, I don't know what to do with your twins. The daycare is threatening to kick them out if you don't pay soon, and I mean real soon" she said, wiping her eyes. Pat inhaled deeply. She wanted to tell Clara how completely frazzled she was. Caring for five kids with four under the age of three, in an apartment, was more than she could handle. She had already said more than she wanted to and definitely more than Clara probably wanted to hear, so, she sat still as she twisted the end of her shirt. Before she spoke again, she took another deep breath and thought carefully about what she should say next—a technique her therapist suggested she use when faced with these types of situations.

"I know this is difficult, but what if I called your mom? She could help you take care of the girls until you felt better."

Clara didn't respond, partially because she was in excruciating pain, but mostly she didn't have any answers for her neighbor. She knew she had asked more of her than she should have, but what else was there to do? The soft spoken lady that never had much to say was her only option. She had no family to count on, to watch after the girls. So, here she was, left to depend on this quieter than usual woman. The few times she'd ever seen Pat excited was when her kids got out of control—which was pretty much most of the time. The moment she started yelling wasn't a pretty sight. No one would ever believe a voice like that could come out of someone so timid.

Clara stared ahead.

"I know not any of this is fair, but if you tell me what to do Clara, I promise I'll make it happen for you," Pat said. Her words came out slow and deliberate. "I've tried to be a good neighbor and friend, I really have. I just don't know what else to do."

Clara stubbornly shook her head. She wished Pat wasn't so weak. "We'll figure it out." Those were about the only words she had for her neighbor before she left.

The next day when Clara called to check on the girls, panic set in. "This number has been disconnected and is no longer in service," the recording played.

Clara looked intently at the social worker and with all the strength she could muster, yelled, "I don't know how either but I'm getting out of here. All I know is that I must go and find my daughters. I have been calling my neighbor for hours and she is not answering. I never expected to be in the hospital this long."

"Calm down, Mrs. Gordon. It's unrealistic to think you can leave the hospital.

You just had your second surgery only twelve hours ago and can't even get around by yourself."

"Do not tell me to calm down! Don't you dare tell me to calm down when my babies are nowhere to be found!"

The room began to spin. The strain of yelling instantly drained Clara of her energy and caused her head to whirl.

"Listen," Jessie said softly, "I'm going to help you work all this out. In fact, I will be leaving shortly to go to the apartment where the kids were last seen," she said.

Jessie had been a social worker at the City Hospital for more than twelve years. She knew Clara's story. Who hadn't heard about the gold-digging, pretentious, ostentatious woman who weaseled her way into the Gordon family only to be left penniless by her husband after his death? The Gordon's story had been the topic of conversation practically at every setting in the city. "It was just no way for a fairy tale story to end," Jessie thought.

"Please hurry, I need to know where my girls are. They are the only thing I…" Clara cut her words short. Swallowing hard, she fought back. "Just get out of here."

"I should know something in an hour or so. I will call you from the car," Jessie said, exiting the room.

When she pulled up to the apartment, Jessie's heart raced. On the curb were piles of trash and furniture. It appeared as if someone was moving or even scarier had moved. She rechecked the address again and pounded on the door.

As expected, no one answered.

She noticed the sign pointing to the manager's office and headed towards it. Walking up to the glass encased counter, she stood, "Excuse me sir, are you the manager?"

Mack nodded never looking up.

"I hope you can tell me whether or not the tenant in apartment 2010 gave any information about where she moved to."

"Ma'am, I cannot give you that information," Mack said, flipping through the piles of paper on his desk.

Jessie switched gears. "Uh, em…," she said, clearing her throat. She slid her business card through the gap in the window. "Do you know Mrs. Clara Gordon?"

She knew that he did.

"I sure do," he said, finally peering at her over his reading spectacles.

"I'm here on her behalf." She told him part of the story she knew he was already familiar with.

He reached for the card turning it over between his fingers. "I will tell you this, the young lady staying in '10 moved in the middle of the night. She still owes me one month's rent." He looked closer at her, "I can't begin to tell you how much the one in the hospital you're talking about owes me. I had to put her stuff out. That's about it. That's all I got for you."

Jessie turned and walked slowly towards her car. She knew his kind. That was the only information she was going to get out of him. She dreaded making the phone call to share the little news she had received. It was going to be more difficult than she expected.

At the hospital, Clara anxiously awaited Jessie's call. The news she shared with her did little for her mood.

"Your temperature is still up Mrs. Gordon," the nurse said, entering her room. "I'm going to have to let the doctor know." She reached for the covered tray and lifted the lid. "You haven't touched your food," she said, moving her tray away. "I'll be back shortly."

Clara felt miserable, her body obviously not responding well to all the injuries. Even though she couldn't
walk and the fever left her feeling exhausted, her
thoughts were on plans of getting out of there. She
hadn't quite figured out how she was going to escape
from the hospital, but she was determined nothing was
going to stop her from getting to her girls.

"I need you to start cleaning your plate young lady so
we can get you out of here," Dr. Owens said, as he
entered the room. "What's this about running a temperature?"

He breezed through her electronic medical record.

Clara turned her head towards the window away from
him.

He gently sat next to her on the bed. "It's going to be
okay," he said. He reached for her hand and held on.
"Now that social service is all over your case, I'm sure
they will have some news about your girls very soon.
Listen," he said, changing subjects. "We've got to get to
the bottom of why your temperature keeps spiking. I
was hoping we would be able to send you home today so
you can get to your kids."

He noticed her somber expression and knew what
was on her mind. "Clara, it's against policy for me to
send you out of the hospital with this kind of temperature. I'm going to run a few more tests to see what's
going on. In the meantime, I will check on you after I
make my rounds."

As soon as he closed the door, she chewed into
her knuckles. Suddenly, thoughts of Eric flooded her
mind. She longed for him. No one could ever make her
feel as safe as he could. He was her friend, confidant,
and lover. He was the answer to all her problems and

protected her from the pressures of life. She was trying to comprehend the thought of him never coming back to her, but when she did, it still made absolutely no sense. Usually, she could fight back from any seemingly hopeless and dead-end situation, but this time, nothing she did took away the feeling of impending doom barreling down upon her.

A soft knock on the door momentarily interrupted her thoughts.

"Mrs. Gordon," the young lady said. "May I come in and visit with you?"

Clara turned her head away and faced the window again.

"I'm here from the chaplain's office. I came by to see if you could use some company."

Clara continued to stare, determined to ignore any and everything that entered those doors. "Besides," she thought, "Who told her to come and see her in the first place. Clearly the hospital had violated her confidentiality rights."

"Mrs. Gordon, is it okay for me to come in?"

Clara never turned her way.

"If you ever need to talk, I'll leave my card so you will know how to get in touch with me. I'm praying for you." She placed the card on the table and slowly closed the door.

"I did not come here for prayer," Clara thought. "You go to church to pray. This is a hospital for goodness sake. I came here to get my body well. If they would just do their jobs and get me back in order, I could go and get my girls. Obviously the hospital gives lousy care."

She suddenly held onto the rails of her bed, lifted herself up, and gasped for air again. She hadn't told the nurse, but on occasion she was finding it difficult to breathe. She knew if she told them anything like that it would prolong her stay. So, she hid it all from them.

Later, the nurse hung her first round of IV antibiotics. She dipped inside the Styrofoam pitcher and scooped out a mouthful of ice. The nurse would be back at the end of her shift to take her temperature, and if it was still up she definitely wouldn't be discharged. With a normal temperature she could leave even if she had to use a wheelchair to get around. So, she crunched on the ice until her teeth chattered. She knew someone would need to help drive her once released from the hospital because of the awkward cast on her leg. Her broken ankle now had several screws holding it together.

"Who in the world would be willing to come to her rescue?" she thought.

"Marty! She would come and see about her. Why hadn't she thought about that before?" She pulled up her list of contacts, scrolled to the *M's* and dialed.

"Clara! Oh my goodness, it's been such a long time. I was thinking about you the other day and wondering how you were," Marty squealed.

"It certainly is good hearing your voice. Did I catch you at a bad time?" Clara asked. She raised her bed higher. It helped her breathe a little better as she spoke.

"Absolutely not, we need to catch up my friend. I am so sorry I wasn't able to make it to Eric's memorial services, but I hope you got the card and floral arrangements I sent."

Even though Clara found it difficult to talk, she stayed on the phone with Marty for hours. When she got to the part about Miriam taking away the money, Marty screamed. "Who can you trust these days?" she exclaimed. She all but lost it when she told her about the girls.

"That's a living nightmare, Clara! What do you need for me to do?" she asked, now shedding a few of her own tears.

"Can you spare a weekend and hang out with me? I'm about to be discharged from the hospital soon. I could really use your help to get around and go find my girls."

"Let me know when and where, and I will be there. It's the least I can do." Marty immediately gave her both numbers to her work and personal cell phones.

As soon as she hung up, Clara forced more ice in her mouth and held it there. It was perfect timing. The nurse was coming through the door to take her temperature.

Chapter 16

Life Altering Times

Preparing for the red carpet ranked right up there as one of the most exhilarating feelings Gwen had ever experienced. Her Yves Saint Laurent, soft bronze, halter gown fit her to perfection. The floor-length formal with a hint of beading sprinkled along the waist flowed with each step she took. It was an original, designed especially for her. The accessories were the perfect touch, especially with her hair swept up the way it was.

"Wow! You look amazing," Rick said, as she gracefully walked into the room. He leaned towards her, gently brushing her lips with his.

"Come on, it's time to go," she whispered.

When they arrived, the night sparkled as flashes from the cameras twinkled all around. A deluge of photographers yelled out her name. While she had finally gotten used to the cameras, she wasn't accustomed to them calling her name like that. She squeezed Rick's hand, occasionally stopping to pose until her assistant signaled them along.

Once inside and seated, the program moved along swiftly. Finally, the time came for the Best Supporting Actress nominees to be announced. She wondered, had it all been a dream or were they really going to call her name?

"The second nominee, Gwen Haley in, Shakers, " the celebrity announcer said.

She took in a quick breath, trying hard to maintain her composure. They had after all just called her name. She managed to force out a smile so that when she didn't win—which she fully expected not to, she would still have a cool expression on her face.

"The Golden Globe goes to-o-o... Gwen Haley in Shakers."

Her legs trembled as she mounted the steps. She did prepare a speech in the rare instance she won, but hadn't actually gone over it. She stumbled through it, finally looking at Rick saying, "I love you baby."

The rest of the awards show was a blur. After all, she was holding her very own Golden Globe.

The post-awards parties were plentiful and she and Rick made the major ones. Rose and William rode along enjoying Gwen's special night.

"I knew you would win," Rose said, shouting over the music. "I didn't want to distract you in any way, but William and I have something special to tell you," she said, holding out her hand. "We're getting married this spring."

"I am awfully glad you waited. I can now focus all of my attention on the two of you—on this wonderful moment. I'm so happy for you guys," Gwen said, squeezing them both.

The night was a mixture of congratulatory remarks, producers whispering in her ear to call, numerous photo-ops, and a host of interviews. It was only when she looked at Rose and saw how happy her baby sister was that she realized—it was family that generated the most pleasure in her life. Gwen understood she was a very fortunate woman.

When they arrived home before dawn, she immediately noticed the lights coming from out of the bedroom.

"What's wrong? Where's Lizzy?" Gwen asked, rushing inside.

"Calm down, she's okay. I had a hard time sleeping," Ellen said. "That's all."

They walked into the sitting area adjacent to the master suite. Gwen knew something had been troubling her mother ever since her last doctor's visit. She noticed how quiet she had become, only brightening up when Lizzy was around.

"What's going on?" Gwen asked.

Ellen hesitated, not in the least bit prepared to deal with Gwen's reaction when she told her the news she had been hiding for weeks.

"I'm going to look for Clara in the morning."

"Oh no you're not! Are you kidding me? No way are you traipsing all over the world looking for her. Have you considered your health?"

Gwen immediately felt guilty. She rarely spoke to her mother in that tone, but the very thought of her looking for Clara caused the spontaneous reaction.

"Gwen, I need to know where your sister is and how she's doing. I must find her. I haven't heard from my child in almost a year and haven't seen her in five. It's tearing me up inside. I cannot go another day without hearing her voice," Ellen said wiping her eyes. "Eric's mother's number has changed and Miriam has been absolutely no help whatsoever. Both Clara and Eric's phones have been disconnected," she whispered. "I hope you understand why I need to go."

"You can't be serious," Gwen said, taking off her earrings. "Clara is fine and believe me, she doesn't want to be bothered with you. It's not as if you're talking about going around the corner, mother. You're talking about an hour plane ride from here or have you considered that."

Ellen sat quietly—much like a reprimanded child.

"Listen," Gwen said, as she curled up next to her. Beaded gown and all, she pleaded, "Don't do this. I never wanted to tell you or Rose about my last conversation with Clara." She inhaled and let it all out. "When we discovered Rose missing, I called her and she was so rude, mother…I can't explain it," she said, turning her head away. "The venom in that girl is frightening." She faced her again. "Let me just say, she made it real clear she wanted you out of her life. I never have cared what she thought about me, but what she said about you and Rose crossed the line. When Clara and I finished talking, I swore it would be our very last conversation."

Gwen looked at her mother, the pain now obvious in both of their eyes. "She is all but dead to me. She wants to break off all ties with each of us and asked that we never call her again," Gwen said.

Those few words unleashed the tremendous load she had been carrying for years. While it didn't necessarily feel good saying it all, the cleansing effect was felt immediately.

"Some people just don't deserve to be forgiven," she continued. "Believe me, Clara fits that mold. You don't treat family, especially your own mother that way. So, if you cannot understand why I don't want you going all over looking for someone who doesn't deserve anything good to ever happen to them, I'm sorry. Mother, let her go," Gwen pleaded. "She is not worth your time or energy. I know you will always love her. After all, you are her mother, I understand that. Just love her from afar so you don't get hurt…but for me, it's over. As far as I am concerned, she will never be a part of this family again."

Neither said a word as they both silently pleaded with each other.

Finally, Gwen shook her head. "Alright, what time am I taking you to the airport?" she said, yielding.

"My flight leaves at six in the morning," Ellen quickly responded. "You don't need to get up that early. I'll have the driver take me."

"No, I want to do it," she said as she stood.

Gwen reached out and pulled her mother close. Wrapping her arms around her waist, she smiled. She couldn't comprehend how anyone could refuse to love someone as special as this. She held on for a while.

"By the way, how are you feeling?" she asked, as they headed for the kitchen. She flipped on the Keurig and made them both a cup of their favorite flavored coffee. "I've noticed you stirring around quite late at night recently, are you having a hard time sleeping or something?" Gwen asked.

"Somewhat… but I believe things will get better once I see Clara. She and Eric may be having problems or it may be as you say, she's absolutely fine. Either way, I must find out."

As morning approached, it was déjà vu all over again. Ellen settled in her seat as the aircraft flew over the harbor, tilting to the left making its steep ascent. Many things had changed in her life, but this time she knew they would turn out differently. She was no longer in denial. The pain in her body wasn't good and she didn't need a CAT scan to tell her so. It was amazing

Gwen hadn't said anything about how thin she'd become. Either she had been too busy to notice or just didn't want to talk about it. Whatever the case may have been, she was glad they had avoided that discussion. It was difficult enough talking about it with her physician.

Dr. Span had always been honest with her, but when she refused the CAT scan, she insisted on doing a quick ultrasound in her office. It showed several shadows on her liver and spleen. She wanted a more definitive procedure to determine what was actually going on and pushed so until she finally conceded. When the results came in, Dr. Span promised she would never keep anything from her. When she asked her to be honest about her prognosis, she was.

There was only one thing she promised herself she would do before she died and that was, to find Clara.

After landing, she rented a car with such a sophisticated navigation system it took a lot of effort to figure out how to operate it. Finally, she mapped out the directions to Eric's parent's estate and headed their way.

"One moment, please," the housekeeper said, when she answered the door.

A tall gentleman walked up. "How may I help you?" he asked.

She couldn't recall this man looking anything like Eric's father. "Although, it had been a long time since she'd seen him last," she thought.

"Hi, my name is Ellen Andrews and I'm Clara's mother. I came by to see you and your wife, Mr. Gordon."

"Oh," he chuckled. "I'm not Mr. Gordon. They used to live here."

Ellen knew it was too good to be true. The guard was so busy he had summoned her into the gated community without any questions.

"I'm so sorry, please excuse me. I didn't mean to intrude," she said.

"No, it's perfectly fine," the middle-aged man replied. "My wife and I never had the pleasure of meeting the Gordon's."

"You wouldn't happen to know where they may have moved to," Ellen asked.

"We are new in town and relocated here a couple of months ago. Wait," he said, reaching for a card inside his wallet. "This is the realtor who sold us the estate, maybe he can be of assistance."

She thanked the nice gentleman, but thought it best to follow the plans she outlined for herself before leaving home. The last thing she wanted to do was visit Clara on her job, but it had to be her next move. She knew it might upset her but she was just going to have to deal with that.

Ellen punched in the address to Carrington Academy.

When she drove up to the immaculately landscaped grounds filled with historic, cobble-stoned buildings, she instantly felt a sense of pride. She expected nothing less from Clara. She told the guard who she was looking for and he immediately directed her to the headmaster's quarters.

"Please have a seat," Mr. Pearson said. "I am the new headmaster and unfortunately I didn't get the opportunity to work with Mrs. Gordon. Several of the teachers who did said she accepted another teaching position. She was fairly private I'm told. I am sorry I cannot offer you much more than that."

"I understand, but perhaps you can direct me to this address," she said, handing him the information. A sense of urgency came rolling in. Why would Clara accept another teaching position? She had gone on and on about the job at Carrington when she initially got it. It was the first in a very long time Clara had shared anything personal about herself.

An hour later, Ellen drove up to the large decorative-steel gate with 'Bradbury' etched inside. A uniformed officer came out to greet her.

"How may I help you, ma'am?" he asked.

"I am here to see Mrs. Miriam Johnson. My name is Ellen Andrews."

"He checked his clipboard. "I'm sorry. I don't see your name on the guest list. I will have to phone the Johnson's first. Wait right here, please."

Minutes later he strolled back to the car. "Ma'am, Mrs. Johnson is not accepting visitors today. You will need to turn your car around in that drive," he said, pointing to the circular area.

"Will you phone her back and tell her it's a must that I speak to her. Please?" She looked up, her eyes begging, "I have to find my daughter."

The guard hesitated, turned, and went to phone again. He walked back slowly to the car.

"I am sorry ma'am. They've left clear instructions…they are not receiving guests."

The cramps in Ellen's stomach gripped her tightly when he offered her the news. "Perhaps she'd had enough for one day," she thought. Besides, she was running out of options.

She pulled the steering wheel to the left as she inched her way out. She had no idea what she should do or where she should go next. Clara had always been so private. She never spoke of any friends—someone she could possibly contact. Ellen also knew Clara had been pregnant and her grandchild had probably been born by now.

"Her grandbaby," she thought.

She braked.

She wasn't going anywhere until she found them. After that, if they wanted her to go away, she would leave them all alone.

She placed the car in reverse when suddenly the nausea seized her body. She tried to breathe, but when she did nothing but bright red blood came up, splattering against the pavement. She hung her head out the car door as she threw up gigantic bright red clots. As the guard ran up to her car she whispered, "Please dial 911."

By the time the ambulance arrived, she was forcing air into her lungs. Being pulled from behind the steering wheel was the last thing she remembered. It all went black.

***

Ellen's cell phone rang and went directly to voice mail.

"Try her again," Rick said.

Gwen handed Lizzy to him, her temp still up. She whimpered as she clung to her blanket.

When the phone went to voice mail again, Gwen placed her hands over her face.

"It's going to be alright," Rick said, comforting her.

"Mother would never make us worry like this. She has not answered her phone in over three hours, Rick."

He hugged her and sighed. "Do you think you should go out there?"

"Yes, I've got to find her. I knew when she left she was in no condition to travel, but nothing was going to stop her from getting to Clara."

Lizzy cried loudly as she rubbed her eyes.

"Are you sure you will be okay taking her to the doctor all by yourself?" she asked, reaching for the baby.

Lizzy laid her head on Gwen's shoulder and slowly closed her droopy eyes. She swayed her back and forth, gently rocking. In a matter of minutes, she was sound asleep.

Gwen could hear Rick in the adjacent room making travel arrangements as she tucked Lizzy into bed.

"I would be going with you if she felt better," Rick said. "Are you sure you don't want to let Rose in on any of this?"

"I'm sure about that. She's in finals and I don't need her worrying. I can do that for the both of us."

The next morning, Gwen left early for the airport. Her plan was to check the local hospitals, then go to Carrington Academy, and if necessary Miriam Johnson's home. There was no doubt in her mind she was going to find her mother.

When Gwen landed, she searched the yellow pages for hospitals with zip codes closest to Clara's and Miriam's estates. She found several and immediately dialed them, but neither had her mother as a patient. She quickly jotted down the address of Carrington Academy and dialed the settings into her GPS.

She phoned Rick.

"No luck just yet. Not any of the hospitals I've checked so far have her listed as a patient. That's a good sign. I'm on my way to the school where Clara teaches to see if she stopped by there. This should be very interesting. I have not laid eyes on my dear sister in a very long time, and I can feel the tension already. I'll keep you posted. What did the doctor say about Lizzy?"

"She has an ear infection and gave her antibiotics. She's fine, already back to her old playful self, eating her favorite snacks again. I'm glad it wasn't anything serious."

"Me too. Kiss her for me. I will call as soon as I leave the school."

Gwen headed for Carrington Academy.

Mr. Pearson didn't quite understand what was going on with Clara Gordon's family showing up all at once looking for her.

"Like I told your mother, I'm not sure where she is. She's been away from Carrington at least two years now."

"What time did you speak with my mother, may I ask?"

"Yesterday, around one-thirty or so. She was headed for Bradbury Estates."

He adjusted his wire framed glasses. Her face looked familiar but he immediately dismissed it. "May I ask what this is all about, ma'am?"

"It's a long story Mr. Pearson and I really don't have time to explain," she said, moving towards the door. "Thank you for the information."

He watched as she hurried out. He wanted to ask her how Clara was fairing after the death of her husband, but thought against it. Everyone in town had learned not to talk about the Gordon saga any more. It was a widely known fact that Clara and her entire family were con artists who managed to destroy a decent family. He picked up the phone to call security. He wanted to make sure she had vacated the premises.

In the meantime, Gwen keyed Miriam's address into her GPS. She turned out of the school's drive and headed east. She was on a mission and needed to have a serious conversation with Clara's sister-in-law today. She refused to go anywhere until that happened.

As she slowly approached the gate, the guard walked up to her car.

"I'm here to see Miriam Johnson," Gwen said, emphatically.

"Sorry ma'am. The Johnson's have left word they are not receiving visitors today. You'll have to turn around," he said, pointing to the circular drive.

"Do you think maybe you could give Mrs. Johnson a message from me then? Tell her I am not going anywhere. I'm looking for my sister Clara Gordon and more importantly, my mother, Ellen Andrews. If she does not help me find them I will wait outside her wonderful gated community until she comes out. I will follow her everywhere she goes. I'll…"

"Ma'am, ma'am, I cannot pass along a message like that. Please, they have asked not to be disturbed. Now, go ahead and turn yourself around. I'm sorry," the guard said.

"Don't be sorry, just help me for goodness sakes," she said.

Suddenly, he pointed, "Hey, aren't you that actress! Yeah, that played in the movie Shakers?"

He bent down, staring into her face.

"Here we go," Gwen sighed underneath her breath. "Yes, I'm Gwen Haley and I am trying to find my mother, my sister…"

"By golly, you did a fine job of acting there. You wouldn't mind signing an autograph for me now would 'ya? My wife would be tickled pink if she knew I was here with you. She dragged me to see that movie of yours twice."

He shoved a small sheet of spiral edge paper in her face.

She quickly scribbled her name.

"Yahoo, she won't believe this," he said, holding up the cherished signature. "Can I please snap one little bitty picture so she can see it really was you in the flesh?"

He ran to get his cell phone before she could object. "Say cheese," he said, aiming the camera at them both. "Hot dog! Now, you can't beat that with a stick," he laughed.

"Sir, will you help me?" she said, sighing hard.

"I sure can Mrs. Haley, what do you need?"

"My mother may have been here earlier trying to get in to see the Johnson's. Do you recall if a lady in her early 60's, grayish hair, around two or three yesterday afternoon came by to see them?"

"Now, we did have some excitement happen around that time yesterday. Lady got deathly ill and I called 911 for her. Wait! She did ask to see the Johnsons."

"Please, what hospital did they take her to?"

"I'm not sure, probably, The City or County General. That's where they more than likely took her."

He gave her directions to both.

"Thank you," Gwen said, her tires screeching.

"Glad to have met 'ya," he yelled after her.

She sped off to The County General Hospital first. The complex maze inside left her breathless. With her baseball cap and dark shades on now, she was barely recognizable.

The hospital had no listing of Ellen Andrews.

Racing back to her car she headed for The City Hospital.

"Here she is, Ellen Andrews," the information clerk said. "She's in ICU ma'am.   Go straight down that hallway, make a left, and take the elevators to three."

Gwen wanted to race down the hall but it seemed something else now controlled her emotions. It may have been that she did not want to face what was at the other end waiting for her or she was in extreme denial. Whatever it was, it pulled hard on the reins of her heart. She walked calmly down the long corridor as she looked up at the large sign that read INTENSIVE CARE UNIT.

"Do you have an Ellen Andrews here?" she asked as she spoke into the intercom.

"Yes, we do."

The door released as she walked in.

"Hi, I'm here to see Ellen Andrews," she said, to the nurse sitting behind the circular desk.

"Are you a relative? We've been trying to contact someone about her all day."

"Is she okay?" Gwen asked the quiver now evident in her voice. "I am her daughter."

The nurse came around to where she stood, "I'm glad you're here," she said, reaching for her hand. "Your mother is very ill and we've done all we could to try and save her. I'll call her doctor so you can speak with him. Dr. Cage will provide more details. In the meantime, why don't you go in and sit with her."

She held onto Gwen's hand as they both walked inside room six.

"She's not breathing on her own at this point and has not responded to any of my commands. I am so sorry this is happening to her," the nurse whispered.

Gwen never said a word as the tears slowly fell.

"You can stay here as long as you'd like. I will be right back."

Gwen sat in the chair by her mother's bed, her hands trembling as she tried dialing Rick.

"She's dying Rick," she cried into the phone. "My mother is dying."

"I'll call Rose," he said panting, the words taking his breath away. "Hang in there, babe."

When she hung up, she stared at the machines attached to her mother. Ten minutes later a tall physician dressed in green scrubs with a surgical mask loosely tied around his neck, approached her.

"Hi, I'm Doctor Cage."

"Hi, I'm Gwen Haley, Mrs. Andrews' daughter," she said standing.

He hesitated for a moment, now fully aware of who she was.

"It's nice meeting you, and I love your work. However, I am sorry we had to meet under these conditions. I need to be very honest with you—at this point, your mother is gravely ill. Her heart is extremely weak and if we removed the tube that's helping her breathe, she would probably die," he said softly. "We have done everything possible to keep her alive."

Gwen doubled over as her body shook hard.

He helped ease her into the chair.

"I won't be far away. If you have any questions, don't hesitate to ask. Take all the time you need to spend with your mother," he said.

When she finally regained partial composure, she knew it was time to talk to Rose.

Dialing her number, she cried, "Hurry, Rose, she's at The City Hospital here in ICU and not doing well."

Gwen glanced at her mother's monitor taking note of how slow her heart rate had become. "Is that normal," she asked the nurse, trying not to panic.

"No, and I have already spoken to the doctor about it."

Gwen was worried that Rose would not make it in time even though her flight was scheduled to leave in an hour. She and Rose had agreed to honor their mother's wishes when the time came and allow her to slip peacefully away. It was one of the hardest things she ever had to do…watching her heart rate decrease from the 60's to the 50's. It was now in the 40's.

Her emotions seemed determined to drain the little energy she had remaining as she rested her head onto her mother's bed.

It startled her when the heart monitor's alarm sounded. She looked up when the nurse came rushing in. There were long pauses between each beat. Her mother's heart rate was in the 20's.

Gwen reached over and whispered again in her ear, "Please know that I love you so much." She cried and held on. "Mommy…"

She lightly shook her. "Can you hear me? Please know that I love you." She held her tightly and wept.

Later, the nurse walked in the room along with the chaplain. They both wrapped their arms around her. Even though Gwen didn't know either of these ladies, she did understand how good it felt to be comforted.

All three watched as her heart stop beating.

Chapter 17

Reversal of Fortune Times

"If you sign here, that should do it," the nurse said.

Clara quickly scribbled out her name, looked up at Marty, and smiled, "Let's blow this popsicle stand," she said, pushing the wheelchair forward.

"Mack will help us," Clara said. "If I give him a couple of dollars he'll tell me where they are. Marty, I hate to have to ask you, but could you lend me a few bucks to give him. I didn't bring any cash with me to the hospital."

She was grateful when Marty handed her a handful of tens, twenties and several crisp one hundred dollar bills. She had already bought her three nice outfits.

It was as if she understood.

Clara eased into the car with assistance from Marty and they were soon on their way. She was surprised when they drove up to her old apartment complex, Mack was actually glad to see her.

"I can't say you look good. Heard you got yourself all banged up there," he said. "I don't know much, but a friend, of a friend, of a friend told me she took those kids all the way to the other side of town.

Here," he said, handing her the name of the apartments he thought she lived in. "You know she squared away her bill last week," he said, peeking over his glasses. "Her conscious probably got the best of her. What about yours? Is your conscious bothering you

Clara? You know you still owe me much more than this," he said, holding up the twenty dollar bill.

"Give me a break will you Mack," she smiled. "As soon as I turn all of this around, you will be the first person I come looking for. I promise I won't forget," Clara said, suddenly very serious. "I appreciate this," she said, holding up the paper with the apartment complex written on it.

When they arrived at the building, Marty drove slowly around the parking area. Clara spotted the car with Pat's personalized license tag.

"There it is! That's her car. Let's go and knock on a few doors."

"Yeah, and when we find her we're going to kick her butt," Marty said.   The first three doors went unanswered. It was a lot of work trying to maneuver up the steps with the crutches they had given her. When she knocked on the door, she could hear the babies crying before Pat opened it.

"Hi, Clara."

"HI, CLARA!! Is that all you have to say to me? Where are my girls?" she yelled.

"Do you want to come in so we can talk about this rationally?" Pat spoke as soft as ever.

"No, I do not want to come in. I want my girls!"

"They're not here, Clara. I called Social Services and they took the girls away. I'm sorry."

Marty stood there fuming. She dared not ask any questions, just ready to take Pat on if she needed to.

"You did what!" Clara shrieked. Her whole body shook. A thin line of perspiration clung to her upper lip as she tightened the grip on her crutches.

"I never thought you would betray me like this. Tell me where they took my girls?"

Pat reached for her purse and handed her the note she wrote the address onto. "I'm told they take real good care of kids here. I made sure of that."

Clara was trying to calculate exactly how she could balance herself on the crutches and punch Pat in the face all at the same time. Suddenly, she became aware of her clothes clinging to her shaking body. She was soaked from head to toe.

"Let's get out of here, Marty," Clara said. As she turned, the dizziness overwhelmed her.

"Are you okay?" Marty slipped her arm around her tiny waist as Clara reeled back and forth. She hadn't realized until then just how frail she had become. It took no effort at all to support her thin friend.

Clara was only able to take in short quick breaths. She tried forcing enough air into her lungs as her limp body fell to the ground.

Marty screamed.

"Here, bring her in here," Pat said, swinging the door open wide.

By the time they got her inside she was starting to come around.

"I'm okay," Clara whispered. "Let's go and get the girls."

Marty had already phoned for an ambulance. "I think we need to get you back to the hospital, Clara. You're burning up. I can feel the heat coming through your clothes."

"No, please Marty, take me to my girls. They are all I have left," she whispered. "I'll be fine. I know I will.

It's just my body trying to adjust to moving around so much again, that's all."

Marty didn't know what else to do. She did realize, however, it wasn't normal for anybody to feel that hot and look so pale.

"Let's allow the paramedics to come and check you out first and then we will go and get your girls," Marty said, clearly not convinced of the latter.

Clara tried begging, but the weakness overpowered her. She had no energy to fight.

The paramedics arrived and took her immediately to the hospital. This time they admitted her into the ICU.

Marty paced the floor until she was finally cleared to go in and see Clara. She was receiving massive doses of antibiotics through her IV site. "You frightened me to death, girl. I had no idea you were this sick. Your temperature was almost 104." Looking down at Clara, she saw the apprehension in her eyes. "Don't worry about a thing," she said, attempting to alleviate her fears. "I'll take care of you now. As soon as I leave here I'm going to search for our babies. These knuckle-heads don't know what they're doing," she said, smoothing out Clara's hair. "Let me 'outta here and watch me have them back to you in no time."

"Thank you, Marty," she whispered as she closed her eyes. She reached for her hand. "I just want my girls."

Marty didn't like seeing her friend that way, lying so helpless in the hospital bed. She knew all about Clara's situation even when they were in college. Although she had come from a different world than hers, she still found her to be an incredibly amazing woman. She loved her tenacity and ability to fit in with the crazy-high-class friends they hung out with. It was fascinating to watch her come from the bottom of the social ladder and climb her way to the top. She had secretly become her own little private project, but as fate would have it they ended up being true friends. The only thing she found strange about Clara was the relationship she had with her family. Since it was clear that subject was off limits, she never bothered her about it. They had a special bond and she was going to be there for her friend no matter what. She set out to find the place where Pat said her girls were.

Marty turned the corner onto a street she only read about in suspense novels. The house displaying the address was surrounded by mostly boarded up homes with large barrels of trash everywhere. A glimmer of light shone through a tiny window at the house she parked in front of. Her heart raced as she glanced back over her shoulder. Everything in her screamed not to get out of the car, but she forced herself to.

Looking around, Marty inched her way towards the fenced yard when out of nowhere, the largest dog ever growled, barked, and banged against it. It was all she could do to keep her three-inch heels on as she ran in neck-breaking-speed back to the car.

What was she going to do? She couldn't get to the door and there was no way she was going to sit there and get mugged. She had no other choice. She cranked the car.

Just as she eased onto the accelerator, additional porch lights flickered on.

She braked.

The door to the house swung open, and a raspy voice yelled out, "Who is that?"

Marty knew her heart rate was alarmingly high as she rolled down the window. "Could you put your dog away please?"

"He don't bite unless I tell him to," the voice responded.

Marty eyed the dark-littered strewn street once again and willed herself out of the car. Stopping in the middle of the street, leaving just enough space to run back to the safety of her vehicle if need be, she yelled, "I'm looking for the Gordon girls."

"What business you got with them," the voice answered.

"Their mother is worried to death and wants to know where they are."

"You come out this time of night to find out about little girls?"

"Yes, I'm sorry to disturb you but could you please tell me if the Gordon girls are here?"

The long pause made her uneasy.

"You alone?" the voice roared back.

Marty wanted to tell the voice she had her 280 pound, 6'6" husband with her, but ultimately gave in to the truth.

"Yes," she said, her bravery now essentially nonexistent.

The voice whistled, "Rusty, come here boy. Let me put the dog away," it rasped.

Marty walked closer to the fence. The voice had gone inside. She eased open the latch to the gate and stepped onto the walk. She stood on the narrow pavement that led to the porch where the voice came from. "What in the world was she doing here," Marty thought to herself. This could easily be a home that harbored a serial killer. They lived in houses that looked exactly like these. She'd seen them on those investigative report series.

The creepy house stared back.

Strong palpitations that plagued her for years were now basically nonstop, causing her breath to come in spurts. She shook her head to clear her thoughts. She had practiced enough karate moves on her exercise tapes to take very good care of herself. As she cracked her neck and with her hand tucked behind her back—she balled her fist hard, taking on the fight position. The adrenaline rush quickly replaced the heart palpitations. She'd made up her mind. She was going to beat the shoes off anything that looked like they wanted to mess with her.

The voice came to the door again. "Come on in," it gargled.

Marty slowly climbed the steps towards the porch, never relaxing the hand that would ultimately deliver the killer blow.

The door swung open and there stood, the voice.

Marty gasped. She wore a thin nightgown on her slim 4'11'' frame, a multicolored scarf tied around her head and pink fuzzy house shoes that overpowered her feet...she appeared to be around 70ish.

"Are you coming in or what?" the raspy voice charged.

"Uh, yeah, I mean, yes ma'am," Marty said, as she walked into the living room of the petite, senior citizen.

"You can call me Betty," she said.

"Hi, I'm Marty."

"What in the world are you doing out this time of night in this neighborhood? That's not a smart move, young lady."

"I know, but my friend is very ill, Betty. She's actually in the hospital right now and as a result, someone else has been caring for her children. You cannot imagine how worried she is. She's a mess! I'm afraid if she doesn't find her girls, she won't get any better." Marty forced out the question, "Do you have her girls? The Gordon twins?"

Betty finally managed a half-smile, "Come here, let me show you something," she said.

As they walked towards the bedroom, Marty's hand tightened again. It instantly relaxed when she saw two beautiful little girls dressed in their Bratz's neon pajamas. Even in their sleep she could tell they were fine.

"They will be up by six," Betty whispered. "After I feed them, we always take a stroll around the neighborhood. The neighbors just love them. They try and give them candy and stuff, but I won't let them. I know they want to be nice, but I like keeping them healthy. After supper, we all head out to church. You should see them clapping their little hands praising the Lord along with everybody else. Marty, tell their mother I said to hurry up and get well. Her girls are waiting for her."

Chapter 18

Crying Times

Rose sprinted through the hospital corridors, finding her way to the third floor. She was on her cell getting directions from Gwen even as she jumped on the elevator. When the doors opened, she instantly knew. She had never seen that amount of sadness on her sister's face before.

"Gwen, is she?"

Gwen reached for her sister and held on tightly as she gently stroked her hair.

From the depths of her soul, Rose cried. She had crossed a threshold of pain a daughter only experiences once in a life time. At that moment, she knew she would never see her mother's wonderful smile again—the one that offered her so much comfort. Most of all, she would never be able to tell her what a privilege it was to be her daughter.

"Come on, let me take you to where she is," Gwen whispered.

When they finally reached the bed, Rose quickly turned away. Regaining her ability to breathe normally, she turned and faced her mother again. She inched her way up to her, "Oh, mommy, I tried to get here," she cried. "I am so sorry I didn't make it."

Gwen held on tightly to her sister now thoroughly consumed by her own grief.

They both cried and talked to their mother for hours as they said their good-byes.

Later, lying on the beds in their hotel suite, neither spoke. William and Rick called every hour, but quickly realized it was very little they could do to ease their wives' pain.

The next morning, Gwen arose early leaving Rose in bed. She went to the hospital as promised to take care of her mother's paper work. After she left the business office, she decided to go back to the ICU and thank the kind nurse. She had been extremely nice and deserved to know how much she appreciated that.

She walked along the shiny waxed floors towards the nursing station.

"Excuse me, Gwen? Gwen Haley?"

Gwen looked up wishing she could avoid everybody today, especially the lady standing in front of her. She tried walking around her, but was blocked, both shifting as if they were auditioning for Dancing With the Stars.

"Oh, my God, it really is you. I would know you anywhere, even under that baseball cap. You were just brilliant in Shakers. I loved that movie."

Gwen wanted to yell, "Don't you know my mother just died!" She managed to calm herself and quietly whispered, "Thank you."

"I said if I ever had the pleasure of meeting you, there would be one thing that I would absolutely have to ask. Did you go to the University of Biscayne with me? Your face always looked so familiar, like a girl that went to college there."

Gwen knew she wasn't going away so she gave in. "Yes, I went there."

"I knew it," she all but yelled. "I'm Marty. Marty Shiner. I hung around the Alpha Kappa's. You must remember me!"

Gwen stared hard. Marty's face was familiar. She slowly began to recall who she was. Clara's sorority…this was Clara's friend. After the one and only time she met Eric, Clara had dared her to ever speak to her again. From that point on, neither of them acted as if they knew each other. As a result, she never officially met any of her sorority sisters. However, she did vaguely remember a few of the most popular and obnoxious ones.

"I must be going," Gwen said, softly.

"Well, isn't this a small world. I have run into and actually know *the* Gwen Haley. Wait 'til I tell the folks back home."

Gwen was finally able to walk around her and was just about to scoot down the hall.

"Wait!" Marty said, grabbing her arm. "One last thing—you must know Clara Gordon. You do remember her don't you? She was Clara Andrews back then, another one of our classmates. She's in room five," she said, "and not doing very well."

"Yes, I mean… I remember her," Gwen said. At that moment Gwen felt as if she had plunged head first into a sea of nightmares.

"I'm here to help her settle some business matters. It's such a sad story what happened to Clara and her entire family. Please pray she pulls through all of this."

Gwen refused to hear any more. "Listen, I must run," she said as she darted around Marty. In a flash she raced down the hall.

Could it be true? Had Clara been in the room right next to their mother's all this time? It had to all be a huge mistake.

When she reached the nursing station, she asked for the nurse who cared for her mother. While they went to get her, she stared ahead at room five. Like a magnet, it drew her in.

There lay a woman with a thin hospital sheet pulled up to her chin. She was much thinner than she had ever seen her, but would recognize that face anywhere. She stared down on the person she hated the most.

"If our mother hadn't come looking for you she would still be alive," she wanted to shake her and yell. Instead, she watched as she slept, the rhythm of her chest moving up and down. It was at that moment she wished it would stop. "Stop breathing," she thought. It would give her the satisfaction she wanted if she took her last breath right before her eyes.

"Were you looking for me, Mrs. Haley?" the nurse whispered, coming into the room.

"Yes," she said, turning.

"Do you know this patient?" the nurse asked.

"Yes, we went to school together." She shifted quickly, "I wanted to thank you for all that you did for my sister and me," she said, as she eased her out of the room.

"Oh, no problem," the nurse said. "I hope you guys are okay. By the way, how is your sister? She was so upset, I really felt for her."

"You know how it is. It will take some time to get through all of this. The three of us were pretty close. I need to run, but I couldn't leave without telling you how much I appreciate all that you did."

"Mrs. Haley, I hate to be a pest, but is there any way I could get your autograph—maybe take a picture with you?"

"Sure, I'll be glad to."

They stood between rooms five and six as they snapped the selfie.

***

Clara awakened with her heart racing again. She knew she was still feverish and extremely weak, but wondered why she had dreamed Gwen was standing over her? She turned over, shivering, as the ravaging fever swept through her body.

***

"Rose deserves to know you've found Clara and that she is in the hospital, Gwen," Rick said. "Even more, Clara needs to know her mother just died for goodness sakes!"

"You just don't understand, she told me she wished mother would die. She hoped all of us would," Gwen cried. "I've never felt this way about anybody in my life, let alone my own flesh and blood. I could never forgive her for what she did to my mother. Never, Rick! She lowered her voice, "I am convinced that her not knowing mother is dead is only payback for how she treated us," she said.

Rick remained silent allowing her to vent.

"I'm afraid if I tell Rose where Clara is, she will head right over there to see her. That's why I don't want her to know. We can have mother's funeral on Friday and get it over with. Besides, Clara is in ICU and she wouldn't be able to attend anyway."

He still didn't respond. He really wanted Gwen to do the right thing.

"I can tell you don't agree, Rick, but I cannot find it in my heart to do right by her now. She's never, ever, done that for any of us. It's what she deserves."

"If that is your decision, Gwen, okay. I can't tell you I agree with it, but...." He wanted to say more, but decided against it.

"What are you going to tell Rose?" he asked.

"Probably something like, neither mother nor I were able to find Clara—or perhaps she's moved to a bigger place with Eric."

"So, you're going to lie to her?"

"Oh, come on Rick, maybe I won't say that, but it will be something to keep Clara as far away from us as possible." When she hung up, she sobbed.

Later on their flight back, Gwen tried to steer the conversation away from Clara as best she could. She adjusted her seat back while they relaxed in their first class seats aboard the aircraft. The trip had been an exhausting one. Early that morning she had arranged to have their mother's body shipped back home, and all the funeral documents completed. The service was in two days.

"I wish we had found Clara," Rose said. "We should have demanded that Miriam talk to us. She knows where Clara and Eric are and it's hard to believe she's being so mean, refusing to see us like that."

"Maybe they all had a big fight. You know how our sister can be," Gwen said.

"Yeah, that might be it," Rose said softly.

Gwen was glad she didn't have to lie, but it certainly did not change matters for her. She still felt the blistering sting of rage when it came to her older sister. She was glad Clara wouldn't be a part of the funeral services and would never-ever see her own mother again. Something about that gave her a sense of satisfaction.

"Let's forget about all of this, besides, I could care less if we ever find Clara."

"No, Gwen, that's our sister and I will never stop looking for her. I will never stop loving her."

Gwen glared over at Rose.

"I don't understand you. She is the sole reason we're here today. She's the cause of all the heartache—all the stress we've found ourselves in. Do you remember how she treated you or has that slipped your mind. You actually want to forgive her, don't you?" Gwen exclaimed.

Rose sat quietly as the whining of the jet's engines hummed.

"Please don't start closing me out again," Gwen said. "I need you to talk to me and this time tell me the truth. I really am confused. What is it that makes you still love that girl?" Gwen asked.

Rose turned and faced her. She knew what she was about to say next would expose the new woman now living inside. "I guess we never have had the time to talk like I wanted to. With Lizzy, Rick and your career, you've been pretty busy. This is a perfect time for me to tell you what I've been wanting to."

She started slowly, "The rehab center where you found me, I met a gentleman there that helped change my life." She glanced away as she spoke…. "I remembered not wanting to go to chapel that day. I didn't feel well, but my friend Marie convinced me to go. I don't know if my heart was soft because of all that had happened to me, but for whatever reason, when I got there I was ready to hear what this man had to say."

Gwen listened intently.

"He told *the* most beautiful story," Rose said, as she eased back in her seat. "There was a woman in the Bible that poured expensive perfume on Jesus' feet. You have to know, this lady shouldn't have been around Jesus let alone touching Him. She had a messed up past and no one saw hope for her future. Yet, something magnificent happened to her that day. When she finally understood the love He had for her, it helped transform her life. So much so, that as she wept, she was able to wash His feet with her tears. She didn't care what the people in the room thought about her or what would happen as a result of what she did…. she wanted His forgiveness….she needed His love, and He gave her just that. When the minister compared our lives with that woman's, I got it. She was forgiven of much, and I knew if Christ could love her so completely, despite all she had done, He could love me too. If that's the case, then who am I not to love and forgive? After that day in chapel, I found a new life—one that's completely amazing. It comes with such peace and joy, it's difficult to describe."

Gwen looked at her sister and burst into laughter. "Come on, are you one of those Jesus freaks or what?" she asked.

Rose smiled, "You may see it that way, and that's okay. All I know, I would not trade what I have for anything. So, call me what you want, I'm like that lady with the expensive perfume. I don't care, I just need His love."

"Whoa, I can't believe you," Gwen said. "What does William have to say about all of this?"

"He's worse than I am," she laughed. "He was raised Pentecostal. Hey, I have one more surprise for you. I've joined his church and teach Bible study to the youth."

"No way! Did mother know about any of this?"

"She sure did, and boy was she happy for me. We talked about it all the time. She even accepted the Lord, and it was wonderful because now I know I will see my mother again."

"Huh?"

"You will have to come to know Him too one day, Gwen. That is the only way we'll get to see each other in heaven."

Gwen laughed out loud. "Nonsense, when it's over, it's over, everybody knows that."

"Not everyone believes the way you do. If you accept Jesus as your Savior, you will also live with Him forever. It's that simple. You've got to love Him with all your heart and soul and love your neighbor as yourself. Those are His rules and it makes for such a rich life. Like loving Clara... that's easy to do. Believe me, it feels better to love than to labor with the burden of unforgiveness—especially when it's towards your own sister."

"Okay, enough," Gwen snapped. "Clara doesn't deserve our love."

Rose turned and stared out the window as she watched the feathery clouds roll by. She knew she'd said enough. Rose began to think about all the good times she had with her mother. "I'll see you soon," she whispered.

The funeral was short. Gwen was quite surprised when it seemed the entire neighborhood came to pay their respects. The tiny church in their hometown overflowed with many of their childhood friends. The minister who conducted the eulogy validated most of Rose's story. He spoke of how much her mother loved the Lord.

Where had she been with all the Jesus talk? Traveling as much as she did, she guessed she missed it. "Well, good for them," Gwen thought. "She wasn't having any of it. As far as she was concerned, what she did to Clara was completely justified. After all, it was what Clara always wanted. Her mother had now been permanently removed from her life."

***

After the funeral, Rose and William had been accepted into their residency programs, and immediately became immersed in their studies. When Rose married William in the spring of the year, she moved about an hour and a half away from her sister's home. With all of Gwen's traveling they rarely got a chance to see each other.

Now the consummate actress, Gwen's life was moving faster than even she was used to. This year alone, she starred in two movies and was being courted to play a major role in a third.

Rick's photography career was booming and his plate was already too full from the many jobs offers.

Despite it all, they adhered to the advice Ellen had given them before she died—they always took time out of their busy schedules for Lizzy.

As Gwen drove along, she glanced at her daughter in the rear view mirror and smiled.

She reached for the ringing phone. It was Rose.

"Hey, sis, how are you? I need to tell you something," Rose said, quickly. "I've found Clara and it's not good."

"Excuse me," Gwen said. She instantly became irritated at the mention of her older sister's name.

"There's this guy in my class who grew up in the same part of town Clara moved to. When I mentioned I knew someone that lived there and told him who it was, he said everybody knew what happened to that family. He told me this horrific story, Gwen. Eric and his parents are dead!"

"Oh my god," Gwen exclaimed. That bit of news did catch her completely off guard.

"It gets worse. Eric's sister took all of her parents and Eric's money, leaving Clara with absolutely nothing."

"Oh, really…."

"I'm not finished. Clara and Eric had twin girls. They don't know where she and the children are," Rose said, her voice escalating.

"That's not any of our concern now is it?" Gwen said.

"Yes, it is our concern and we have to go and find our sister and nieces. Oh my goodness…they may be homeless or even worse, Gwen."

"Clara has always been able to take care of herself Rose, and I'm sure she will bounce back once given the chance. In the meantime, you need to concentrate on your studies so you can take care of all the little sick babies you plan to see after you graduate," Gwen said. She tried her best to steer clear of the troubling conversation.

Rose did not respond.

Gwen breathed hard into the phone keenly aware of her silence. She knew she had done the right thing not telling Rose she'd found Clara, and as predicted, the first thing she wanted to do was go and look for her.

"Are you still there?" Gwen asked.

"We need to find our sister and as soon as I get a break, William and I are going out there to search for her. I was wondering if you wanted to join us."

This time, Gwen didn't respond.

Chapter 19

Transforming Times

"Good news Mrs. Gordon, you can be transferred to a regular room today. Now that they have found your girls, what are your plans when you get out of here?" Dr. Owens asked, as he placed his orders into the computer.

"Just discharge me first for heaven's sake and then I'll figure all of that out. Besides, I've already discussed this with the social worker."

She didn't mean to be so snippy, but she was frustrated and in pain. No matter how much medication she took, her ankle throbbed. Clara took in a deep breath and settled somewhat. "I have a little cash stashed away so it will be easy for us to stay in a hotel until I find a nice place."

Dr. Owens didn't push the matter as he typed in a few more orders. "If your temperature stays down like it has, I believe we can send you home tomorrow. Hey, and no more tricks with the ice. Deal?"

"Alright," she snapped.

The next day, just as he promised he discharged her. She was packing the few items she had accumulated when Jessie entered the room.

"Here's the address to where your children are staying. I have already filed the appropriate paperwork so you can go and get them whenever you'd like. Are you sure you don't want me to try and arrange some housing assistance for you, Mrs. Gordon? It's not too late for me to help you with that."

"Nope, I can handle it," she answered abruptly. "My girls and I have special requirements where we choose to live. After all, they are still Gordon's," she said, rolling her eyes. They had already given her a voucher for a free cab ride and that was about all the assistance she was going to accept from them.

As a social worker, Jessie had seen just about everything. She dealt with having to make arrangements for temporary housing, obtaining food, or even helping get medications for her patients. She had to admit, most were extremely grateful to get the assistance she offered. This time, however, she discovered something quite different about her job. There was one thing she would never get used to dealing with from any of her clients. It was their pride.

"Here's my card if you need anything," she said, handing it to her.

"Put it over there," Clara said, never looking back.

Jessie eased the door closed and walked away.

"Mrs. Gordon, are you ready?" the nurse asked, pushing the wheelchair in.

"Am I? I was ready the moment I stepped foot in this place." She held her head down as the nurse pushed her along the hospital corridors. "She hoped she wouldn't recognize anybody in this charity hospital," she thought. As soon as they reached the front, she motioned for her to stop.

"I can make it from here," she said.

It took a little maneuvering adjusting to the crutches, but she finally worked her way inside the awaiting cab. She felt a sense of accomplishment as they drove away.

"I'll need you to stop by the bank on 25th and Waverly," she told the driver. "It will only take a few minutes."

She wanted to withdraw the little money she had left in her account. In her estimation, it would be enough for a nice hotel room until they found a permanent home. She was also going to need to rent a car for them to get around in, which threw a kink in her plan. Since hers had been demolished, a small portion of the money would have to be set aside for that.

She felt sick to her stomach when the teller told her the balance. "How can that be?" she whispered. "I know how much money should be in there."

"Calm down Mrs. Gordon, let's take a closer look. We have three checks written lately, to a grocery store, a storage facility and for day care fees."

"That's not my signature," Clara said. She knew exactly whose it was. Pat had gotten hold of one of her checkbooks and helped herself to the money.

"If that's not your signature, then we need to investigate this matter further," the teller said, looking closely at her.

"That won't be necessary," she finally said, as she faced her harsh reality. She knew Pat had used the money to take care of her kids, and there was no argument she could make about that. She turned and hobbled out the door.

When the cab drove into the neighborhood where her girls were, her pulse quickened.

"That's your address ma'am," the cabby said.

"I know they did not place my babies in a dump like this," she thought. She gave him the voucher and slowly slid across the leather seat, careful to avoid the huge crack in it. The large dog was paying close attention to her every move and barked violently as she approached the gate.

"Who is that, Rusty?" someone called out.

"Hello," Clara shouted.

"Yes! What do you need?"

"I'm here to get my girls. I'm told they are here," she yelled, over the barking dog.

"Sit, Rusty." He immediately stopped barking and sat obediently. "You can come on in now, he won't bother you."

Clara slipped the latch to open the gate and eased past the now calm dog. As soon as she hopped up the steps, she saw her girls. Dropping the crutches, she grabbed them and held on tightly. The urge to cry came tumbling in, but she quickly pulled it together as she kissed their cheeks over and over.

"Mommy really missed you," she said. "I believe you've grown a couple of inches since I've seen you last." She drew them close again. "I'm never going to leave you. Never!"

"I believe they missed you too. Hi, I'm Betty," she said.

"They look awfully nice," Clara said, with a moderate amount of sincerity as she stood.

"They told me you would be coming," Betty said.

"So you dressed them up special to see their mother. That was kind of you."

"No, I didn't dress them up because of that. They look this way every day," Betty boasted.

"I have to admit, when I drove up I had my doubts about what I would find. I must say, I am quite surprised," Clara said, scanning the room.

"Most people are. Rusty always gives them second thoughts about coming up here, though. The outside may need a little more work, but inside is where I spend most of my time anyway," Betty said.

As Clara glanced around, she had to admit the home was spotless and well decorated with the most up to date amenities. She noticed the large flat screen TV that sat inside the beautiful entertainment center, the focal point of the room. The couch was a nice plush one accented with large decorative pillows and the house smelled clean and freshly painted. After she saw the smiles on both her girls' faces and the nice warm home, it actually made her feel better knowing they had been here instead of with Pat.

"I heard you were in a bad accident," Betty said. "Are you feeling better? You are looking awfully thin there. She pointed towards the couch, "Here, have a seat."

"It's my ankle that's giving me the most trouble. Trying to get around on these," she said, holding up one of the crutches, "Can be difficult to say the least."

"You seem to have the hang of it. You climbed those steps pretty good."

There was an awkward silence between them for a moment.

"I really appreciate you taking in the girls. If you gather their things, I can get them out of your hair."

"They have been no bother at all. I loved having them around. When Miss Jessie, the social worker found out they were with me, she was relieved. She knew I would spoil them rotten," she said laughing. "They love 'Mama Betty.'" She reached her arms out as the girls ran and embraced her. "Now," she said, placing them on her lap. "You're both in your favorite spots." She looked over at Clara, "Where will you and the girls be staying?" she asked. "I would love to keep in touch with them."

Clara sighed hard. "We've got to figure that out, but for now I'm going to find us a hotel until I can arrange somewhere decent to live."

"Wow, it must be nice to be able to afford a hotel room. They're awfully expensive."

"Quite," Clara said. "You may have heard of my family, I was married to Dr. Eric Gordon."

"Oh yeah, I heard of the Gordon's," Betty said as she shifted, taking a closer look at Clara.

She didn't like her staring at her like that. "I think we should be going now, and thank you for taking care of the twins." Clara stood and almost immediately her head began to spin. She reached for anything to steady herself as she regained her balance. "Whew, I may have been on my feet too long already."

"Here, let me help you. Between those crutches and that big 'ole cast on your leg there, that's a lot of weight to carry around for a little girl like yourself."

Betty grabbed her under the arm as Clara plopped back down hard on the sofa.

"I was just about to make the girls some dinner and fix me some as well. Why don't you eat yourself something before you leave?" Betty said.

"No, it's already getting late and I really do need to find a nice hotel on the other side of town. If you gather their things, we can get going. As soon as I get there I'm going to take the longest, hottest bath ever. I can't wait to soak for hours," she said looking down at her cast. "First, I need to figure out how to keep this thing from getting wet."

"Nonsense," Betty said. "The girls have to eat. They get cranky when they don't. I will make sure you get to your nice swanky hotel after that. Sit back and relax."

"Her persistence was beginning to aggravate her, but she wasn't about to challenge the lady who had seen after her girls," Clara thought. She laid her head back on the couch to decrease the whirling motion. A few hours later, she awakened to something she hadn't felt in quite a while. At first she thought she was dreaming, but it was the smell of smothered chicken that caused her stomach to rumble. She sat up straight and immediately spotted her girls as they both waved. They sat in high-chairs, their faces grimy with potatoes and gravy.

"It's good," one of the twins said, displaying her sticky hands.

"I'm so sorry, I didn't mean to fall asleep," Clara said. "It's the pain medication I'm taking for my ankle that keeps me this drowsy. Oh my goodness, it's dark outside. We must get going. I knew we should have left earlier."

"Yep. Here, take your food and try and eat yourself something before you leave," Betty said, placing the tray in front of her.

"I haven't had much of an appetite since all of this happened to me," Clara said. She took small bites at first. "Boy, this is good." She proceeded to eat everything on her plate.

"You keep eating like that and you'll fatten up in no time," Betty said later, removing the tray.

"I don't want to get too fat," Clara said, reaching for her cell. She needed to call for a cab, but the black screen quickly reminded her that her phone had been disconnected this morning. She slipped it back inside her purse. Her ankle was aching and the frustration mounting. She had no idea where she was going or how she was going to get there.

"May I use your phone? I need to call for a cab. The girls and I really do need to be on our way."

"It's already late, why don't you stay here for the night?" Betty said. "I have a nice guest bedroom back there."

"Listen," Clara said, her fuse now lit. "Just because you think you know what happened, don't you go judging me too. My husband was a good man and would fix all of this if he were alive. I'm so sick of people like you believing all the lies. Why would you think I would need a handout from you anyway," she yelled.

Her voice raised another octave.

"As soon as I get myself back on my feet, I will show this town something they have never seen before. My girls will be exposed to nothing but the best because guess what…I'll make sure that happens," she said, pointing to her chest. "I have done it before and believe me, I can do it again. So don't you go trying to feel sorry for me, I can take care of myself *and* my girls just fine."

Clara was now screaming.

Betty counted to ten and then drew in a deep breath. "Like I said…….. Why don't you stay here for the night?" She used every ounce of self-control possible as she spoke.

Clara stared back at her, not expecting a response quite like that. She knew the cab fare would take a large portion of the only money she had in the world. Besides, what decent hotel would allow her and the girls to stay there with only a couple of hundred bucks in her pocket? It would take at least a week to figure out living arrangements. Even at that, how was she going to get around—she had no car. No one could contact her if they needed to because her cell was disconnected. She couldn't get around easily because of her dumb-broken ankle. The doctor had advised her to keep it elevated as much as possible. Running after two little girls and trying to get around when she still felt so weak, propping it up was going to be next to impossible. The fleeting thoughts scampered through her mind.

"If you let us stay one night, and I mean only one night, I will be out of here before day," Clara said.

"No problem, I'll call for the cab myself," Betty said, walking away.

In the meantime, neither of them said anything to each other as Betty busied herself putting away the dishes. Clara tried playing and talking with her twins but finally gave up as they followed Betty everywhere she went. She sat in the living room alone.

"Here take this," Betty said, walking in and handing her a large fluffy towel.

Clara stretched, "I must have dozed off again. What's this for?" she asked, reaching for the towel.

"Follow me," Betty said, as she led her down the long hallway to the bathroom.

When Clara looked inside, she was pleasantly surprised. The large, sparkly, clean bathroom had a Jacuzzi size tub filled with sudsy water.

"The stool beside the tub is so you can prop your cast up to keep it dry. Enjoy your bath," Betty said, closing the door.

Sliding into the warm, soothing water felt magical. Since she had not bathed in weeks, it seemed her body screamed with delight the moment she placed her foot inside.   She soaked for hours, often releasing the tepid water only to replace it with water as hot as she could stand it.

Betty gently tapped on the door, "Are you alright in there?" she asked.

"I'm fine. I'll be out in a minute." She stayed there another hour. A brand new toothbrush, a pair of pajamas along with slippers lay neatly on the counter. She assumed they were all for her as she brushed her teeth and dressed. Tying her hair up, she finally hopped out and sat on the couch.

"Here," Betty said, handing her a cup of tea.

"Gee, thanks. I appreciate your hospitality and I know the girls will miss you once we leave in the morning. Is this herbal?" she asked, blowing into the cup.

"Yep."

They sat back and watched TV before Betty bathed the girls and put them to bed.

The quietness in the old, yet modernized home along with the pain medication was a soothing combination for Clara. It was something about the soft pillows and the thick comforter that made her sleep so well.

The next morning she awakened to a wonderful aroma of coffee and something else that smelled awfully good. She slowly shuffled into the kitchen and spotted her girls eating.

"That's your plate," Betty said, taking another mouthful of eggs.

"Thanks," she said softly. Clara sat quietly as she ate her eggs, blueberry pancakes and bacon. She never mentioned anything about a cab.

As she helped Betty tidy up the extremely neat home, seeing it for the first time in the daylight gave her an even better perspective. It was actually much larger than she realized. Each room was arrayed in the latest new home design. The bedrooms and den were beautifully decorated with matching décor and the spacious kitchen had the latest features including a very nice island. She was somewhat impressed.

Later, she hopped into the large laundry area and washed a few of the girl's clothes. As she sat folding them, they watched Wheel of Fortune on the large flat screen TV.

"Ummm... Give Me Liberty or Give Me Death," she shouted out.

"Gee, you are good," Betty said. "Vanna hadn't turned but four tiles and you got the answer already."

"That was pretty easy," Clara said.

Betty prepared her bath again and this time Clara washed her hair the best she could. Another set of clean pajamas were awaiting her. She read the girls a bedtime story as she sipped on her herbal tea. When the twins climbed in bed with her that night, it felt good to finally snuggle with them. She knew then her body was ready to heal.

The following week at breakfast, Clara said the one thing she had been avoiding. "You know we can't stay here forever, Betty."

"I know," she said, reaching into the pocket of her apron. "Here's a list of apartments that you may approve of. I'll drive you to check them out if you'd like."

"That would be nice. I promise when I get this stupid cast off and get back on my feet, I will pay you..."

"Hey, let's not worry about any of that," Betty interrupted. "Now that the color is back in your cheeks, I think you will be able to handle the girls fine all by yourself."

Betty looked up at the clock, "Oh my goodness, I have got to get out of here. We have a special church meeting in an hour." She took the last bite of her toast. "By the way, we are going to service later. Would you like to join us?" Betty asked.

"No thanks. I think I'll pass on that. Besides, I haven't been inside a church in forever."

"Okay," Betty said, leaving her eating the very large meal she prepared.

Later, as darkness settled in and Betty dressed for church, Clara didn't think being left alone was such a good idea after all. She wasn't convinced the neighborhood was as safe as she liked it to be, even though they had an elaborate alarm system and a huge guard dog. In fact, it did little to ease her mind when she recognized the kind of security system Betty had installed. It was the same kind she had when she was married to Eric. "What would a house of this value need with such an elaborate alarm system?" she thought. Plus, she had seen two men parked outside the house when she peeked out.

"I'm taking the girls with me to service if that's okay. The folks at the church love them and will want to tell them good-bye. We won't be long," Betty said, as she fiddled with the clasp to her skirt. Looking up, she suddenly stopped. "Well, aren't you all spiffed up there," she said, looking Clara over. "Going somewhere?"

"I've changed my mind. I think I'll join you," she said, standing, smoothing out the wrinkles in her dress. "I hope this is okay."

"You look just fine," Betty said.

Clara was pleasantly surprised. Even though the church was only a few blocks from Betty's cluttered street, this part of town was extremely nice and very well kept. The sanctuary and other buildings stood tall as they spread across acres of the neatly manicured lawn.

"Will we be long?" Clara asked. She could feel the nerves settling in. It almost didn't feel right going inside a church now. She had not prayed or even thought about God since the last time her mother forced her to go to Sunday school.

"No, we won't be long at all, and we'll leave if your ankle gets too uncomfortable."

"I would appreciate that," Clara said.

Betty took them mid-way into the large sanctuary as several of the members waved and blew kisses to the girls when they passed by.

After the choir sang, "Grace and Mercy", a very tall, stately minister in a long white robe came to the podium.

Clara wanted to leave, but since no one else was walking, she sat still.

The minister opened his Bible and began to read about a man who was extremely wealthy…"Then, he lost everything, including his children," he boomed out in an expressive tone. "He even lost his health. His name was Job." In graphic detail, he described Job's plight.

"I sure can relate to that," Clara thought, and so far, he had captured her attention.

"Even his friends turned on him, offering him bad advice, but he did not turn on God. When Job prayed for his friends," the minister preached, "The Lord turned the captivity of Job around. God restored to him double for all that he had been through. Some of you have had Job-like experiences and need the Lord to turn things around for you. He can do it, you know, but all you need to do is trust Him."

No longer concentrating on leaving, she folded her arms and listened. Clara had never heard anyone speak quite like that before.

"Why don't you allow God to help change your circumstances? If you are tired, even feel that you don't know what to do... trust that He does. Job trusted Him and He did something for him no earthly man could do. He blessed him greatly both spiritually and naturally. He's a friend that sticks closer than a brother. Why don't you try Him for yourself....What a friend we have in Jesus," he began singing.... all our sins and grief to bear....what a privilege to carry.... everything to God in prayer." His rich, melodious voice sent chills down her spine, each word seeming to find its way into the center of her heart. It was the next few lines in the song that caused the tears in her eyes to shine ..... "Oh, what peace we often forfeit...Oh, what needless pain we bear...all because we do not carry....everything to God in prayer," he sang.

Betty reached over and patted her hand.

Later that night, Clara lay in bed, unable to close her eyes. "What was it that happened at Betty's church?" she kept asking herself. There was no denying the pastor's message had stirred up something deep inside. She tried rationalizing it away, but finally understood the questions she had were not going anywhere. So, she hopped out of bed and toddled down the hall.

"Betty, are you asleep?" she whispered.

"Yep."

"Sorry to wake you up, but I couldn't sleep." Clara hesitated, "Never mind," she said, as she turned to hop back to bed.

"Well, you got me up now. What's on your mind?" Betty called out. She reached over and turned on the light. "My goodness, it's three a.m. You really couldn't sleep."

"I cannot stop thinking about what your minister said and what I felt at your church. Do you believe God can fix anything…that He can truly turn things around like He did for that fellow Job?"

"Yep."

"Betty, tell me, what makes you believe in someone you can't even see?"

"You're up aren't you?"

Clara looked puzzled. At this point, she was trying real hard to grasp what was happening. Deep down inside, she knew it was something more to it and she needed to find out what it was.

Betty sat up. "You see Him every day, you just don't acknowledge it," she said softly.

She pulled back the curtains. "See those stars…that's His creation. Look at those trees…He did that too. Take a deep breath in…He's responsible for that. The fact you couldn't sleep, that's His doing, stirring you up and all. God is everywhere, Clara. All you need to do is open your eyes and see Him."

"Betty, if you don't mind, I think I may want to go back to church with you," she said. "I would like to take it all in one more time. I still can't believe what I'm feeling is real."

"Yep. Good night," Betty said, turning over, switching off the light.

Clara was ready for Sunday morning service before Betty. They sat on the pew they had the first time she came. The same minister preached again. This time, he said he wanted to talk about, "An Easy Yet Complicated Love". "Jesus loves us so much, that while we were yet sinners He died for us. He had the ability, the power, and the opportunity to avoid death, but He never denied His fate. Marred, ridiculed, beaten, and scourged, He withstood it all. He did not come down from the cross," he preached…"because He loved you and me. It's the kind of love that supersedes our intellect—that surpasses our knowledge—that exceeds all of our expectations. It's hard to imagine how someone who knew no sin, loved us enough to die for our sins. Someone who offered His life for those that deserved to die. I may not be able to adequately express why He did what He did….. because it's sometimes difficult even for me to comprehend a love like that. Yet," he cried out, "He did it all for you! He did it all for me! Come to the altar and find out more about Him," he boomed out, as he began to sing one of Andre Crouch's most famous hymns…. "The blood that Jesus shed for me ….. Way back on Calvary….Oh, the blood that gives me strength, from day to day…It will never… lose its power…..," he sang.

This time, tears that had been bottled up in the secret caverns of Clara's heart flowed freely. She wasn't used to the strange-warm sensation, but knew something life-altering was taking place. Despite all the hurt she experienced as a child, for years the tears had refused to fall. In the face of the trauma that tore through her life, they still never fell. Today, for the first time, they spilled out everywhere and it was nothing she could do about it. The more they came, the more something untangled inside. She had always been daring, so, she thought, "I may as well go to the altar and see what happens next." In less than a minute, the life she once knew was no more. Her heart was suddenly caressed and massaged by a love so deep, the feeling literally took her breath away. When she finally maneuvered her way back to her seat with the help of a few of the church mothers, Betty reached over and hugged her.

"I would never believe God could love me and allow me to love Him back," she said.

Later that afternoon, as Clara sipped on her herbal tea, she acknowledged the delightful feeling that refused to go away. "Betty, this is wonderful," she finally gushed. "I've got to know more about Him. I feel so light....so free."

"You will get to know Him better," she said. "Just remember, the one thing God wants from all of us is to love Him and love each other."

"Like the kind of love you've shown me and my girls," Clara said softly.

"Yep."

"I want to be able to show that kind of love now." Clara looked warmly over at her daughters, "I really do," she said.

"You can, just start with loving yourself, keep loving those girls, your family and all the people God places in your life. That will keep you busy for a while," Betty said, smiling.

Clara sat quietly, memories of her family flooding her mind. Finally, she confided in the one person she knew she could.

"Betty, I've done some pretty horrific things to my folks, especially to my mother. I disconnected myself from them…I thought I was too good…I wanted a different family—one with class and status."

The choppy words were liberating as she choked on the never-ending stream of tears.

"Boy, have I made some awful mistakes. I had everything I needed in the family God gave me and I threw it all away. My mother really loved me and was willing to do whatever it took to make me happy," Clara said, as she sobbed. "She and my sisters moved to New York and I have no idea where they are. I need to find them and apologize….to tell them how sorry I am." She looked up at Betty and said, "I hope they can forgive me for being such a horrible, insensitive daughter and sister."

"I'm pretty sure they will," Betty said. She knew there was a lot more to her story as she sat and listened.

Clara started from their father exiting their lives, all the way to Eric's death. "I don't know, I really messed up," she sighed. "Hey," she said, blowing her nose. "Let's pray that I will find them soon. It's time for me to get them back in my life. My girls need to know their family."

"Yep."

As the weeks passed by, Clara read her Bible incessantly. The highlight of her days was going to church and learning more about the God she now served. There were at least two services during the week she attended faithfully. While she had not officially joined the church, it still didn't stop her from allowing the twins to take part in all the youth activities.

"This afternoon, we are having a special church meeting," Betty said, drying her hands on her apron. "I would like for you to join me. You're pretty savvy about business matters and I think we may be able to use your expertise.'"

"I would love to help in any way that I can, but I have a doctor's appointment this evening. There's just no way am I going to miss getting this thing off," she said lifting up her cast.

"What if I go to the doctor with you and then we head over to the meeting afterwards?" Betty asked.

When Clara walked inside the church for the first time without her crutches or cast, she felt free. Even though they had given her a funny looking shoe to wear, she knew it was better than the confining plaster.

Sitting in her customary seat, she watched as the pastor walked to the podium. Adjusting the microphone, he briefly began to discuss the importance of embracing the community in which they lived.

"I would like Miss Betty Anderson to come to the platform at this time," Reverend Brown stated, proudly.

Clara was surprised when he called for her friend. She watched as she stood and gracefully stroll to the stage.

"You have done an exceptional job in assisting our neighborhood revitalization program," Reverend Brown said. He looked out over the congregation. "Ever since the church purchased all the homes on Miss Betty's street, we have remodeled the inside of most of them. While many are still boarded up, the plan was to get the inside finished before the weather changed. Miss Betty was our first occupant," he said, laying his hand on her shoulder. "As long as she had her trusty dog Rusty with her, she didn't mind living there."

The crowd laughed.

"We want you to know Miss Betty, because of what you did, it helped us to get the mayor and his committee's attention," he said, kissing her cheek and handing her the plaque. "We would like to thank you for the courage, commitment, and dedication you have shown your community."

Thunderous applause erupted.

"When the mayor realized we had someone actually living in our remodeled homes, he finally took us seriously. Deacon Hill and Deacon Jones, will the two of you please come up here."

He handed them their plaques. "These gentlemen, as you know are police officers by profession. On their own time, they provided security for Miss Betty and those homes. As a result of the dedication from these individuals and others, we can now afford to finish the project in its entirety—we can complete the outsides of the homes and even build a Christian Academy, community center, skating, bowling, and a movie theater in the area. That's because we were awarded the full grant we applied for," he yelled.

The entire room jumped to their feet and screamed. It escalated to the point of tears for many, and the hugs were ample. The community board led by the efforts of their church, had been finalist as potential recipients of a specially funded federal grant. The competition had been extremely stiff, but they had just succeeded in securing one of the largest revitalization endowments offered in the country.

"Not only will this create a wonderful environment for our families and children, jobs will become available in our community as a result of these efforts," he said.

Clara had not been involved in any of it but cheered along as well. She finally put it all together…the clutter on the street and boarded up homes…the two strange men she would occasionally see when she peeked out—all of it was a part of the revitalization plans. She marveled at the boldness and courage of the police officers and her friend Betty.

"Now, let's have a few words from Miss Betty," the pastor said, handing her the microphone.

"I always have believed in this community. When I first heard Reverend Brown describe his vision to us, I knew we could do it. However, I understood believing was not going to be good enough. I had to get involved in some other way. That's when I made up my mind I was going to live there. It did not bother me one bit to be the first to move in. Yeah, the street was a little isolated, but I knew I was safe. God is my protector."

The audience cheered.

"All of this is just a beginning. A beginning to something wonderful and I can see God's hands all over it," Betty said. She continued on and eventually thanked them for their love and support.

After the meeting, the congregation met in the adjacent fellowship hall for a fabulous celebratory meal. Clara sat with her girls and ate as she watched Betty greet her church family. All of them were extremely happy for her while they took time to offer their congratulations.

"Excuse me. It's Clara, isn't it?" Reverend Brown said, approaching her table.

"Yes, Clara Gordon," she said, reaching to shake his hand. She had not seen him coming.

"Miss Betty tells me you are a school teacher and actually taught at 'The' Carrington Academy. Now, that's pretty impressive."

She smiled politely and nodded.

"I was also told you have plans of one day starting your own school. Now, that would be awesome."

"Yes, it's all true. It has been a lifelong dream of mine." Clara sat back, wondering when Betty had the time to share all that information about her. "One day I hope it will all happen for me," she said.

"I'll be praying for you." He paused for a moment. "Mrs. Gordon…. I was thinking, perhaps you might be interested in being on the development committee for our Academy here," he said. "The grant approval came faster than we anticipated and I haven't had time to get all the appropriate committees together. We could benefit greatly from your expertise."

"Wow," she said, hesitating, clearly not expecting the offer. "Well, I don't see why I couldn't assist in some way."

He described the designs while she shared her ideas. They talked for quite a while.

She didn't mind. She loved his smile.

Chapter 20

Unforgiving Times

"Lizzy, Auntie Rose is here," Gwen said, racing out to meet her. "I was beginning to think they would never give you guys a break. I have already written administration to complain," Gwen giggled, rushing up to her.

"Look at how much you've grown," Rose said, swinging Lizzy around. "I'm so happy to see my little munchkin, I can hardly stand it." She hugged and snuggled her close. "All that studying has my brain in serious need of rest and I'm ready to have some

F-U-N." she said, facing Gwen. "I couldn't think of a better place to do that than being here with all of you."

"Believe me, you will not leave disappointed," Gwen said, wrapping her arm around her sister.

William opened the latch to the Explorer and removed the bags. "Come on inside," Rick said smiling. "I've got the game on, a bowl of popcorn and a great big 'ole Pepsi waiting just for you."

It wasn't long before the men were in Rick's man-cave. Gwen and Rick had just moved into their new home overlooking the hillside of an exclusive suburb in upstate New York. The mansion sprawled over acres of hilly terrain and provided all the privacy Gwen's now very public life demanded. It was hard even for her to believe, the girl in the baseball cap was now a Hollywood star.

"You can get lost in here," Rose said, wandering from room to room. "This place is unbelievable. Oh my goodness Gwen, your closet is as large as one of my bedrooms. God has definitely been good."

"I would like to think it was the hard work that did it," Gwen said, not looking up at her sister as she unzipped the bag, helping her to unpack.

Rose knew Gwen wasn't ready to hear what now consumed her life. She had so much she wanted to share with her sister. As soon as they graduated, she and William were going to open their practice in an underprivileged area. He had also accepted a position as the associate youth pastor at their church. There was one other thing she wanted to let Gwen in on—a subject she could no longer avoid. A thin film of moisture rested on her hands when she thought about it. She did not want to upset her, but it was time to share her news.

"Hey sis," Rose said, as she joined her later on the terrace. The cool mountain air made her gather her jacket close.

"Okay, what's up? Whenever you call me "sis", I know something is definitely on your mind."

Rose smiled as she drew near. "You know me well. I would like for us to talk about Clara." Rose didn't give her time to respond. "I'm going to look for her when we leave here. I wanted to spend a few days with you first and then start on my quest to search for our sister."

There was a surprising calmness as Gwen spoke. "Well," she said, "Now that's quite interesting. Somehow I can't say I'm not surprised. I guess if you want to waste your time and your vacation looking for someone who doesn't have any desire to see you, I'm not going to try and talk you out of it. I'm just glad we are getting a chance to spend some time together."

The beauty of the mountains drew her in. It was such a captivating view, and what Rose needed to relax. "I was hoping, perhaps I could convince you to join me?" she asked, as she stared ahead. Her question was a half-hearted one. She already knew the answer. What did take her off guard, however, was Gwen's ability to discuss 'the Clara' subject without getting overly upset.

"I can't ever see that happening, Rose. You know... I don't think about Clara much anymore. I gave her what she wanted—us out of her life. Besides, she treated mother like trash," she said, staring out over the balcony. "Good luck trying to find her."

That was the extent of their conversation and for the next three days the subject was successfully avoided.

They had such a blast, that when it came time to say goodbye, Rose found it difficult to leave. They toured places in New York she had never even heard of and enjoyed a family picnic in a private park and beach area. The highlight of the trip was the day they took a quick flight to Washington D.C. and attended an invitation only dinner for the President.

"Boy, this is harder than I thought—leaving and all," Rose said, rolling her suitcase along.

"You don't have to go," Gwen said, softly. "You can stay and enjoy your family. Plus, I have so much more to show you."

"I really wish I could, but we need to get on the road."

"Do you have any idea how you're going to find her?" Gwen asked.

It was the question Rose hadn't seen coming. She wasn't expecting to talk about Clara again determining that the subject was off limits—at least on this trip.

"Yes, I do," she responded. "Well, not exactly," she confessed, "but I know I'll find her. God has promised me that I will."

"There you go again with that religious stuff. Please convince me, even if you don't mean it, that you've worked out a plan because you are my smart-creative sister…and that's how you are going to find her. It will help eliminate my worrying and make me feel a whole lot better about you and William traveling all over the country looking for Clara."

Rose turned to Gwen and smiled. I love you my dear sister and I am very proud of you too. I believe real soon, the three of us girls will be back together again. That's what she wanted to say, but somehow, she ended up with, "We'll be okay."

After saying their long goodbyes, Rose and William traveled along the interstate listening to Kim Burrell's latest gospel CD. "I don't think I can ever recall seeing my sister so happy," she said. "Between Lizzy, her career, and having the love of her life with her forever, she's one blessed mother, actress, and wife. God is going to have to do a special work on that hard shell surrounding her heart, though."

William smiled, "She always has been one tough cookie," he said. "In my estimation, Rick is the only one who seems to be able to penetrate that impermeable wall she has up. Speaking of Rick, he and I had a long discussion about our church. He told me as soon as we get settled into our new home, he's going to bring everyone to visit and definitely wanted to go to church with us. He was raised by a grandmother that took him to Sunday school. He says he misses that and wants Lizzy raised in a family that worships together."

"Now, that will be the miracle I have been praying for. I'll look forward to the day when I see my sister walk inside a church," Rose chuckled.

As they drove into the city, William punched the address into the GPS. It took them directly to the doors of an extremely large, upscale office building.

They walked up to the information desk and were given directions to the Administrative Offices. Taking the elevator to the 23rd floor, they entered through the glass doors of the office area.

"We are here to see Mrs. Miriam Johnson," William said, handing the large sealed envelope to the receptionist. "There's a very important message inside for her."

"I'll give it to Mrs. Johnson as soon as she's available," she said.

They watched her tear open the package, both noticing a slight change in her expression as her eyes skimmed the first few lines of the letter.

William nudged Rose, thankfully snapping her out of her trance. They quickly turned to find seats in the lobby area.

"I hope she gives her the envelope right away," Rose said, fiddling with her earphones.

"Let's just pray this works like we've planned. All we can do now is wait and see what happens next," William said.

Suddenly, Rose sat up straight as she stared into the face of a woman who looked like she was on the hunt for something.

"Excuse me, Miriam? Miriam Johnson?" Rose said, walking up to her.

"Yes," she said, as she bristled away.

"Hi, my name is Rose and I am looking for my sister Clara Gordon. Perhaps you can help me."

Miriam eyed Rose from head to toe—twice.

"Do you think you can give me any information about where I might be able to find my sister? Any word you may have of her whereabouts would be greatly appreciated."

After a long, silent pause, she said, flatly, "Come with me."

"This is my husband, William," Rose said, following close. "We've come a long way and we certainly would appreciate your assistance."

She led them into an enormous corner office. "Have a seat," she said, pointing to the two-high back chairs. "Did you just deliver this?" Miriam asked, holding up the letter.

"Yes, I did," Rose said, "Let me explain." She started slowly, "My sister has always had an estranged relationship with her family. We rarely got to see her, in fact, we didn't even get a chance to attend her wedding," she said, dropping her eyes. "She was always so proud and, well…self-sufficient. She didn't need anything, nor did she ever want anything from us. So, we tried to respect that and give her the space she always demanded. That was, until we heard what happened to her. Miriam, my mother traveled a long way to try and find her daughter, yet it seemed no one would help her when she got here. My mother shouldn't have been traveling because she was quite ill. I'm told she came to see you and all but died at the gate to your home. In fact, my mother did die that day," the emotion in Rose's voice now evident.

Miriam's facial expression relaxed, even softened.

Rose forced back the tears and continued.

"My mother needed your help. While she was in poor health I believe if she could have just laid eyes on Clara, things may have gotten better for her. Who knows?" The tears inched their way closer. "When she died in your local hospital, we began our search for Clara. We wanted to let her know about our mother so that she could at least attend the funeral. More than anything, we wanted to see how she and her family were. That's why we are here today, to see if you can help us with that."

Miriam glared, holding on to the letter she'd received. She remembered Clara's mother, the quiet lady that sat alone at the bridal party. They all thought it strange she didn't show up the following day for the wedding. She knew Clara had always acted as if her side of the family never existed, yet, she virtually took over her mother and father...and of course Eric. Now, she was beginning to understand why. She wanted nothing to do with her own. She wanted a different one. She wanted the Gordon family.

"So, I'm here to ask for your help to find Clara," Rose said, interrupting Miriam's thoughts.

Miriam continued staring ahead, wondering if she should discuss or share any of what she knew. Whenever she brought up the subject about her family, it left her feeling miserable for days. Even though it had been five years since the accident, the pain of it all was still too real. She was just now beginning to deal successfully with the grief the tragedy left behind. This time, however, she figured she had to say something. Someone connected to it all in a strange sort of way was sitting here before her. She heard about the lady getting deathly ill at the gate to her home. Well, it wasn't her fault Clara's mother had not called ahead and asked permission to see her like most normal people would have. Driving up uninvited like that, she had every right not to let her in. Still, the guilt washed over her like the evening tide.

"I don't know how much you've heard," Miriam finally said. "It has been over five years since the accident, and neither my parents nor my brother survived." She gasped for air as the pain of mentioning it punched her hard. She breathed in deeply and continued. "Clara moved away from the home she and Eric lived in and I have no idea where she is. We never kept in touch after that." She pushed the words out as fast as she could.

"You haven't heard anything about where you think she might be," Rose said. "I was hoping to get a little more information from you."

"Sure, I've heard plenty of rumors. At one point, I heard that she died in a terrible car accident," Miriam said. "Then the next month, I heard she was living in the projects. It has been all over the board, so I quit listening to any of it. I'm sorry, I wish I had more to offer."

Rose sighed, "Thanks for seeing us. I realize you didn't have to. If you hear anything that may be useful, here's my number," she said, handing her the card. "You can call me any time, day or night. I'm going to search a few other places before I leave the city. Maybe something will turn up."

Rose and William stood, thanking her again.

"Wait, before you go." Miriam turned and faced Rose. "If you find Clara, please tell her that I would like to speak with her." She paused, grappling with her jumbled emotions.

"I was very angry when my brother and parents died. Clara was the easiest target I suppose," she said, slowly. "We never did get along and I guess I took all my frustrations out on her. I was so upset I lost all perspective, especially when it came to Eric."

"Whenever I need to make an important decision about the company, inevitably someone will say, Eric would have wanted it that way. He frequents my dreams," she said, glancing up, her eyes deep and haunting. "He always leaves me saying, I would have wanted it that way. At first I didn't understand." She paused and looked at Rose, "Let me just say I need to settle some things with Clara too. It's the only way I believe I can find peace. Eric would have wanted me to. He truly loved her."

"Would you like to help me find her?" Rose asked softly.

Finally, Miriam smiled. "Let me make a few phone calls."

Every place she sent them to, however, no one had heard from Clara in years. Miriam was beginning to believe the rumors. "I won't give up, Rose. I'll call you whenever I find something out," she said.

As Rose and William headed home, they drove along in silence. He knew her heart was breaking. She still hadn't found her sister.

Chapter 21

Moving Times

Despite a few hiccups in the plans, the Academy and community center were now in full development. Clara had been made project manager over all revitalization efforts for the church and added the much needed organizational expertise required.

"Reverend Brown, I think we're prepared to meet with the mayor. We can't afford to put it off any longer, it's been over a year and the plans are solid—the figures good. If we get his approval, we should be opening the Academy in the spring of next year."

"I believe you're right, Clara. It's going to blow him away when he sees how well you've integrated the Academy and community center concept. Masterful!" Reverend Brown stood, holding up the business plan. "There's one set of figures, however, I think we still need to discuss before we proceed," he said, scratching his head.

She was taken aback at his comment—even slightly aggravated. She had gone over those numbers countless times and knew them like the back of her hand. They were rock-solid and she dared anyone to challenge her about them.

"May I ask which ones have you concerned?" she asked, trying hard to conceal the defensiveness sneaking its way in.

"It's the transportation part, uh, the buses you budgeted for. The community center is right around the corner from the school. Will we need that many?"

Before Clara could answer, he held up his hand.

"Why don't we discuss this over dinner, I'm starving. I know a wonderful little place that's quiet and private. It's a perfect spot to go over the numbers there."

"Okay," she said. "Let me grab my briefcase."

He pulled in front of the nice Italian restaurant and they were seated immediately.

When she tried explaining the figures, she noticed he never challenged any of her budget-performa assumptions. She went ahead anyway, making the point that her calculations were exactly right.

"If we are projecting the number of kids in the next two to five years to grow as we anticipate, we will definitely need these many buses. Here's the bottom line," she said, pointing to the page of numbers. "We can afford it."

She glanced up waiting on his response. "Are you okay with my calculations now?" she asked.

"I believe you've covered everything," he said, softly. He meticulously folded his napkin and laid it aside. "This has been an extremely long day, Clara, why don't we just relax and enjoy the rest of it," he said, smiling.

"Okay-y-y," she said, slowly closing the folder. She smiled back and shifted to a more comfortable position. "I agree, why don't we enjoy ourselves?" As she raised her goblet filled with water, a hint of what he might be up to gradually sank in. "Here's to ending our day relaxing for a change," she said.

He picked up his glass and brushed it softly against hers. "Yes, a real nice way to end the day."

The conversation was light at first, but by the time the dinner ended, they were absorbed in ideas they each had for the community center.

"Miss Betty has always been a great judge of character," he said. "Her discernment is keener than anyone's I know. When she suggested you for the project manager, she was practically reading my mind. She told me you and the girls would be around for a while until your ankle healed."

"My ankle has been fine for over a year now," Clara said, laughing. "She just doesn't want my girls out of her sight, that's all."

"She sure does love those twins and you too I might add. When she mentioned your desire to open a Christian Academy, I knew you were the woman for the job."

"Betty is a real shining star in my book," Clara said. "Honestly, I never would have made it without her."

They talked until there was only one other couple remaining in the restaurant.

"I was wondering," Reverend Brown said. He stopped mid-sentence, "I hope I'm not being too forward, but Miss Betty told me you were looking for somewhere for you and the girls to call your own. I know it may not be exactly what you've been used to, but, I was wondering if you would be interested in living in one of the homes we're remodeling. The one I'm speaking of is almost complete and will easily be my favorite— definitely a model for the neighborhood. Those newly planted trees and brand new lighting will add a spark to the street it's on." He cleared his throat, "It's very nice. Would you consider living there?"

She knew she was just as nervous as he was when she burst into hearty laughter. "That's the best news I've heard all day, Reverend Brown.   It would be my pleasure to do so and I think Betty will finally be satisfied," she said. "Whenever I talked of moving, she always has a million reasons why it wasn't the right time or the right place. Besides, it's not too far from both my jobs."

Clara had found an assignment in one of the city schools teaching math and in the evening worked tirelessly on the revitalization project.

"Living with Betty has allowed me to put a little bit of money aside. I should be able to afford it."

"That's great, I'll draw up the paperwork right away," he said, smiling. "I certainly have enjoyed our dinner tonight, Clara." He hesitated and then stammered, "Do you…uh… think we could… uh…. do this again? Not business, but something like a real date."

She laughed out loud again. She knew she had to work on that. Ever since her transformation, she was just down-right giddy.

"You're not used to asking anyone out are you? Of course, I would love to go to dinner with you Reverend Brown and leave the figures at home. Now, see, that wasn't so bad."

He wiped his forehead. "You made it easy. Let's get out of here."

They slipped pass the other couple as they headed towards the door.

"Clara Gordon?" the young lady called out from her table. "I thought that was you," she said coming towards them. "Hello, Reverend Brown, I'm Christy Belmont from Bradbury. Clara and I worked together at Carrington. Well, well, well… I haven't seen you in ages," she said, turning to her.

Clara hadn't realized the only couple left in the restaurant was an adversary from her past who hung out with the old gang.

"It's nice seeing you again," Clara said, politely.

"I must say, you look fantastic. You're as skinny as ever!" Christy said.

Clara paused, trying to recoup from the awkward moment. She fought hard to think of something positive to say. Christy had to have gained thirty pounds since she'd seen her last.

"Thanks," Clara said, smiling. "It was good seeing you." She turned quickly and headed out the door. She refused to let bad memories destroy a perfectly good afternoon.

Brushing the encounter aside, she enjoyed the ride home as they chatted, both making an extra effort not to discuss work.

"May I ask you a question?" she said, as they pulled in front of Betty's home. "Your wife, what happened to, Mrs. Brown?"

"I'm surprise you haven't heard that story already." She watched his eyes as a hint of sadness eased its way in. "My wife and daughter were killed in a car accident five years ago. One of the most horrific days of my life I might add. After that, I didn't know if I would make it, Clara…but God showed me that I could. He has been my Comforter and help through it all. He kept me sane. When I talked to Him during that time, I wanted to know what in the world He was doing," he said. "I'd served Him well. I'd been faithful, so why did He let that happen to me. The normal questions I guess anyone would ask. I just didn't understand it all until one day He let me in on a secret He had been keeping. He explained that my wife and child were a temporary gift He allowed only me to have. I was the person He could trust to take care of them in such a short period of time. Since they weren't going to be with us very long, He wanted to make sure every day was a special one for them. He said I was the man for the job. Little did I know that the promise I made my wife shortly after we were married—to make as many memories with her as possible—was my way of fulfilling His plan. Every day that we were together, I tried to make them special. Needless to say, I thought we would grow old together when I promised her that...but, I did keep my word. I even ramped up the stakes when our daughter was born. We all had great times together the short while they were here." He gazed softly into her eyes. "Those precious memories with my family, I will cherish forever. So, when I preach about what God can do, it's because I really do know that He can. The messages come from here," he said, pointing to his heart.

The tears in Clara's eyes sparkled. She leaned back and told him her story.

***

"Reverend Brown, you and Clara have done an incredible job," the mayor said, swiveling around in his chair. "I am going to see to it personally that each project is voted on by the City Commissioners during the next session. You shouldn't have any issues with that because I'm supporting this endeavor all the way. It could be the model for revitalizing every underserved community in this city," he boasted. He stood and shook hands vigorously. "I'll see you two at the vote."

As soon as they turned the corner, no longer in the sight of the mayor's staff, they faced each other and hugged. "I knew you could do it," Reverend Brown said. "I just knew it," he said, punching the air. "Everyone says if he approves the first phase, all the other plans are a go. Here's to Christian Academy," he said, pointing to heaven.

"Let's hurry and get back to the office. We have tons of work to do," Clara said, picking up her pace. "We still have a deadline to get the plans signed off by the City Inspectors Office this week." She adjusted her briefcase. "Then we have to…"

"Whoa, slow down a minute," he said, reaching for her arm. "Don't you think we deserve to celebrate at least this one major accomplishment? Clara, you have been working virtually non-stop ever since all of this began. Let's face it. We may not have too many opportunities to relax after this. Why don't I take you to a very special place of mine?" he said.

She slowed and faced him. He seemed to have a knack for helping her keep things in perspective. She felt calmness—a peace she hadn't experienced since Eric suddenly passed away.

An hour later, they sat eating hot dogs on a secluded park bench overlooking a sparkling blue pond. The mild breeze along with the sunlight created the only necessary conversation.

"I often come here whenever I need to relax and spend time alone with God," he finally said.

As soon as the breeze stroked her arms, Clara understood why he'd chosen that spot. She breathed in the fresh air. "Is this our second date?" she asked.

"Nope," he said, biting into the hotdog bun. "This doesn't count. I still want to show you what a real date with me is like."

At the end of the week, he kept his word. As she slipped into her dress, she admired herself in the mirror. She loved the way it fit, a hint of pink, perfectly accenting her skin tone, the beading on the high collar giving it just the pop it needed. She fiddled with her hair as she eased into her black heels.

"Mommy, you're so pretty," the twin said, skipping into the room. She patted Clara's hair.

"I've never seen you this dolled up," Betty said. "If it ain't a hoot….you and Reverend Brown."

"Now, don't you go teasing me about that. I'm such a nervous wreck. I haven't been on a date in a very long time. I can hardly believe this is happening," Clara said.

"Well, I can. I saw it coming a long time ago."

"No, you did not. How? When? Was I too pushy?"

"It wasn't you I was worried about at all. It was the Reverend I had my eye on," Betty said. "He kept asking me… how is Clara getting along?" she said, in an exaggerated tone. "Then sometimes he asked about your girls and would causally sneak in…oh by the way, how has their mother been doing? Now, thank me young lady that I always gave him a very good report."

"I owe you a lot, Betty. I really do," Clara said laughing loudly.

After putting her sparkling earrings on, they all sat in the living room. The twins chatted as they combed their baby doll's hair.

"Stop in the Name of Love," Clara called out.

"You really are good. I'm telling you, you should go and audition for that show. You would spin that wheel right into a ton of money," Betty said.

When the doorbell rang, she looked up as Reverend Brown walked in—standing tall in his gray Alexander

Vanquish suit. She thanked God she had worn her special dress for the evening.

"You two have a great time," Betty called out as they walked to the car.

Right after their magnificent meal, he took her to one of the hottest tickets in town—a play entitled, "No Other Help I Know". She was stunned, slightly embarrassed when he reached over and held her hand. The night was turning into one she often dreamed about. It had been a real long time since she felt so alive and beautiful.

***

While Clara enjoyed Reverend Brown's company and loved spending time with him, the race for building the Academy and community center was on. The Commissioners voted to approve all components of the revitalization plans. They scurried about week after week to ensure deadlines were met and spent countless hours pouring over contracts. Clara found herself formulating design teams, altering the blueprints and managing the architectural schematics. She was now officially employed only by the revitalization committee and was slated to be the headmaster of the new Christian Academy.

She was dressed in her hard–hat so often, she accidently wore it home one day. The mayor took note of the level of detail she brought to each assignment and began requesting her assistance with other city projects. Racing from board meetings to construction sites, she barely found time to move into her newly renovated home.

"This Saturday, I have the moving crew all lined up. Gracie, Karen, Randal and Tommy are coming over. We'll move with or without you, take it or leave it,"

Betty said. "You will never get moved if you don't slow yourself down, girl."

"I guess meeting with the architects can be rescheduled for Monday," Clara said. She texted her assistant and looked up…"Tell them, it's a date."

When moving day finally arrived, she watched as the men unloaded her newly purchased bedroom, living room, and kitchen furniture. The twins darted in and out of each room, carefully dodging the movers. She stood there momentarily allowing her thoughts to carry her away. It had been five years since Eric's death. In that short period of time, her journey had been a long one. She had been homeless, in poor health and loaded with pride…a deadly combination that should have killed anyone, but God, had graciously placed Betty in their lives. She'd gone from a penniless, frail, angry woman, who was ready to take on the world, to one who stood rich in the things that mattered most. She had family, friends and above all a God whom she loved and knew loved her. She gazed up at the two-story brick structure and thought, "and now, we have a home." Life was good.

"Quit your daydreaming and tell us how you want these things arranged," Betty called out.

"I'm coming," Clara shouted back as she ascended the steps.

As soon as the move was complete, she and her design team were moving at break-neck speed. Electrical and plumbing inspections were scheduled and the contractors were still making last minute adjustments. The late nights continued as they poured over paper work… financials, determining to come in under budget.

The opening date for the Academy and community center was in two weeks.

"Good night," Melissa called out. "If I don't get home on time, my husband is going to kick me out! We're celebrating twenty five years tonight," she said, flashing her wedding band.

She was Clara's assistant and knew as much about each project as she did.

"I'll be right behind you once I tweak this last letter and fax it over to the attorneys," Clara said, staring into the computer. "Here, take a look at it before you go," she said, handing it to her.

"Alright, but I'm telling Charlie it was your fault I'm late again." She quickly scanned the documents. "I would change this sentence," she pointed. "Spell out our name instead of saying *we* and that should do it."

"You're right." Clara said hitting the delete button.

"I've got to get going," Melissa said, grabbing her bag. "Don't stay too late and tell Reverend Brown I'm locking the side door," she said, racing out.

When Clara finished making the necessary changes, she printed the document and placed it neatly inside a folder. She grabbed her bag as she walked out, closing the door behind her. She climbed the stairs and knocked softly on the Reverend's door. "I'm calling it quits for tonight. It's been a very long day," she said, walking in. "Can you take a look at this document before I leave? Once you sign off on it, I'll fax it over to the attorney's office."

He perused the article, signed it, and handed it back to her. "Good to go."

"What a load off of our shoulders. That's the last of the paperwork the City Inspector should need," Clara said, as she left to fax the letter.

"Goodnight," she said, peeking back through the door. "They should have the plans on their desk first thing in the morning." She turned to leave but stopped. "Don't forget we have a meeting with the transportation committee at eight. Oh, and I almost forgot, Melissa has already locked the side door." Suddenly aware he was staring at her, she paused. If he hadn't been smiling, the intense look would have made her uncomfortable. "What?" she asked, raising both hands.

His smiled widened, "What is it about you lately? You have to be exhausted but you still have this…this glow," he said. "It really brightens up the place."

"I can't imagine what you're seeing right now. I'm so tired and I know I must look a mess." She blurted out that nervous laugh of hers, as she smoothed over her hair.

"See, it's that laugh and little move you just made that makes you so beautiful, Clara. Never lose that."

"Thanks, Phillip… I'll try and keep that in mind." At that moment she wanted to kick herself. Why hadn't she been honest with him? She was glowing because for the first time she understood who she was and what it took to make her happy. He, made her happy, but she knew now wasn't the time to tell him. So, she walked away.

"Clara."

"Yes," she said, her heart slightly racing. She hadn't realized he'd gotten up and was now walking towards her.

Their eyes locked.

"I didn't mean to startle you," he said, smiling and embracing her softly. "Are you okay?"

"Well, it may be the right time after all," she thought. "Yes, I'm fine. I guess I wanted to thank you and let you know—well—you make me happy. The glow and all, thingy." She smiled, circling her face with her finger.

"Oh, I see," he said, moving closer. "I'm glad I make you happy because guess what…you make me happy too." He gazed into her eyes and hung there for a moment. "I'm in love with you, Clara."

"I know, and I'm really glad," she said.

He kissed her goodnight. "I'm looking forward to our date tomorrow," he whispered.

She smiled.

***

The next day, his thoughts were mostly of her. They'd spent a great deal of time together recently, and yet it wasn't enough for him. Even though they had been with each other going over contracts early in the morning, it was their special date tonight that filled his mind.

"It couldn't come soon enough," he thought.

"Miss Betty, that has to be the most famous smothered chicken this side of the Mississippi," he said, coming through the door later that evening.

"I've got a special piece just for you," she said, scooping the gravy on top of the savory meat.

"Please save it for me, I've planned a special dinner for Clara and me tonight, but I'll probably want to snack on something later."

"Let me pack it up then," she said, as she hummed, 'His Eye is on the Sparrow'.

"I hope you two have a great night," she said, packing the dish and handing it to him.

"I'm pretty sure we will." He smiled and quickly kissed her on the cheek.

Thirty minutes later, they pulled in front of a small restaurant on the south side of town.

"Is it open?" Clara asked, as they walked towards the door. "It doesn't look as if anyone's inside," she said, peeking in."

At that moment, a young man appeared, "Right this way, ma'am" he said, opening the door wide.

Walking in, she noticed a lone table draped in white linen in the center of the room. Two flickering candles stood tall on each side of a bouquet of red roses—resting in the middle. Reverend Brown walked her to it, pulled out the chair as she slipped in.

"Thank you," she whispered, yet very much stunned.

"We have the place all to ourselves tonight," he told her.

A mild glow eased its way in—warming her from the inside out. She reached for his hand and gently held on.

"You've been working so hard, I thought I would surprise you with a special night…just the two of us. I hope you enjoy it," he said.

Clara thoughts outpaced her words. She sat speechless, completely amazed at his generosity and kindness.

The gospel music in the background played softly. The soothing ripple of the waterfall resting in the corner, added an additional spark to the already romantic evening. The server moved swiftly filling their glasses with orange blossom-peach-mango tea.

She looked all around and then back at Reverend Brown, "How could I ever repay you for making such a difference in mine and the girls' lives?" she asked, softly.

"I can think of one way you could start," he said, reaching for her hand.

He pulled out the two carat diamond ring. "If you accept this and agree to be Mrs. Phillip Brown that would be a great start."

Tears instantly sprang to her eyes. "Yes, oh my god, a million times, yes."

The server smiled.

Chapter 22

Mending Times

The car zipped through traffic along a stretch of highway. "Please slow down, Rose, we have plenty of time," William said.

She looked down at the speedometer and eased off the pedal. She hadn't realized how fast she was going until he pointed it out. The only thing on her mind—this may actually be the day she gets to see her sister again.

"Can you believe this could really be it, William? After months of searching, we may have actually found her. Miriam told me she's almost one hundred percent sure this is the correct address. Someone spotted her at a restaurant and they were able to trace her here."

"This is a pretty big city, Rose, let's just get there safely."

William didn't need her getting her hopes up again. He knew how disappointed she had been the last time they hadn't found Clara. They'd driven out two times before with no luck. He was going to suggest they quit for a while if this turned out to be another dead end.

They pulled in front of the quaint, two-story brick house, accented with an array of multi-colored flowers neatly lining the walkway.

"There it is," Rose whispered.

When she spotted the swing-set and a large Barbie doll-house in the backyard, she took in two deep breaths. She didn't know if the nervousness had to do with at long last finding her sister or how Clara would react when she saw her. She could only imagine her throwing a fit and forcing her away as she'd done before. "Don't you ever come to my home uninvited again,"… she could actually visualize Clara screaming that. She had been so unbelievably cruel the last time they had spoken, she could still feel the sting from her words. According to Gwen, Clara never wanted to see any of them again. It was strange though, somehow she was okay with that. She was willing to deal with the rejection and the hurt. Something else much stronger was driving her now—she was prepared. What she wasn't ready for, however, was not finding her sister today. They hadn't seen each other in over six years and she knew without a doubt she would be devastated if this wasn't her home.

She pushed the doorbell in slowly and released it as the chimes echoed inside. At that exact moment, she could feel the stubborn tears, refusing to go away. William slid his hand into hers and squeezed.

"Yes," Clara said, opening the door. She stopped abruptly. "Oh, my god Rose."

"I've been looking for you for a very long time," Rose mumbled. She felt that same sense of inadequacy slowly creep its way in when she suddenly faced her older sister.

Clara threw the door open wide, grabbed Rose and held on tightly, clinging to her as if she could make up for all the years they had been apart.

The warm embrace of Clara's now loving arms was what Rose had longed for ever since she was a child.

They buried their heads together and wept.

"I prayed you would come and you did," Clara cried, pressing out her words through the tears.

Rose instantly knew she wasn't as prepared as she thought she would be. Was this the sister that had mocked her these many years? The one who ignored her every move? Was she dreaming or was Clara actually hugging her back? It took a moment for her mind to adjust to it all. Finally, she took a good look at her sister and smiled, "I'm so glad I've found you," Rose said.

Clara gently held Rose's face and lightly wiped away her tears. "I'm glad you did too."

"Who's that, mommy?" one of the twins asked, peeking from around her leg. "Are you okay? Why are you crying?" she whimpered.

She stooped down and held her. "No, it's okay. This is your Auntie Rose and she came all the way out here to see us. This is mommy's sister," Clara said. "Mommy is happy, that's all."

She ran yelling, "Mommy's sister is here! Mommy's sister is here!"

"Oh my goodness, Rose, how's mother? How's Gwen?" she asked, facing her. "Where are they? We have so much to talk about. Look at how skinny you are!"

"I know," Rose said smiling widely. "First, let me introduce you to my husband." "This is unbelievable, your husband!" Clara squealed as she hugged William. "You mean I have a brother-in-law!"

"You have two brother-in-laws. Gwen's married too."

"It feels as if I'm dreaming," Clara said. "Somebody please pinch me, I've prayed so hard for this moment" she said, hugging Rose over and over again.

They laughed, talked, and cried for hours.

At noon they dined on Clara's homemade broccoli and potato soup along with a garden salad.

"This is really good," Rose said. "I almost forgot you could cook." She placed her spoon down, "I have something for you—pictures I brought in case I found you." She grabbed the small album from her bag, "Here, this will help you get caught up faster." She evaded any question the best she could about their mother, shifting most of her attention to Gwen.

Clara turned each page carefully, admiring every photo. "I can count on one hand the number of times I've gone to the movies in the past three years. I rarely get to watch television. I guess that's why I didn't know. I haven't seen Shaker's, but I have heard about it. I've even heard the name Gwen Haley. I just can't believe she's my sister. Gwen is lovely," she said, shaking her head in disbelief.

She softly rubbed the picture of Lizzy. "You mean I have a niece," Clara said. "She's beautiful." Tears filled her eyes once again.

"That's it! Go and get your things from the hotel. You and William are staying here with me. We have too much to talk about."

As soon as they heard that, both girls grabbed William's hands yanking him towards the guest room as he pretended to let them drag him along.

Clara moved closer to Rose, "My life has changed so much," she said, reaching for her hand. "I prayed each day that God would let me find you. I didn't have much luck looking for you guys in New York. I called the operator hundreds of time," she said, laughing, "Asking for Ellen Andrews. I called the Bronx, Upper Manhattan and Queens. It was the one in the Bronx that got to me the most. This is Ellen Andrews," Clara said, in her thick Bronx accent. "I said, never mind, and hung up the phone. I gave up after that." They laughed and then instantly searched each other's eyes again. Neither spoke for a moment—both understanding the messages their hearts were now sending.

"I'm sorry, Rose," Clara finally said.

"No, don't," Rose said.

Clara gently brushed her fingers onto her sister's lips. "Sh-h-h, please allow me to do this. I must. I've waited a long time for this moment... to tell you how truly sorry and ashamed I am for all that I've done," she said softly. "I shouldn't have been so mean—so selfish. It was all my fault what happened to us. I know that now. I also know that God has given me a second chance to get things right. Believe me Rose, I plan on doing that. I know how to do that now."

Rose reached over and hugged her tightly. Never in a million years did she ever expect to find such a transformed Clara. She could see and feel the drastic change taking place in her life.

"I love you, and I'm thrilled that we're back together again," Rose said. She held on for a while and then looked up, "I need to share something with you about mother," she said softly. She had no idea why she picked that particular moment to tell her, but knew it was the right time.

"You're making me nervous, is she okay?" Clara asked.

Rose shook her head.

"No, Rose, oh my goodness, no!" she said, clutching her chest.

"She passed away three years ago. I tried real hard to find you to let you know."

Clara sat back, gasping for air, squeezing Rose's hand as the pain ripped through every inch of her heart. The shock of it all wouldn't allow her to utter a word no matter how hard she tried. So, she sat there and cried.

"She will never know how sorry I was…I am," Clara sobbed. "I want my mother…I need my mother, Rose."

"I know…I know," Rose said, trying hard to console her.

The twins came running in and rested their heads on their mother's shoulders.

"Are you okay, mommy, please don't cry," they said.

"I can't help it right now. Mommy will be better in a little while."

She cried all the rest of the day.

Rose tried all she could to help her sister, but nothing worked.

Reverend Brown gently wrapped his arms around her when he came over. "I know it hurts, Clara" he whispered. "God's going to see you through it."

All during the night, Rose could hear Clara silently weeping. She checked on her frequently, but nothing she said seemed to ease the heartache she was now experiencing.

The next morning, when Clara took the girls to school, she came back and apologized for being such a poor host. She excused herself, went back into her bedroom, curled up in bed, and sobbed.

Rose was becoming increasingly concerned about Clara when she refused to eat. As she was about to check in on her again, she was startled when the front door pushed open and a tiny woman came marching her way in.

"So, you're Clara's sister, Rose? Hi, I'm Betty, her friend and neighbor."

Betty walked past Rose towards the bedroom.

"She's quite upset, don't you …"

Betty reached out, gently slid her hand into Rose's, and kept on walking. As she eased the door open, she walked into the dimly lit room and sat next to Clara now curled up in bed. The puffiness in both eyes stunned her.

Clara looked up at Betty and burst into tears.

"Okay," she soothed her. "Now that's a terrible hurt you got yourself there, and it's a wound that deserves every tear," Betty said, softly. "Can't tell you not to cry. Nope. Just keep the reason you're crying clear, dear. You will miss your mother and you didn't get a chance to say good-bye is what the tears are for. I know you had a lot to tell her—to apologize for." She rested her hand under her chin and gently lifted her head, "Clara, listen to me. Your mother knew you were a wounded little girl, but she also knew this day would come. It always does. That one day when you would mature and realize what a wonderful mother you had and how much you loved her. She was just waiting on you."

"Betty, do you think she knew I loved her?" she forced out.

"Without a doubt."

"I did and said some awfully mean things."

"Listen, she knew that was the wounded, young girl talking, not the mature woman I'm speaking with today. Your mother would want you to forgive yourself. I believe that would have made her very happy."

"I really loved her so much. I just wanted to tell her that and I can't."

"Call me old-fashioned, but some kind of way, I believe she already knows."

"I pray that she does. Oh, how I pray that she does," Clara cried.

"She's looking down at us now," Betty said, pointing upwards.

For the first time since she heard the news of her mother's death, Clara smiled. "Thank you, Betty," she said, hugging her tightly. "Thank you for everything."

"Why don't you get up and try and eat yourself something there," she said, flipping on the top light. "You don't need to lose those few pounds you finally gained. Have you told Rose about the Academy you're about to open?" Betty asked, as they all paraded into the kitchen.

Rose stood in awe of the small woman. Like magic, Clara never really cried again. The next few days they enjoyed sightseeing and reflecting back every chance they could about their childhood. A couple of times Rose noticed the sadness trying to creep its way back in, but the twins always seemed to somehow drive it away. Staying an additional day with her also gave Clara a little more time to deal with the lingering grief.

"Tell Gwen as soon as she's back from Africa to please call me, I really do need to speak with her," Clara said.

Rose didn't have the heart to tackle that subject right then. "It would just have to wait," she thought.

"I can hardly believe it's time for me to leave," Rose said, as she reached the handle to the car door.

"Promise me, you and Gwen will be here for my wedding. I couldn't do it without the two of you," Clara said.

"I wouldn't miss it for the world," Rose said.

"As soon as the Academy opens, the girls and I are coming to New York to visit you," she said.

"Promise?" Rose said, hugging her.

"I promise. We'll talk every day. I am so glad you came," Clara said, holding onto Rose's hand.

"Me too," Rose said.

They said their last goodbyes. Clara dried her eyes and waved as they drove away.

Chapter 23

Traveling Times

It was Gwen's favorite role yet. While she received numerous awards from other movies, this one was by far the most memorable. Most of the filming had taken place in the remote areas and villages of Kenya. The people there had been warm and friendly and the African scenery remarkable. It was a once in a lifetime experience and she had made life-long friends while there. Without a doubt, Gwen promised to bring her family back to Africa so they could enjoy all she had the opportunity to see.

When her plane landed, she quickly gathered her belongings. Stepping outside, she spotted them. "There's my little bunny rabbit," Gwen said, as Lizzy came running into her arms. "I've missed you two so much. Hi honey," she said, kissing Rick. "Look how much you've grown," she said, twirling Lizzy around. "That's it! I'm never staying away from the two of you again. Six weeks is way too long. You're so big I can hardly carry you anymore, Lizzy," Gwen said, pouting.

"I got all smiley faces today on everything," Lizzy said, holding her arms out wide.

"It's all on the table for mommy to see," Rick said. "You look different, are you okay," he asked, reaching over, tucking her hair behind her ear.

"I must admit this trip really tired me out. I made them promise the rest of the production would be here in

New York. Hey, I'm starving, can we stop by Gables?" she asked, quickly diverting the topic away from her appearance.

While they ate, Lizzy chattered non-stop as she told Gwen all about her plans for her up-coming birthday party. Gwen got a chance to describe the safari adventures she went on. "It was at night when the lions would feed. The poor zebra never had a chance."

The long drive home was relaxing. While Lizzy was now completely absorbed in her Disney movie, Gwen felt it was a good time to tell Rick what she had been dying to discuss with him while she was away. The distance was too great to talk about it over the phone and she didn't need him worrying about her any more than necessary.

"I need to discuss a few things with you," she said.

"I knew it, I could tell something was wrong the moment I saw you."

"If you call being two months late wrong, then I won't bother talking to you about it," she smirked.

"You mean what? You think you're pregnant!"

"I'm almost ninety-nine point nine, nine, nine percent sure. I knew something was wrong the minute we landed in Africa. I was waiting to get back to the states to confirm it," she said. "Now you should see your face." she laughed. "Hey, you may want to pull over if you're going to keep staring at me that way."

He continued to stare.

"Rick, keep your eyes on the road, for heaven's sake!"

"Yahoo," he finally yelped. "You mean I'm going to be a daddy, again."

"I believe so. We will know as soon as we can check it out with one of those kits. I'll make an appointment with Dr. Grant tomorrow."

When they arrived home, Rick paced outside the bathroom door.

"Hello, daddy, again," Gwen said, holding up the stick that confirmed her pregnancy.

They fast forwarded the production when she told her producers the news. The question about a baby bump was already beginning to surface.

The movie was a huge success and the next script was already waiting for her. While on set, Gwen reached for her ringing cell. It was Rose.

"Hey sis, are you busy?" she asked.

"Not for you! How's hospital life?" She had just stretched out on the couch in her trailer trying to squeeze in a much needed nap.

"You're speaking to next year's chief resident, thank you very much."

"I knew you would get it," Gwen screamed, bouncing up. "You're one of the smartest people on this planet. I'll tell you, that school's finally gotten something right."

"Stop it," Rose laughed. "You know it's one of the most competitive in the country and I'm blessed to know they have that kind of confidence in me."

"If they want to keep being ranked number one they'd better have that kind of trust in you," Gwen said, joking.

Rose was anxious about what she had to say next, so, she stalled. "Are you taking your prenatal vitamins every day? You're not working too hard are you?"

"Yes and No. I'm fine."

"Gwen, I found Clara," she blurted out.

"You've actually spoken with her on the phone?"
She was surprised to hear the news.

"I did speak to her on the phone, but I also saw her at
her home," Rose said.

"That's interesting. I assume you told her about
mother."

"Yes, I did. You already know about Eric and his
parents being killed, right?"

"Yeah, and I was sorry to hear that," Gwen said.

"All of that has changed her. She's not the same person we once knew. She's a totally different Clara and is
about to marry a minister. She's…"

"Wait, wait, wait," Gwen said. "I am sure he's some
kind of snooty, upscale character that I'm certainly not
interested in meeting or better yet discussing right now.
Knowing that chameleon, she's probably already transformed herself into a high-class preacher's wife. You
never saw her perform like I did when we were both at
the University. Believe me, I'm nowhere near the actress
in this family. I'm sorry for her loss—Eric and his
parents and all. I'm also happy you've accomplished
your mission in finding her. That's what you wanted.
Now, let's not talk about her anymore."

"Please, one last thing," Rose said. "Clara is coming
here next week and would very much like to see you."

"No, I'd appreciate it if you wouldn't do that, Rose. I
don't ever want to see her again. I want to stay calm and
peaceful during my pregnancy. I could not imagine
anything that could upset me more than seeing Clara. I
hope you understand that."

"I understand," Rose said, now thoroughly disappointed. She had desperately wanted a different response.

After they finished talking, Rose began to pray. She prayed throughout the night.

Despite the temptation to phone and plead with Gwen to change her mind, she turned her attention to Clara and the girl's visit. It was only a few weeks away.

When the day finally came, she headed for the airport with thoughts of how to explain Gwen's reaction to Clara lingering in her mind.

"Auntie Rose," the twins yelled as they ran towards her in the terminal.

"How was your trip? Did you guys enjoy the plane ride?" Rose asked, squeezing them.

"It was fantastic, but it took a long time to get here though. Yeah, I thought we would have been here by now," the other twin joined in. She found it amusing to watch them finish each other's sentences.

"How's mommy?" Rose asked, as she stood hugging Clara.

"Let's just say, I am glad to be on the ground."

"We're going to stop and get some ice cream at my favorite ice cream spot before we head home. How about that?" Rose asked the girls.

"Yay," they cheered.

Volcano hot-fudge sundaes with homemade ice cream, brownies, and caramel toppings were ordered. The twins talked non-stop about what each wanted to see while in New York. As soon as Rose pulled into the drive and parked, they spotted William.

"Uncle William," they yelled, jumping from the car.

"Hey, you're in for a good time," he said hugging them. "Guess what, I have a surprise for you two." When he opened the door, he reached down and picked up the tiny golden Labrador retriever.

The squeals could be heard down the street. He looked up at the ladies and smiled, "That should keep them entertained for a while. It seems you two may need a break."

"Thank you," Clara said, nodding in agreement. "Careful girls, he's just a puppy."

They were already off like a flash.

"How's Phillip?" Rose asked, pulling the suitcases along.

"Wonderful. We've been very busy lately. In fact, I didn't think I would find time to come and visit, but he insisted that I didn't miss the opportunity to get together with my sisters. Speaking of... when is Gwen coming over?" she asked, as she unpacked their clothes. "I'm dying to see her."

Rose tried to cover up the silence, but couldn't think of anything to say that would spare Clara's feelings. "We need to talk," she finally said.

"She doesn't want to see me does she?" Clara said. Her voice softened—the rejection now evident on her face. "Every time I asked you about her, you would either change the subject or look away. I realize Gwen and I had a rocky, oftentimes stormy relationship. I didn't expect she would embrace me fully but I thought as time passed, we could eventually patch things up."

"I want that for the two of you so much," Rose said, now teary eyed.

"Do you think if I asked her to meet my girls, she would at least come over and visit?" Clara asked.

"I don't know. She's five months pregnant."

"Wow, I would love to see her."

"She's invited William and me to the opening of her new movie this weekend," Rose said. "I'll call and let her know you're in town and would love to attend. She's into this peaceful, chaza thing. I don't understand it fully, but it teaches you how to remain peaceful even in stressful situations," Rose said.

The next morning as soon as the sun rose, Rose slipped out of bed. "I hate to call you this early, Gwen," she whispered.

"Is everything okay?" she asked, careful not to disturb Rick. "You are still coming tonight aren't you?"

"Yes, we'll be there." She paused….. "I wanted to let you know Clara and her girls are here with me, and they would love to come to your opening tonight. She's such a changed person now you would never have to worry about her upsetting you again. In fact, she says you don't even have to see her, she just wants you to at least meet your nieces," Rose blurted out.

"It's way too early to talk about any of this. I'll call you back," Gwen said.

"Thank God! At least she didn't say no," Rose thought.

While Rose chauffeured Clara and the girls around New York, Gwen was on her mind most of the time. It was almost noon and she still hadn't called. Around two o' clock, her special ring tone finally chimed.

"I have been busy all day, but I thought about what you said this morning. I guess it wouldn't hurt for them to come with you. I don't mind meeting Clara's girls, but I'm not ready to deal with her. I still can't believe she's sincere. I've seen too many of her performances to know better. So, I would appreciate it if she stayed away from me."

"I'll let her know," Rose said. That was the best she could hope for. At least she would get to meet her nieces.

***

They were all finally ready and off to the opening night of 'In a Moment', starring, Gwen Haley. Clara chewed on her nails—the mixture of emotions causing her stomach to churn. While she was excited to see her sister for the first time in all these years, she was extremely heartbroken that she wasn't going to be able to speak with her.

The twins had such a busy day that by the time they got to the opening, they were sound asleep. They tucked them into one of the cozy Barbie bunk beds at the nearby child-care center Gwen had suggested. Lizzy slept in the other.

Clara noticed Gwen the moment she stepped out of the Limousine. "She really was as stunning as she appeared in all her photos," she thought. She was completely enthralled by her sister's riveting performance. No one moved a muscle during the part when Gwen tried escaping her tormenters. Clara had the perfect seat to watch her sister's reaction. She loved the way Gwen laughed and even cringed during particular scenes. It was when she tossed her hair that she noticed how much she looked like their mother. As Gwen stood to thank everyone for coming, she knew she'd spotted her in the crowd.

She stood back while Rose and William went to congratulate her. It was then that she replayed what Betty said right before she left. "It's all a process. You may have to go through some difficult times in order to get to the good stuff, but it will all be worth the journey."

"She always knew what to say," Clara thought. The advice, however, only softened the blow as she watched her sisters warmly embrace. "God," she prayed, "If you ever give me the opportunity to have both sisters back in my life again, I will do whatever it takes to keep them there. I'll love them with everything in me."

At that very moment Gwen looked over at her, turned her back, and walked away.

While they went inside to get the girls, she sat alone in the running car left only to imagine what could be happening when the twins met their Auntie Gwen for the first time. When they finally brought the sleepy-eyed twins out, they climbed in and immediately curled up next to her as they drove along.

William chattered about his favorite parts of the movie. "I think this is her best film ever," he touted.

It did little to help the tremendous rejection she felt inside.

The following day as they packed to leave, Rose knew Clara had been a lot quieter ever since she'd seen Gwen. "Give her more time. I know God is going to fix it. She's just really hurting right now. You know how Gwen was about mother. It's taking her more time to get through this. It will work its way out…it always does."

As Clara looked up at Rose, her heart screamed of how incredibly blessed she was to have such a warm, loving and caring sister. "I'm not going to give up," she said. "I pray she doesn't wait too late like I did. I was so foolish," Clara said. "I just want to be a family again." She turned and hugged Rose. "I'm glad I have you,"

"I'm awfully happy about that too."

As they gave their final hugs and scurried through security, it was difficult moving the girls along. They kept looking back at her. "Bye, Auntie Rose."

"Bye! Love you. I'll see you at the wedding," Rose said, waving.

Chapter 24

Community Times

"Mr. Mayor, I'm so excited you were able to come," Clara said, opening the doors to the Academy. "Now, boys and girls I need you to be on your best behavior," she whispered, as Reverend Brown escorted the mayor and his entourage throughout the building.

"You are the first in the city to become a paperless-virtual classroom," he proudly, yelled into the microphone. "That is an astounding feat and I can tell you the eyes of the country are upon us here. The curriculum you've developed, I can see success written all over it. We will not disappoint them," he said, pounding the podium.

The children were so impressive and on their best behavior, the media wanted to interview them all.

"Mayor, we appreciate you taking the time to come and see what the city has so graciously supported," Reverend Brown said.

"I wouldn't have missed it for the world. I'm telling you Reverend Brown, what you have done here is a model for others to follow. The ideas you have in place, takes this school—this community and this city to a whole new level," he said, waving his arms.

"I really can't take the credit, Mayor," he said, pulling Clara forward. "I couldn't keep up with this young lady and all the ideas she had. She led the project with such ingenuity and creativity, I'm not surprised at all how it has turned out," he said looking proudly at her.

Later, as they ate lunch, the mayor lowered his voice and leaned in. "Reverend Brown, I know Clara is very busy these days with the Academy and community center development. I'm told there's a waiting list for the school already. That's good, but there's something else she needs to do for her community. I would like to appoint her to the revitalization and zoning committee."

"That's a mighty powerful committee, Mayor," Reverend Brown whispered.

"Yes it is, but hold on a second, I'm not finished. I also want you to run for the school board next year. It will be a perfect match. I heard through the grapevine you two are quite an item anyway," he said, bellowing out his signature laugh. "I will give you one hundred percent of my support. Meet me tomorrow in my office to talk about it all," he said, shoving the last bite in his mouth. "I've got to run."

"He wants what!" Clara said later that evening.

"I know it's hard to believe, but he's invited us to lunch tomorrow to discuss the offer. I've given it some thought and I'm beginning to think it's not such a bad idea."

"What about the wedding and all the other things we have going on," Clara said. "The girls' piano recital is coming up soon. We want to do a good job at whatever it is we do." She drew in a deep breath. "Do you think we can fit something this major into our lives?"

"We know what to do," he said as he pointed up. God will direct us."

After they prayed, she relaxed. "I spoke with William today," Clara said. "He's excited about his role in their church and wanted some guidance on a few things. He has a great head on his shoulders and such a wonderful spirit. He's particularly interested in the Academy and the community center concept, and you know what…our revitalization efforts may actually work right there in New York City."

"That is good news. By the way, how's Gwen?" Reverend Brown asked. Clara had avoided talking about her ever since she'd come home.

"I believe she's fine. You know that's a work in progress," she said. Hesitating for a moment, she looked into his eyes, "She still blames me for our mother's death. She feels if mother hadn't come looking for me she could possibly be alive today. I can't say she's not right, but I've forgiven myself for that. Given time, I pray she forgives me too."

"Let's go to lunch," he said, wrapping his arms around her. "We can talk about it more if you'd like. In the meantime, we'll pray for her."

While they dined, his comforting words helped. Now, thoughts of how she was supposed to share her limited time with another committee was on the forefront of her mind. Later that night, Clara tossed and turned, dreaming she was in a very large neighborhood surrounded by tattered-clad children begging for help. She was trying to escape, but two of them—with tears streaming down their faces, stopped her in her tracks. There stood two beautiful twin boys pleading with her to come and help rescue their family. Thoughts of the dream lingered with her for days.

As they sat in the mayor's office, he complimented them both on all the hard work they were involved in at the church and in the neighborhood.

"I'm glad you have decided to join the real efforts of this community, Clara," he said. She didn't miss the rub. He was taking a shot at her past life.

"You both are shining stars and for all the right reasons," he bragged. After he explained the time commitments the appointments required, they agreed to the proposal.

"This is great," the mayor said, slapping Reverend Brown on the back. Clara knew the night of her dream she was going to accept the offer.

Reverend Brown didn't have to campaign much. Name recognition went a long way and the mayor was doing a great job supporting him as he promised.

The wedding would take place right before the election. Rose and Marty were Clara's only two bride's maids and Reverend Brown's brother was his best man. He had a fairly large family, his parents and six siblings were all members of the church along with their spouses and children. Between his family, Betty and their friends, the wedding was going to be larger than planned.

Clara dialed Rose's cell…"Will you give me Gwen's address? I want to send her an invitation to the wedding. I know she may not come but I still feel the need to try."

"Who knows, she might," Rose said. "Anyway, my dress is gorgeous and it fits perfectly. I am so excited for the two of you. I really like him, Clara. He seems to be such a good man. Most of all, I love the way he treats my nieces. Speaking of my nieces, how are they?" Rose never liked lingering around the 'Gwen' subject too long.

"They can't wait to see you. Well, it might actually be a tie," she laughed. "They really miss Jazzy and now they want a puppy just like that."

"You've got a nice back yard for a dog. By the way, where are you planning on living once you're married?" Rose asked.

"Phil has a really beautiful home and the girls will have their own bedrooms. It definitely needs a woman's touch but it's very nice."

Clara and Rose talked so frequently now, their phone bills were enormous.

"We have never really talked about Eric and the elaborate past you left behind with him," Rose said. "Do you miss that lifestyle?"

"I miss Eric and he was definitely a wonderful husband. Looking back, I know I wasn't such a good wife. I was not honest with him and the stress of deception made my life miserable. I never want to be in that kind of bondage again nor do I want to treat anyone else I love that way."

"I understand," Rose said.

As she told her all that happened after Eric's death, they talked until dawn. "I'm glad it's the weekend, perhaps I'll sleep to ten today," Clara said laughing. "I would like to know what that feels like for a change."

***

Even though the work days were long, it seemed in no time the wedding had come. It was a beautiful day and an even more beautiful setting. The classic wedding gown fit Clara's body to perfection. The church was packed with family, friends and a few of the 'inquisitive'.

While Clara stood atop the flower covered podium, she caught a glimpse of her mother's smile. As the minister pronounced them husband and wife, she knew at that moment, Ellen was pleased—and so was she.

At the reception, Clara would occasionally glance over at Rose and William. From the looks on their faces she could tell they were having a really good time. They sat in the middle of Reverend Brown's family who kept them in stitches. The very large clan immediately welcomed them as part of the family.

"This is the most fun I've had in a long time," Rose gushed.

Clara and Reverend Brown enjoyed themselves in Paris while Rose and William babysat the girls. When the newly-weds phoned to check-in on everyone, the twins described their theme park rides, sleep-over's and exciting church activities they were enjoying.

As soon as the honeymoon was over, they returned to their very hectic schedules, with the twins' activities filtered in.

"I'm leaving early," Clara said, looking over at Melissa. "I promised the girls I would be home for a change when they got in from school. So call me if anything should come up." She reached for her handbag and headed down the steps. Driving home, she pulled into the market and quickly inspected the fresh produce. She had a new recipe she wanted to try out for dinner tonight. She got home just in time to have the girl's favorite snack on the counter as they came crashing through the doors.

A few hours later, supper was on the table.

"That was scrumptiously-D-delicious," Reverend Brown said, leaning back in the chair, rubbing his stomach.

"Can we go to our rooms? We've got homework," the twins said in unison, downing the last of their milk.

"Can't you sit with us a few more seconds?" Clara asked.

"Mom, we need to get started and then practice."

"What do you have to say, dad?"

He shook his head and smiled.

"Alright-then, go!" she exclaimed.

They dashed off to their rooms.

"I'm glad we had the chance to enjoy our meal to-gether," she yelled after them as they raced down the hallway.

"We've got to make time to do this more often," Reverend Brown said, pointing to the empty plates. "I've got the next one."

"I can't wait," Clara said as she reclined in the easy-boy chair. She had just closed her eyes when the phone rang. Before she could say hello, she could hear the mayor explaining why he needed to meet with her.

"I'll be there the first thing in the morning," she said.

"The mayor is calling an emergency meeting—something about the city's plans for re-zoning" she said. "Apparently a portion of the revitalization project on the East Side crosses boundaries with the old community and they are all up in arms about it. The banks are throwing their support behind the occupants there."

It was her old neighborhood that was in the middle of the controversy. She couldn't help but think of Miriam leading the charge. She could vaguely remember the committee discussing the project when she first joined the board.

Later that night, with thoughts of the mayor's con-versation still on her mind, she peeked over at the clock—3:00 AM. She slipped out of bed and pulled the re-zoning plans for the area they would be discussing.

The revitalization project was well on its way and resided several blocks from where she and Eric used to live. She guessed she'd been so lost in her old *'storybook world'* she never once realized how close the area was to those that needed restoring. She read her notes and as best she could tell, the plans were solid. She double checked them and then... she saw it. Lightly tapping the paper, she realized the controversy was where they were proposing to build the Academy. The Bradbury neighborhood had set aside that parcel of land for an exclusive membership only Academy. The revitalization project was now occupying that property too. "Oh no," she thought, "The mayor had signed off for the revitalization committee to build on the land." She knew that Bradbury group. They were never going to let that happen without a fight.

The mayor filled her in the next day. What she discovered last night was true. He had given his support to the revitalization project on that very land. The ownership and rights to the property was turning into a complex and delicate matter for him.

Later, he dropped the bombshell she was in no way thrilled about. She would have to lead the meeting on tomorrow as co-chairman of the committee. He had an emergency session out of town that could not be postponed.

When she walked in the following morning, as expected the chamber was overflowing. It made her uncomfortable at first seeing so many familiar faces from the old crowd she hung out with. She knew she looked differently to them. While her simple yet classy business attire was nice, it was a far cry from how she used to dress. Her hair was neatly pulled back in a nice bun and she wore her black-hard rimmed glasses. Clara could feel the stares as she took her seat. She sat up and looked back into the faces of the people she once lived among. She pulled the thin microphone towards her, leaned into it, and called the meeting to order. She took care of a few old agenda items that required the committee's vote.

"All in favor please indicate by saying, *I*," she said. One by one they all assented to the motion before them.

"The *I's* have it, so moved," she said, banging the gavel. "Who's the spokesman for the revitalization committee?"

A woman with long dreads stepped up to the podium.

"Please state your name and explain to the committee what brings you here today," Clara said.

The articulate woman spoke with such passion they all immediately understood why she was chosen to speak for the group.

"We've successfully turned our community into a safe and beautiful place to live, where parents can finally feel comfortable raising their children," the woman said. "It didn't just happen overnight either. Through much prayer and divine direction, we were able to transform our neighborhood into a community we can all be proud of. One of the final initiatives attached to our revitalization plan is the Academy and community center project modeled after the one in your neighborhood Mrs. Brown. In my opinion, it's one of the most important components of the program. The Academy and community center will allow our children to have a first class education while at the same time recreational facilities to enjoy. They will be available to all children within the community and surrounding areas to utilize."

The representative went on to talk about what it meant to be one community. In the delivery of her heartfelt speech, it was clear who the members on the opposing side were. Clara watched their taunt faces, the men loosening their ties and women occasionally shifting in their seats.

When the woman graciously sat down, Clara spanned the crowded room. "Is there a spokesman from the Bradbury community?" she asked.

A short, stout gentleman who wiped away beads of sweat, walked to the podium.

"Madam Chairman, my name is Mr. James Hinson," he said with a very distinct southern drawl. "I would like to first start by thanking the mayor and his committee for addressing this sensitive yet very important matter. Secondly, I'd like to acknowledge that warm and compassionate speech given by colleague." He nodded and smiled at her. "She did a magnificent job of describing for the committee what has generated so much concern among us loyal citizens. She is absolutely correct regarding one community and how important it is for us to embrace that concept. I believe everyone here understands that. Unfortunately, that's not the issue at hand. What actually brings us to these chambers is the parcel of land they are proposing to build their Academy and community center on. The land was purchased and has been owned by the Gordon family, who as you are aware, is one of the premier families in this community. Several years ago, the Gordon's gave the Bradbury community exclusive rights to that property and we are offering a different purpose for its use." He wiped his forehead with the handkerchief.

The quiet chamber now rumbled with whispers. "Quiet please," Clara said, into her microphone. Her heart quickened. It was the first time she had the opportunity to talk about her father-in-law in public since his death.

"Here is a document from Mr. Randy Gordon," the southern gentleman said, handing it to her. "His desire was to build an exclusive Academy for his community which would not only educate his grand-children but educate future generations to come. It was never his intent to have the land under the auspices of the city. It is a private- funded matter and it should be directed that way by the board of governors in this fine community. I am the president of the board of directors for Mid-South Trust Bank and we have been given charge to ensure his wishes are carried out. Ironically, our ideas are similar for the use of the property…"

"No they are not!" someone from the audience yelled, interrupting him.

"Ladies and gentlemen, you will have an opportunity for rebuttal, but we must maintain order," Clara said.

The chatter instantly ceased.

"Please proceed."

"Thank you, madam chairman. As I was stating, the ideas for the property are similar. However, there will be a screening process for those interested in applying into the Academy we are proposing. Students will be selected based on strict criteria."

One of the committee members leaned into their microphone, "Can you elaborate on the screening process, please?"

"Certainly. The children whose parents are a part of our community association will of course have priority for enrollment. Should slots become available after that, the screening process will be based on academic aptitude and quite frankly, the ability to afford the tuition. Let me add, we have decided to award a few scholarships to deserving parents that may not be able to afford the tuition. The community insisted that be a part of the selection criteria."

A gentleman representing the opposite side was recognized by the chair.

"I would like to elaborate more on the differences between what we are proposing verses what Mr. Hinson has just articulated. The only criterion for admission in the school we have before you is the ability to house the number of students enrolled. The selection process in Mr. Hinson's proposal is very restrictive and I'm afraid many students would never be able to attend or should I say, be accepted nor afford their Academy."

The noise grew—the contention evident.

Mr. Hinson stood, adjusting the tight belt that circled under his protruding abdomen. "I can put all of this into perspective madam chairman. The issue is not the restrictive practices or the affordability of the school, but who holds the rights to the property the school will be on. Here is the language from the letter Mr. Gordon wrote prior to his demise." He handed a copy to Clara.

"I am writing in regards to the land located at 23 Bradbury Place. This property has been owned by my family for many years. Now that I am a proud grandfather of three, I would like to see this acreage utilized as a place where my children and those within the community may receive a quality education. I will allow the community association to be the executor of this property as long as it is utilized in that manner. I am also leaving a substantial portion of funds that will assist in erecting an educational facility that will rival those who boast of offering world class educational services. I will ensure the plans for this campus is of superior caliber since my grand-children will also be educated there."

Clara's hands shook as she read it. She laid the paper on the desk so that it wasn't so evident. She thought of the Gordon family. Was Miriam in the room? Had she overlooked her?

After clearing her throat, Clara pushed the words out, "Is anyone here from the family that can attest to the fact this property belongs to the Gordon family?"

"Here's the deed," Mr. Hinson said laying it down before her. "It will affirm that the Gordon's are the sole owners of this property."

"Excuse me," a man from the other side said standing. "We also have a signed affidavit that describes the re-zoning efforts prior to the purchase of the land. Based on that schematic, the city has the rights to approximately one-half of it. That portion was never signed over to the Gordon's," the man said.

"All of that land has been in the Gordon family for years. Everyone knows that," someone cried out.

"It may have been, but certainly not legally," was the immediate response back.

"We will take into consideration all parties' concerns and re-convene at our next regularly scheduled meeting to discuss the matter. This meeting is adjourned," Clara said. She couldn't wait to get out of there.

"Can you believe this mess?" Mildred Cotton said storming up to her.

She had tried to inch her way through the crowd the moment she made eye contact with her, but it was too late. "Why the mayor appointed her to the re-zoning committee was still a mystery to her," Clara thought. Everyone knew she was a drama queen—known to exaggerate.

"I'm sure it will work its way out," Clara said, shuffling around.

"You are always such an optimist. The Gordon's were kind, respectable, and upright people. That land belongs to them and it's not fair for anyone to try and take it away. You of all people should know that."

"I see you've already made up your mind should we need to vote," Brian said, walking up.

He'd rescued her. "Thank you," Clara mouthed silently.

"I have been told the zoning for the city took place after the Gordon's purchased the land," Mildred touted.

"Where did you get that information from?" he asked.

"Never mind that, the mayor just needs to fix this. The whole city is talking about it and people don't want the Gordon's disrespected any more than they already have been," Mildred snapped.

"Why would anybody think something like that?" Brian asked.

"The bankruptcy…oh, just forget it. I need to make a few phone calls anyway," she said marching away.

"Is it me or is she crazy?" Brian asked. "She has to know you were a part of that family."

"She knows," Clara said. "That's why I'll be glad when the mayor gets back in town. With a mouth like Mildred's he'll have a real catastrophe on his hands if he doesn't handle this real soon. Channel 8 has already picked up on it."

"Then it's just a matter of time before we'll all be bombarded with questions," Brian said.

"You're right, so it's best to tell everyone to direct all media to either yourself or John until we can get further instructions from the mayor," she said.

"Got it. Call me when you hear from him," he said.

Clara sat in the car and massaged her temples. She knew her father-in-law had great plans for his grand-daughters. He was a kind, loving, gentle man. She vaguely remembered the property in question. Eric had only spoken briefly about it when he considered using it to build a large medical complex. However, his father and mother had other plans. It was the Academy, the one she was supposed to help put on the map for the community.

"It's funny how life changes," she thought to herself, driving away. She now firmly believed all things were working together and that good was coming out of it all. Since Miriam kept the money, she now lived a much richer life. She'd substituted revenge and malice for integrity and truthfulness. Most of all, she had a life overflowing with love. If she ever saw Miriam again, she was going to thank her.

The ringing phone cut into her thoughts. It was the Mayor.

"We certainly have been playing telephone tag lately," he said.

"I'm pretty sure your assistant has given you the heads up on the Gordon property situation," Clara said. "There's a real stalemate and neither side is willing to budge on this one. I'll give you the specifics about the zoning at the time of purchase when I see you," she said.

"I have already heard an earful from Mildred," the mayor replied. "I believe that woman has psychiatric issues, but there's nothing I can do about it now. She's the governor's first cousin. Listen, I need you, John and Brian to meet me first thing in the morning so we can figure out how to handle this. Call Madolynn. She'll give you the time and place."

"Okay, I..."

He had already hung up.

She sped thru traffic to get to the girls' piano recital. As she drove up, Reverend Brown was pulling in at the same time. Racing from their cars, they grabbed each other's hand and rushed inside.

The twins' eyes sparkled when they spotted them.

Clara nodded.

Perfect timing—they were next.

Sitting with their backs to each other, their tiny bodies dwarfed by the large baby- grands, the twins began playing. The tiny fingers floated across the piano keys mastering them like only skilled, experienced pianist should. Tears filled Clara's eyes as she watched them play so effortlessly. The audience was silent, the twinkling keys mesmerizing them. She knew they had choreographed the selection in a way only her gifted twins could pull off. As one climbed the scale, the other filled in, embellishing—accenting the ensemble to perfection. She watched her twins lose themselves in the moment—completely absorbed by the eighty-eight keys.

It garnered them the only standing ovation of the night.

Later, the twins spotted them in the hallway and ran to where they stood.

"You guys are the best," Clara and Reverend Brown said, hugging them.

The piano teacher scurried up trying to find a private spot away from all the congestion. "I think we need to talk about your girl's future. They've outgrown me," she yelled over the noise, the other parents lingering by. "Here, take this. His name is Monsieur Finevest," she said, handing Clara the card. She turned and was immediately engulfed by the crowd.

"Can you believe how talented they are?" Clara said when she and Phillip were finally alone. "I can play a little by ear, but nothing to write home about. That gift had to have come from Eric's side of the family."

"I believe great things are awaiting our girls," he said.

It was true. Under the tutelage of Monsieur Finevest, they had been the opening performances for many high profile concerts. An invitation to perform at Madison Square Garden at their classical music-fest had also been extended to them.

Chapter 25

Convincing Times

"Mayor, what are we going to do?" Clara asked. "It has been well over a year and the matter still hasn't been resolved. I don't know how many ways they are going to have to prove to you the property did not legally belong to the Gordon's before the area was re-zoned and before they purchased the land. It was the property of the city," she exclaimed. "The revitalization committee is right, Bradbury does not have legal access to it."

"The Gordon's and their community are tremendous players in this city," the mayor shot back. "They are threatening to stop supporting the very grants that helped build your Academy as a result of all of this. I know you don't want that! I can truly say I'm not sure what to do about this disaster." He reached up and loosened his tie. "Since it is so confusing, Mildred is urging me to re-zone the area to settle it. She's pulling out all the stops this time," he said, his voice dropping. "I'm afraid she's convinced many on the committee to go along with her. Her argument being, it's too risky not to have the Mid-Trust Bankers in our corner. They are behind too many important projects."

"I just cannot go along with that, mayor. They can't win this one. The revitalization committee has the proof."

"Not if I re-zone. I believe I have the votes to accomplish that."

"It would not be fair. Need I remind you, you are up for re-election next year?" she said.

"I know," the rowdy, mayor said, now suddenly restrained. She knew she'd struck a nerve. She paused slightly to settle her own emotions. "Listen... if you revitalize that area, then the entire community benefits," Clara said, "Not just a select few. I'm afraid we are divided on this one.

For the next few days, Clara couldn't ever recall the mayor's demeanor being so tamed. She had barely slept herself the night before, her stomach in knots. The matter was in the forefront of the community and when they walked into the packed conference room, it was all too evident as the crowd spilled into the hallway. It was rumored Mildred had already persuaded three of the seven members to vote along with her.

The most eloquent and knowledgeable speakers addressed the audience. They were all thoroughly convincing, and essentially it came down to a vote on whether or not to re-zone. It was a tie...hers being the deciding one.

"Before Mrs. Brown votes, Mr. Mayor," Councilwoman Cotton stated, "There is one other person I would like the committee to hear from. I think it would be unforgivable if we didn't let someone from the Gordon family speak. They are clearly the ones who can shed more light on this complicated matter."

"Mildred Cotton just wasn't giving up," Clara thought. She noticed whenever she spoke how straight she sat. The corner of her mouth tight, eyes flickering with every other word.

Ted walked slowly to the podium and faced Clara. It was the first time they had seen each other in years.

"Good afternoon," he said in his distinctive, lawyer-like voice. "I would like to speak on behalf of my in-laws. I believe I'm qualified to represent them, seeing this property has been in our family for years. Everyone knows how much support the Gordon family has given this city and today is just another example of that. It was my father-in-law's desire to build an institution of higher learning on the land in question that would help educate the children in the community it was designed for. Presently, our surrounding schools are extremely over-crowded, and this Academy would be the necessary addition our children will need to help make my father-in-law's dream come true. The revitalization committee already has a school in its neighborhood. I'm told it's a highly successful one and while it is slightly over crowd-ed, I believe it should still suffice. Re-zoning would solve all of this. Clara, I hope you take that into consid-eration," Ted said.

Calling her name jarred her momentarily but she quickly regrouped. A silence fell over the room as Clara adjusted her microphone.

"What is your vote?" the mayor asked.

"Nay," she said.

Those on the revitalization committee jumped to their feet and screamed in delight.

The mayor sat still, the wind completely taken out of him.

"Order please. Let's maintain order," he finally said.

"Mayor I have something I would like to say," Clara said. Despite the fact she knew she'd just delivered a blow to the Bradbury community, she still didn't like leaving them that way.

"Go ahead," he said in a tone she wasn't accustomed to.

"Our Academy was virtually overcrowded the first day it opened its doors. That's because parents are seeking safer places for their children to get a quality education. I'm told this newly proposed Academy will accommodate all the students in the community and give everyone who wants to have a stellar education the ability to do just that. I want the people of Bradbury to know my vote not to re-zone was based solely on what I believe to be right. I respect and love the Gordon family. Mr. Randy Gordon and his wife Gloria were two of the kindest people I ever had the privilege of getting to know. I loved them and their son dearly and I would never do anything to disrespect or dishonor their memories. Yet, knowing them the way that I did, I believe they would want to embrace any community that's set itself on transforming into one filled with really good people... where their sons and daughters can get to know those in the Bradbury community and vice versa. I'm sure those affected will soon find out they have more in common than the differences they perceive to have. Just give each other a chance and a few years from now, this will all be a distant memory."

"You can't do this." Mildred snapped, jerking her microphone down and covering it with her hand. "You of all people should know the property belongs to their community and no one should be allowed to take it away from them. Bradbury's children are in need of a different type of education. Perhaps you don't get it," she sneered. "Since you never came from a family exposed to the lifestyle they're talking about. It may be too difficult for you to grasp." Her eyes flickered, "It's what their kids deserve."

Clara sat stunned, but still she felt a strange sense of compassion even for Mildred. "I wish we would give each other a chance," she said. "I guess I don't expect you to understand."

Clara lowered her head, trying hard to avoid the faces of those with Mildred Cotton's sentiments.

"She's exactly right," the voice from the back of the room cried out.

Clara lifted her head as she watched Miriam in all her grandeur step into the aisle. She hadn't expected to see her there. This time, she slowly placed her head back down, the weight of her past settling in on her.

Mildred Cotton smiled widely, sitting straighter than ever—extremely glad to see her old friend, Miriam. It was the showdown she had been waiting for.

"Why can't all of our children go to school together?" Miriam asked.

Mildred gasped as Clara slowly lifted her head again. Both women now unsure the direction Miriam was going in.

"I don't believe there is one person in this room that doesn't want the same thing—a quality education for their love ones. Isn't that the reason we're all here. Isn't that what we're all fighting for," Miriam asked the crowd as she walked forward. Lowering her voice she continued to speak, "How can I deny my nieces the right to go to a school simply because they live in a different neighborhood? I recently read an article of these two gifted-straight A students who are only nine years old, and are slated to be featured at Madison Square Garden in a few months. They attend one of the Academy's we are talking about. Are these the kinds of students we're trying to keep out of the school my father longed to build? Some of you may want that, but I don't," Miriam said. She stood in front of Clara as they both stared into each other's eyes. "I've been so foolish," she whispered.

The room stood still with the only noise coming from the news reporters scurrying about capturing every word.

"There, now you see," the mayor said, as he eased his way into the conversation. "I have been successful bringing these two sides together just as I expected," he said, clasping his hands.

"Oh, sit down," Mildred demanded.

"No, you sit down. In fact, why don't you excuse yourself from this committee, permanently." he whispered, wrapping his hand around the microphone.

Mildred clutched her chest.

He quickly glued a grin back on his face and smiled at the audience. "Your mayor has tried everything to keep this great city together. This is just another example of that happening!" His voice rising.

The audience politely clapped.

"I am appointing a special committee to look into how we can effectively bring both sides together as we offer our children a quality education in a community where everyone benefits."

The audience clapped louder.

"This meeting is adjourned," the mayor said rushing into the crowd.

The people in the room instantly surrounded Miriam and Clara.

However bad they wanted to, both women knew it wasn't the time or place to address each other.

Later that evening, the day's event was the primary topic of conversation at the Brown's dinner table.

Reverend Brown bragged, "Girls, you have a wonderful mother and you should be very proud of her too. She fights hard for everyone."

When they were alone, Clara rested her head in her hands, "You're such a good man, Reverend Brown. Have I told you how much I appreciate all that you do for the girls lately?"

"It all comes naturally, Clara. It's easy to love them."

"Do you think if we had another child they could possibly be as smart as our daughters?" she asked.

"Without a doubt," he said.

"I guess in about eight and half months, we will know."

He stared…suddenly overwhelmed with emotion. Finally, he rubbed both hands over his head. Tears filled his eyes. He drew in a deep breath. "Are you telling me…?"

"Yes I am," she said, softly.

He walked over to where she sat. Reaching for her hands, he gently helped raise her to her feet. "You have made me the happiest man in the world," he whispered.

The girls were ecstatic when they found out the news.

"I hope it's a boy. I really, really want a brother."

"Me too," the other twin joined in.

The baby news was momentarily pushed aside as the buzz surrounding the twin's debut at Madison Square Garden's began to circulate. The interviews started flooding in and even the mayor himself secured them as his special guests at the annual Christmas party he hosted. It was a move that sent the already crowded gala into an over-capacity event.

***

Miriam knew they were scheduled to perform at the Christmas party and it left her on edge. As soon as she arrived, she scanned the room. Even though the ballroom was extremely crowded, she spotted them the moment they walked in. She had not seen her nieces since they were babies. Never taking her eyes off the pretty identical twins—who were relatively tall for their age, tears filled her eyes. They performed several numbers while the crowd surrounded them, completely mesmerized by their blend of ensembles.

As soon as they completed their sonatas and taking their bows, they joined the other kids in a room set up especially for the mayor's guests' children.

Miriam noticed Clara when she exited the ballroom heading for the place where the kids' festivities were being held. She quickly slipped out of her seat and headed towards her.

"Hello Clara."

Clara was startled not realizing anyone else was in the long empty hallway. She turned only to face Miriam.

"How are you?" Clara said. "It's been a really long time," she said softly.

"It sure has." Miriam hesitated…everything she had planned saying to Clara—just that quick, she'd forgotten. "Well….I wanted to tell you how completely amazing your girls are," Miriam finally said. "You know momma could play the piano like that. Her parents invested a lot of money in her lessons. She just never pursued it…always had too many other things going on, I guess." She let out a nervous little giggle.

"I knew it wasn't my side of the family that had that kind of talent. I'm pretty proud of your nieces," Clara said.

"You look great," Miriam said trying to jump start her brain and move pass all the formalities.

"You do too. How are Ted and the boys?"

"Ted's great. The boys are in there with your daughters. I believe your girls are actually taller than they are," she said fidgeting.

"The girls get their height from Eric. He was such a handsome man." Clara said.

The unpleasant quietness crept back in again.

"Well, I must go and check-in on the girls," Clara said, turning to walk away.

Miriam reached out and touched her arm, "Before you go I need to say something." She looked away, suddenly finding it difficult to face her. She turned back slowly.

"I'm sorry Clara…I…." She stumbled at first but then let it all out. "After the accident, I went into a spiral of depression and anger that almost killed me." She hung her head, "When you left, we had no one else to enjoy…to call family. Every day, I wished I could take it all back. I was wrong for what I did to you and I wanted to let you know that," she whispered.

The sincere apology caused her to reel. She quickly readjusted and said, "Miriam, I need to say something as well. I said if I ever saw you again, I would actually thank you."

"I don't understand," she replied. They searched each other's eyes.

"We were both hurting when we lost our family and I wanted the money for all the wrong reasons," Clara said. "It was a good thing I didn't get my hands on it. My world would have never ended up like it is today. While having everything taken away from me was one of the hardest things I've ever experienced in my life, it actually put me on the path to finding the real Clara. I'm completely happy now, Miriam. Something I wouldn't trade for the world. Not having that money helped me teach my girls the value of hard work and what loving and respecting others is all about. So, I accept your apology... that is if you are willing to accept mine."

Miriam extended her hand.

Clara slowly squeezed it as they shook. Immediately, the tension slowly began to fade—replaced by a strange sense of closeness.

Walking back down the hall towards the ballroom Miriam said, "How's Reverend Brown? I've heard of him and his outstanding work on the School Board. You two look very happy," she said.

"He's a wonderful man and a great father to your nieces. We can't wait for the new arrival in five more months."

"Are you kidding me? No way, are you pregnant. Where are you hiding it?" she asked, facing her.

They laughed as Clara pulled her gown closer outlining her growing stomach.

"I see. Congratulations!" Miriam said. She suddenly stopped, "Clara, two years after you and the girls left, I began setting aside their money. I was able to turn the company around and I'm proud to say it's doing quite well. Now, I want to make certain the girls get every penny of what they deserved a long time ago."

Clara knew she was talking about a very large sum of money.

"I'd remember the time I would have jumped at that opportunity, Miriam, but honestly, we don't need it. Hey, but I do have a suggestion for it, though. If you could make a donation on behalf of the twins and me to The Bennington Child Care Center and Patricia Hudson, I would really appreciate that." Even though she had already repaid Mack, her old apartment manager and friend, three-fold, she still wanted to help support her old community. They were aggressively involved in giving themselves a much needed facelift. Clara was now on the board of directors of the day care center and knew they could use the money as well. She had also vowed she would assist her old neighbor Pat. Looking back on things, she was truly grateful for all that she had done for her. So, she'd already seen to it that a college fund was set up for each of her kids. The additional money would also help solve her housing situation.

"Something is really different about you," Miriam said. She stared at Clara, understanding for the first time a huge change had taken place in her life.

"An experience with Jesus is the best way to describe it," Clara said.

"You need say no more," Miriam said. "Can you believe Ted is a deacon at our church and I sing in the choir?"

"No way!" Clara said.

"It's true, and the boys help lead praise and worship for the youth services. You should hear them sing and play their instruments. They are great."

They stood there for a moment—smiling—something neither expected to happen, not even a year ago.

As the quietness settled back in, Miriam gazed up, the years of sadness still there. She allowed her heart to have its say.

"It was after the accident that I became completely desperate. I was willing to try anything to pull myself out of the depression I found myself in. Actually, it was Ted that suggested church—probably the best and only brilliant idea he's had in years," she laughed. "I needed to shed the guilt, to get rid of the grief, but it just wouldn't go away. Not until I had a real experience with Christ," she said, "That's when my life changed forever. I've learned how to cope now."

Clara shook her head, "Would you have ever thought our lives would end up this way, me a minister's wife, and you singing in the choir? If anyone told me that in college, I would have offered them a free ticket to the Brookfield Mental Hospital."

They sat on the decorative bench in the hallway. Miriam knew it was time to tell her what she had wanted to for years. "I met your sister, Rose, Clara."

Her eyes grew large. "You did ….. When? She never told me that."

"She came looking for you and found me. She had a letter delivered to my office from the actress Gwen Haley. It stated she was your sister and would take me to court if I didn't tell her where you were. It was interesting because at that time, I had actually been trying to find you myself."

Miriam paused, "That's when it finally sunk in how incredibly cruel I had been. In fact, this whole town was. How could no one, I mean absolutely no one, know where you were with those two little girls. Karen, Shannon and the gang told me about an accident or something you had. After that, it was if God Himself removed you from the face of the earth. When people found out I was looking for you, they thought it was to do you harm. The rumors started flying, and I knew then they would take hold of a good thing and attempt to destroy it. So, I thought it was best to let the rumors die down and start over again. The next time I started my search, I didn't tell anyone except Rose. Not even Ted. Anyway, after my assistant handed me the letter, Rose and I put our heads together and with the help of a private detective, we tracked you down."

Clara sat stunned. She knew it was Rose who had written the letter and used Gwen's name to get Miriam's attention.

"So, the award winning Gwen Haley is your sister?" Miriam said.

"Yes, she is. That's another interesting conversation we'll have to sit down and talk about one day. We have so much to catch up on," Clara said. She could tell the hard years had softened Miriam, but God's comforting Hand was on her now. She gently reached over, "Would you and the boys like to come to New York to see the girls perform?"

Miriam gasped, the offer being a dream come true. "I couldn't think of anything better I'd rather do," she said.

"Phillip's mom and dad aren't going to be able to travel as they had planned. That's two available tickets. I'm sure I can get more. I'm told it's an already sold out performance."

"Why don't you let the girls stay over at least one night in our condominium we have there," Miriam said.

"That would be a great way for them to get to know their cousins a little better."

"That's a wonderful idea," Clara said. She looked up as Reverend Brown came racing down the hall.

"There you are. I have been looking all over for you," he said.

"I'm sorry, honey. Phillip, this is Miriam, Eric's sister."

"It's nice meeting you but when you have a pregnant wife missing for over an hour, you get a little worried," he said, hugging Clara.

"I understand and I had better get to Ted, not that he's worried or anything. He has probably looked at his watch a million times," she chuckled. "I had to pull him by the ear to get him here tonight. I'll call you next week, Clara," Miriam said, walking back to the ballroom.

"What in the world was that all about?" Reverend Brown whispered as soon as Miriam turned the corner.

"I will tell you all about it on the way home. Let's get the girls. I'm exhausted."

When she gathered the twins, she immediately recognized Little Teddy. He looked exactly like his grandfather.

Chapter 26

Fame Time

"The Academy Award goes to....Gwen Haley." It was no surprise. "Two Sides to Every Story" had been number one at the box office for months. She had been favored to win by all the critics. Even though she'd just given birth to a beautiful baby boy, she was back to her normal size. The gown she wore slipped effortlessly over her slender-toned body.

"You look wonderful and congratulations on your newest addition," the entertainer commentator said. "Who are you wearing tonight?"

"So'leing Thoreux," Gwen said. "An up and coming designer I'm sure you will hear much more about."

The next day Gwen was highlighted in all the magazines and papers. She was the fan's favorite. They loved her witty, down-to-earth personality and touted her as one of the most beautiful women in movies today.

Gwen was soon scheduled to begin shooting her next role, but took time out of her busy schedule to attend Roses' and William's graduation. With much coaxing, she even agreed to go to the first service William was scheduled to officiate at his church. He'd also just graduated from seminary.

"Where's Auntie Rose?" Lizzy asked, as they looked for her in the crowd. "There she is," she exclaimed, running up to her.

After the graduation, they ate at Edward's Garden. Gwen's personal security ensured their meal wasn't interrupted by her gawking fans and kept the Paparazzi at bay. They were only able to get a few pictures of her as security quickly whisked her into the awaiting Hummer. They finished the rest of the night's celebration at Roses' new home.

"This is absolutely gorgeous," Gwen said, as she wandered from room to room. "It's so much larger than you described."

She was proud of her little sister. Her home was hidden in an alcove surrounded by large oak and pine trees. It was the perfect get-away from the paparazzi and all the commotion they generated.

Sprawled out on Rose's den floor, Gwen picked up the photo album and slowly turned its pages. "I didn't know you and William went on a cruise. When in the world did you find the time?"

Rose ignored her comment, secretly hoping she would move on to another topic.

"Who are these women in the pictures with you…friends from the hospital?"

"No, those are other friends of mine."

Just then Gwen spotted Clara in one of the photos, her arms wrapped around Rose's neck, kissing her on the cheek. She fought the urge to say anything but finally gave in. "So you went on a cruise with Clara?"

"Yeah—I started to tell you about it, but you had asked me not to mention her to you, so I didn't. This was our girl's only adventure we had planned. We all left the husbands home while relaxing in Montego Bay."

"What husbands?"

Rose took advantage of Gwen's curiosity and quickly said a silent prayer.

"Remember, I told you Clara is married to a wonderful man, Gwen. I was the matron of honor in her wedding two years ago. We met some of the most amazing people ever. Her sister-in-laws are three of the kindest women you would ever want to meet. Clara has a mentor who virtually helped change her life named, Betty. Her roommate from college, Marty, and my mother-in-law also met us there. Those are the women in the photos and we had a blast."

Gwen slowly turned the pages. "So this thing with Clara hasn't gone away, I see," she said, looking up.

"Did you honestly think that it would?" Rose asked.

"Yes, I did. Clara could never change and I cannot believe you are falling for her trickery. You will go and get yourself hurt for sure, just because you've chosen to be so stubborn."

"You have no idea what you're talking about," Rose said. The words rung out like a bell and she could instantly tell they stung. "I'm sorry...I didn't mean to ...it's just that... I don't want to see you miss out on something so special because you refuse to forgive your sister. It's not hurting Clara much anymore, she is happy and loving and has become a great sister, mother and wife. Time is your enemy Gwen and you are wasting it not getting to know the person completely the opposite from the one you have conjured up in your mind."

Gwen slammed the album shut and stormed into the other room. A few minutes later, she eased back in. "I'm sorry. I shouldn't have."

"That's okay," Rose said.

"I don't know how to forgive her, Rose. In my mind, she's the reason mother is no longer with us and I can't get past that. I miss her so much I can hardly stand it. When I receive each award and look at myself on the screen, I'm thinking mother should be here to enjoy this. That's the only thing that stands in the way of me being totally happy. With Rick, Lizzy, and now Rainey in my life, in addition to all of my success, I feel such peace and contentment. There's only one thing missing— mother. If I see Clara again, I know the pain of losing mother will come pouring in again. It's just not worth it."

"Would you please listen before you completely shut me out? Please," Rose pleaded.

"Okay! I'm listening. Go ahead," Gwen said, wiping the steady flow of tears.

"You will never be able to heal the kind of hurt you're talking about on your own. Only God can do that. He is the one who turned Clara's life around. She loves Him so much and it shows. Clara lost everything, Gwen," she said, standing. With an inner passion she spoke. "Miriam took it all from her. She was homeless and in poor health due to an awful accident. Miss Betty took them in and introduced her to Christ. She went to church one day and had an experience there that changed her life forever. Her light now shines so brightly I guess that's how she ended up marrying a preacher," she laughed. "Seriously, she has forgiven Miriam and now actually appreciates her for keeping the money she knew she so rightfully deserved. She doesn't care about any of that any more. She's not the flashy, sassy dressing, Clara I'm sure you still have in your mind. Instead, she is the smart, articulate, loving, and kind sister, whom you should get to know. Only God can help you do that, Gwen." She blurted it all out before she gave her a chance to respond.

Gwen sat quietly, suppressing her thoughts.

Rose made her next move. "Clara will be in town in a few weeks with the girls. You have two beautiful and talented nieces that are being featured at the Classical Music Fest at Madison Square Garden. I've wanted to tell you about their overnight success for a while. They were featured on one of the local shows in town and spotted by Mr. Simon Cantrell himself. The next thing Clara knew they were headed for Madison Square Garden. Her whole family will be here and it would be a good time for you to meet them," she said.

"I don't think so," Gwen said. Rose's passionate speech did little to change her mind. "I'm afraid to let my guard down when it comes to Clara. I can never imagine her being anything but what I know her to be—a horrible person."

***

As the months swiftly passed and the twin's debut neared, there was turmoil swirling about the camp.

"Rose, for goodness sake, its Lizzy's birthday," Gwen chided. She had become completely flustered at Rose's continued conversation about the piano concerto.

"I know, but I promised I would go and see the girls perform. It's a once in a lifetime event, Gwen. I thought you would understand that. I did not know you were having Lizzy's birthday party when I agreed to chaperon on the same date. Hey, but I've thought of an idea that can settle all of this. Why don't you invite her guest to the twin's performance at Madison Square

Garden? They would love it and have a wonderful time."

Gwen tried counting to ten, but it did no good. What was Rose thinking? She had always been a major presence at each of Lizzy's parties. She knew exactly what it was that caused her to forego their plans. Clara. Again! "Well, she wasn't about to change things because of that fox's manipulation," she thought.

"We've always allowed Lizzy to plan her own birth-day parties," Gwen said. "She has already given me names of eight little girls that will be invited over that day. They would have a horrible time at Madison Square Garden. That's a place for older adults anyway, not children and especially not for a birthday celebration."

"That's nonsense. The concert has been advertised specifically for kids. Clara told me how many schools have secured tickets for their students. That's one of the reasons it's an already sold out event. Kids are coming from around the world to hear your nieces," Rose said. "It would be an ideal birthday celebration for Lizzy. Her friends would melt with envy when they discover the twins are her cousins."

"Lizzy wouldn't enjoy anything like that. Besides, I hate changing her plans."

"It's not Lizzy's plans you're changing. It's your own. You don't want to go, just admit it. I know my niece. She would love something like this."

Rose knew Gwen wasn't used to the kind of attitude she was giving—challenging her back that way.

"Can't you see, Rose? She's doing it again," Gwen whispered. "Only Clara could cause you and me to fight with each other this way. Nothing could ever convince me she has changed. Not only do I not want to be around her, I don't think it's a good idea to expose Lizzy and Rainey to someone like that either. Besides, they are not even aware they have another aunt. The only one they know about is you and I would prefer keeping it that way. How could I explain to Lizzy that I have a sister she has never laid eyes on? She will ask too many questions. I don't want her to know there's someone we could not permit into our lives just yet. I will tell her about that when she is older and better able to understand it all."

"Gwen, what is it going to take for you to forgive Clara?" Rose asked, softly. "At this point, the unforgiveness you're harboring is not hurting her anymore, it's slowly destroying you. I have had this conversation with you so many times, but I do believe this will be the last. You are missing out on one of the greatest gifts God is trying to give you. If you choose to throw it away that will be something you will have to deal with."

Rose took in a deep breath, stumbling over the last few words. "I wish... I would... love all of my nieces to meet each other. What a perfect opportunity it would be for them to grow up together and learn to live and love as a family should. That would be the beginning of something wonderful, something special that could change their lives forever. God is shifting things around and I want you to be a part of it. Mother would have wanted that for you too, that's one thing I do know. However, it's up to you. Your kids are growing up and will miss out on a blessing that you chose for them not to receive. Although, I have a feeling they will rectify that all in due time. They will make it right for themselves one day."

"I'll talk to you later," Gwen mumbled.

Rose could tell she was crying.

Hanging up, Rose cleared her head and then dialed Clara.

"Are you sure you have enough room for all of us?" Clara asked. "Miriam has been kind enough to let two of my sister-in-laws and their families stay in one of their condominiums. The last time I counted, twenty of our family members are coming. At least one hundred people from our church are flying in as well."

A small pain pricked Rose's heart when she heard Clara talk about her family. It was the Brown family that she spoke of so fondly. They had completely embraced her as their own.

"I have plenty of room. We are going to have tons of fun," Rose said. She tried hard to cover up the fact she had been upset just minutes ago.

"The girls are excited about spending time with Aunt Miriam but they can't wait to see their Auntie Rose," Clara said. "She wants them to stay with her while we are in New York. She has planned shopping trips, tours and the whole nine yards. They want to stay with you," she whispered.

"Encourage the girls to spend some time with Miriam while they're here. They will always love Auntie Rose. I'll forever be their favorite aunt," she laughed.

"You are exactly right. I couldn't believe how well the girls knew Little Teddy and Buddy. They screamed when they found out they were cousins. "They are so cool. All the girls just love them," Clara said, in her tiny voice, imitating the twins. "They cannot wait to spend more time with each other."

"Are you ready for this?" Clara said the excitement evident. "Miriam, Ted and the boys visited our church today. Betty helped me cook a wonderful meal for everybody afterwards. Rose, it is truly unbelievable. Miriam is such a changed woman. I guess she was thinking the same thing about me," she said laughing.

"I'm happy for the both of you," Rose said. "We have quite a whirl-wind of a week-end ahead. We will have to factor in some relaxation time for you, mommy," she teased Clara. "Are you sure you'll be okay? You can't get around as fast as you used to."

"Are you serious? Just watch me."

Clara was in her seventh month and had no plans of slowing down. "Believe me, he lets me know when it's time to rest," Clara said.

"You said he," Rose exclaimed. "Oh my goodness, you said, he," she repeated.

"Yes, we're having a boy."

"Ahhh," Rose screamed.

Clara beamed. "No one else knows except Phillip, not even the girls. So, please keep it under wraps for now."

"I will but that's so super cool. Our family is growing and I can't wait until we're all together again."

"I can't wait either," Clara said.

While they didn't mention her name, they both understood, 'coming together' also included Gwen.

"The invitation I sent to Gwen and her family should be arriving any day now," Clara said.

***

As Gwen browsed through the mail, she spotted the decorative envelope almost immediately. She gently eased it open and unfolded the newspaper article that came along with it. "The brilliantly gifted Gordon-Brown twins will be featured along with Master Pianist, Nina Tendral and The New York Symphony Orchestra, conducted by Maestro Oliver Front at Madison Square Garden. At ten years old, they are two of the youngest concert pianists to ever grace the stage, having performed since the age of four. It is a sold out performance."

There was a picture of the beautiful, identical twin girls attached. "They look just like Clara," she thought. "I hope they don't act like her." She walked into Rick's office and slid the invitation across his desk.

"Wow, there are four tickets here. I wouldn't mind going," he said. He avoided making eye contact with her.

Gwen could feel the anger mounting. She tried hard to deescalate. "Do you really want to go? Even when you know how I feel about Clara?" she asked.

"I know how you feel, but don't you think it's time for you to settle your differences," he said, looking up at her. "Do you recall the night I told you about Jessica? I didn't have any idea how you would react to a newborn baby coming to live with us. Remember what you said to me after I shared the news? You made me promise we would always take care of family. Well, Gwen, I kept my end of the bargain."

"Clara hasn't ever acted much like family," she said.

"Neither did Jessica back then, but that didn't stop you from making me see things in a different light. Besides, you don't know how Clara would respond to you now. Many years have gone by. She could be a totally different person. Do you really believe she would send you four tickets if she hadn't changed somewhat?"

"I don't know. It's not the tickets. She may have…," Gwen stammered.

Rick walked over and reached out to her. "What's really bothering you, babe?"

The tears quickly formed. "I cannot forgive her for hurting my mother. I know Clara is the reason she died so quickly....so awfully... and I am afraid if I see her again, it will only bring back the memories I've tried desperately to bury. It took me years to get over the grief from her death. I don't think I would be able to handle that kind of pain again." She rested her head on his shoulder. "Anyway, how can a daughter, your own flesh and blood, do something like that to you?"

He knew the pain of losing her mother was at the root of the problem, but he also knew something else was troubling her. "As I recall, nothing was going to stop Ellen from looking for Clara. She did the same thing when Rose was missing. She was going out there to find her no matter what. Clara couldn't stop that."

"If she was a half-way decent person, she would have come to see her mother instead of making her travel across the country looking for her," Gwen cried. "That's not the way anyone with any kind of morals should behave. I'm sorry Rick. She was a horrible person and an awful daughter."

When she was that emotional, he understood it did absolutely no good to try and reason with her. He thought about suggesting that he take Lizzy to the concert, but knew she wouldn't go for that either. So, he did what he knew she needed most. He rocked her in his arms.

"Rose won't be coming to the birthday party for Lizzy either. She told me she was going to the twin's concert."

They both looked up at that moment as Lizzy charged through the door, plopping her book-bag down hard. "Kelly is going to the concert on my birthday. So is Bria and Trina. They can't come to my party."

"What concert?" Gwen asked.

"Some kids featured at Madison Square Garden. Teacher said it was something we should all go and see. That's what happens when you work hard at something, she kept telling us. It's just some 'ole dumb piano," she said, stomping off to her room.

"We can change the date of the party," Gwen yelled at her.

"That's not my birthday," she yelled back.

Rick looked at the tickets on the table and slid them towards her as he exited the room.

"Are you trying to tell me something?" she yelled at him. "I think I got the message," she mumbled to herself.

She picked up the phone.

"Of course I'll call her," Rose said, trying hard to suppress the delight. "They are going to have a wonderful time at the concert. How many little girls does she want to invite?"

"It's five of them that have been together since kindergarten. Plus, the two Woodrow's kids and Bailey's little girl. That makes eight, no, nine with Lizzy."

"Do you mean *the* Kelsey Woodrow and Cassie Bailey?" Rose asked.

"Yes. We had our kids on the sets with each other ever since they were babies."

"So we need nine tickets for the kids and two for you and Rick. What about Rainey?" Rose said.

"He can have my ticket."

Rose ignored the remark and continued. "Okay, I'll call Clara and let her know. Hey, I have another suggestion for the party. What if we let the girls meet each other after the concert, take pictures with the twins and then we all go to the dinner you've planned." She held her breath.

"We'll see," Gwen said. "I will talk with you later."

Rose made no comment. She absolutely did not want to push her luck.

Gwen knew in order to sell the idea to Lizzy she would have to toss in a few extra perks. "Personally meeting the twins after the concert may actually work," she thought.

"Lizzy, honey, I have something to ask you about your party," she said, sitting down next to her on the bed.

Lizzy turned onto her back, revealing the sad look now evident all over her face. Gwen knew most of it was theatrics.

"What if we rearrange some things on your birthday?" She told her about the concert, meeting the twins and dining at Pretty in Pink, one of the most coveted places for little girls to have their birthday parties.

The huge smile slowly found its way onto her face.

Gwen knew then it was a go.

"Okay, let mommy make a few phone calls and see how we are going to re-arrange all of this. Don't worry, it's going to work out," she said, kissing her on the forehead.

She called Rose to let her know the change in plans. Rose in turn quickly phoned Clara.

"Are you kidding me? She's actually coming," Clara screamed. "I need to tell the girls about Gwen. They will be excited to meet her again."

"Uhmm…before you do that, let's make sure she's coming," Rose said. "I spoke with Rick. He's definitely bringing the girls to the concert but mentioned something about meeting Gwen and Rainey later."

She hated to tell her that.

Clara didn't respond.

"I know you are disappointed," Rose said. "God will work things out. He always does. He is going to fix it and we won't have to do a thing. Just you wait and see."

"You really do have faith. Whoa, you have great faith," Clara whispered. "It was the wonderful gift our mother gave to you, Rose. When she believed in something, you couldn't make her change her mind no matter what."

That was the first time in a long time they had spoken about their mother.

Both of them hung on silently for a brief moment. Rose knew it was time to just let her talk.

"I didn't know mother was looking for me," Clara said, softly. "I was so sick physically, mentally, emotionally—in every possible way. In my heart, I wanted mother to come and take me home. I needed her," her voice shook as the tears fell. "I wanted to see my mother as much as she wanted to see me. Now, it's too late."

"I know. I know," Rose said, trying hard to settle her. "We have each other Clara. That's what mother fought so hard for."

"Yeah, you know how grateful I am about that, Rose. I couldn't imagine my life without you. I thank God every day for allowing me to have such an amazing sister… but I still need to talk to Gwen. I believe our reconciliation would accomplish something very important to me…something that would have made mother extremely happy. When I saw Gwen at the premiere, she looked so much like mother I almost found it difficult to sit there. I wanted to hug her and tell her how much I missed her, but she turned her back—she turned her back to me," she cried.

"It's okay. Clara it's okay," Rose said trying to console her. "The day will come when she won't ever do that again," she said.

"I love your faith," Clara whispered.

Chapter 27

Settling Times

The plane ride was an event all by itself. Trying to coordinate twenty people, including eight children through airport security was quite a challenge. Four hours later, the group headed for Madison Square Garden had all arrived on time, including their luggage. The twins were a bit of a celebrity in their own right. Their pictures were taken by local photographers when they de-planed and many promising a nice article about the concert the following morning.

"Auntie Rose," they yelled, running to her as they entered the baggage claim area.

"We've missed you so much," they both said.

"Not as much as I've missed you two," she said kissing them.

"Okay, listen up everybody," Rose said, over all the chatter. "The cars are lined up according to each family's destination. Once we get you all settled in, we have a scrumptious meal planned at my home."

"I'll be the judge of that," Betty said, coming around the corner.

"Oh my goodness! Betty! I had no idea you were coming. I'm so glad to see you," Rose said, hugging her.

"I came so you could show me New York," she said, in her rough voice. She reached for her hand and held on.

"I'll see you all at my house around six," Rose said. "However, you young lady, are coming home with me," she said, squeezing Betty's hand.

Later that evening the entire clan gathered at Rose's home. The food was delicious and plentiful and the conversation lively as the men gathered around the TV yelling for their favorite teams. It was the NFL playoffs. The kids played an intense game of Taboo and when Rose went in to check on them, she stopped at the den's door and smiled. Her only wish was that Lizzy had been there to enjoy it all.

Even though the day was a long one, it was still difficult trying to get everyone to leave. At two a.m. Rose finally climbed into bed.

Early the next morning, Rose and Betty prepared a breakfast that caused everyone to stir.

"Boy, that smells good," Clara said. She stretched and yawned as she leaned onto the kitchen island. "Can you believe Miriam has invited all the kids over after the concert for a sleep-over? That's a bunch of kids," she said, reaching for a slice of the turkey bacon.

The doorbell chimed. "I'll get it," Clara said.

"Marty! You've made it. I'm so glad you could come," she said, hugging her tightly. "Where are Jack and the boys?"

"I left them at the hotel, grabbed the keys to the rental, programmed the GPS and here I am. I wouldn't miss this for anything in the world," she said, heading straight for the kitchen.

Reaching for the homemade roll, she picked up the knife and proceeded to butter it. "Ouch, Ouch," Marty said, shaking her hand from the hot bread. "Well, look at you mommy. Aren't you the cutest pregnant person ever," she said, rubbing Clara's stomach. "How's the doc?" she asked, kissing Rose on the cheek. "Miss Betty, I pray God blesses me to keep my figure when I get your age. You are just too cute," she said, stuffing her mouth with the now much cooler roll.

"This week-end is going to be wild," Marty said, waving both hands in the air. Her exuberant personality always ramped up the atmosphere whenever she came around.

"Let's get the girls to rehearsal," Clara called back down to Marty as she climbed the stairs. "We don't know our way around this town and we'll need to leave in plenty of time to get back by one o'clock. The girls must have a good nap before the concert."

"Are you sure you don't need me to take you," Rose shouted out.

"No, we will be fine. Marty is a great driver and fantastic with directions," Clara said.

After they whisked the twins off to rehearsal, the house began to settle. Soon after they returned, however, and everyone napped, they were busy getting dressed for the concert.

"Here they are," Reverend Brown said, descending the stairs. He moved aside, proudly displaying each twin. Their long curls bounced as they spilled onto the cobalt blue gowns with the long satin bows cascading down their backs.

"You guys look amazing," everyone gushed.

"I'm so nervous, honey," Clara whispered.

"I know, but we can't let the girls see us this way. We've got to keep it together," Reverend Brown said, wiping his brow.

The ride to the venue was relatively quiet until they all noticed the marquee. "There's our name," the twins yelled.

Clara was glad when they drove around the building to the reserved parking area. The crowd and all the lights caused her butterflies to increase. She couldn't imagine how the girls must be feeling.

The excitement intensified as they were directed into the dressing room and given last minute instructions. Master Pianist, Nina Tendral gracefully entered the room. "My precious accompanists, two of the most gifted young ladies I've had the pleasure of working with. We will have a marvelous time out there. Please try and enjoy the performance." She kissed them both.

"It's a sold out crowd, Nina" Clara said. 'I can't tell you how much we appreciate you agreeing to let the girls perform with you. This has done marvelous things for their young careers. We will need to sit down and decide where we go from here." Clara knew her chattering had everything to do with the nervousness that simply wouldn't go away.

"Three minutes to curtain," someone yelled.

"Come here girls. Let's pray before you go on stage," Reverend Brown said. "I would like you to join us, Ms. Tendral."

"It is my delight, Reverend Brown."

"This is a special night and we need to thank God for what He's doing in our lives," he said, as they all held hands. "Father, we thank You for Your goodness and the abundance of grace You have showered upon us. We thank You for our family and friends and everybody You have brought together safely here to Madison Square Garden. Most of all, thank You for the gifts You've given our beautiful daughters and Ms. Tendral. Let them be used tonight so that some child, some young adult or even an older adult may understand just how wonderful and good You are. Let all that occurs tonight be for one purpose only, and that is, that You be glorified. Also, please calm everybody's nerves. This we ask in Jesus Name. Amen."

"Ladies, it's time for you to take your places," the attendant said, rushing in.

"Mommy will be on the front row. Now, don't worry, you are going to do so well," Clara said, as she kissed them, smoothing their hair and hugging them tightly. She kept looking back as Reverend Brown nudged her gently on.

"We're okay mommy," they said.

Clara and Reverend Brown slipped into their seats as they held on tightly to each other. The orchestra began with several Mozart selections. Once their performances were complete, Master Pianist, Nina Tendral waltzed onto the stage in an elegant ball gown and curtseyed, her head bowed as if it would touch the floor. Thunderous applause erupted. When she took her seat, she gracefully, almost effortlessly began to play. Gently floating across the keys, each hand alternating over the other, she massaged, hammered, and even tinkered the ivories over like only a skillful pianist could do. The audience was already enchanted, evident by only the alluring sounds of the concert-grand piano filling the room. On cue, the soothing sounds of the orchestra carefully blended in with the pianist, synchronizing magical musical harmony.

It was the beginning of a magnificent evening.

Clara could feel her heart racing as Nina finished her third selection and moved from behind the piano and floated center stage, the curtains slowly closing behind her. She positioned herself in front of the lone microphone and thanked everyone for coming. She began her introduction of the Gordon-Brown twins.

The curtains pushed back, revealing three beautiful pianos aligned in a row. Everyone knew this was partly the reason they had come tonight. The girls walked out, hand in hand, bowed and took their seats.

Clara took in small, short breaths. They looked so lovely with the soft spotlight shining down on them. Tears glistened in her eyes as they began playing.

Like magic, they started with quick movements, their hands running simultaneously along the keys. They took turns improvising, one with a slow free expressive style, while the other exploded into a burst of faster, quicker movements. It all combined and blended together to create a sweet sound of harmony. At the height of their ensemble, their hands had now become a blur, their eyes intensely focused on the keys they had learned to master—their heads bouncing each time they struck them. Reverend Brown whispered to Clara, with tears in his eyes, "Only God can do that."

It was the final selection that caused the greatest stir of the night. Master pianist Nina Kendral took the lead as she softly played the first stanza of Amazing Grace. The twins eased their way in, each taking turns playing their selected parts as the other two improvised along. Magically, all three somehow suddenly blended together the triad, and began playing, "When we've been there, ten thousand years, bright shining as the sun, we've no last days to sing God's praise than when we've first begun." A spirit like none other swept through the room. The orchestra right on cue joined the heavenly symphony, drawing the audience to new heights. As if the atmosphere couldn't get more glorious, suddenly the cymbals crashed in transitioning into a soulful-symphonic gospel version of, "Praise God… Praise God… Praise God…Praise God…" Instinctively, the audience joined in and sang as they rose to their feet. The emotions squeezed the hearts of everyone in the place. There wasn't a dry eye among the adults in the arena. For some, it was a life changing moment. No one would have ever believed a piano concert could end that way.

When the music's thunderous finale came crashing in, the clapping, bravos and yells became so deafening, the echoes bounced off the rafters inside. When the announcer with his deep baritone voice proudly intro-duced the twins as New York City's special guest artists, the clapping became so intense the girls squealed and hugged each other with delight. The dozen long-stemmed roses they cradled overpowered them. It was several ovations later that they finally exited the stage.

For the next few moments, it became next to impos-sible to get to the twins. The newspaper reporters, magazines and TV stations were all pressing to interview them.

"Clara, Clara," Rose tried yelling over the swarm. She wanted to let her know Gwen had shown up with her family. As she inched her way through the crowd, she finally reached her and whispered the news in her ear.

Clara quickly turned and spotted her sister from across the room. Their eyes met. Clara hesitated a few times, but then slowly, not so sure if she should, lifted her hand and waved.

Gwen ignored it and walked up the aisle.

***

Clara stretched back in the recliner on the shaded patio. It was a beautiful, clear day and she was finally able to take the long awaited break her expanding body longed for. "What a mind-blowing week-end this has been," she said, reaching for the tall glass of water. "You know this would have been impossible without you Rose," Clara said, giving her hand a quick squeeze.

"I wouldn't have missed a moment of it. Watching my nieces mesmerize a crowd with those tiny hands will forever be etched in my mind."

"Miriam's reception for the girls was way beyond anything I could have ever imagined," Clara said. The governor and the mayor both coming by was unbelievable. Can you believe how the place exploded when David Partovi walked into the room? The young man is still very humble despite having won the coveted Gold Medal Beethoven Award," she said.

Rose smiled, as the welcomed breeze blew lightly across them. All the reviews for the performance had been extremely positive, each article raving about the gifted twins. Franklin Allen from the New York Times repeatedly called them musical geniuses.

The wind kicked the aroma from the barbeque pit towards them, leading an enticing trail of savory spices their way.

"Hurry up with those steaks," Clara called out to the men gathered around the smoky grill. "We're starving," she said, pointing to her stomach.

"They're almost done," Reverend Brown yelled back.

The long picnic tables were filled with large dishes of potato, tossed and pasta salads, baked beans, fresh corn on the cob, baked potatoes and numerous casserole dishes. All the relatives, friends, and neighbors finally sat down for a huge old-fashioned, backyard barbeque.

"I was glad to actually meet Robin in person," Rose said, biting into the roasted corn. "Thanks for letting me tag along."

"I think being interviewed by her on Good Morning New York, has clearly been one of the highlights of the trip," Clara said.

Neither of them mentioned the Gwen incident. Rose could tell Clara was probably getting used to the fact that talking with her sister wasn't going to happen. She was just grateful the twins had a chance to meet Lizzy. She couldn't help but notice the curiosity all three had when the introductions were made.

The next morning, managing to get everyone to the airport was another coordinator's nightmare.

"Where are the twins?" Clara called out to Rose from the SUV. The last time I saw them, they were upstairs," Clara said. "I just can't climb those steps again to look for them."

"Stay put, I'll find them." Rose searched each room and finally located the girls in the middle of her bed, dressed in their pink and black matching jogging suits.

"Okay, you want to tell me what this is all about? Everybody is waiting for you two downstairs," she said.

"We're not moving until you promise we can spend the summer with you and Uncle William. Please," they pleaded. They both rubbed and hugged Jazzy as if they would never see him again. He snuggled trying hard to share his attention with them both as he stretched across their laps. "We promise we'll practice every day while we're here. We just love being in New York with you, Auntie Rose."

A huge smile lit up Rose's face. "I'll tell you what, we'll meet at Disney World and after that you can come home with me."

They tore down the steps with Jazzy close on their heels and charged outside. "Mom...Dad, we're spending the summer with Auntie Rose."

Clara looked up at Rose, hunched her shoulders, and threw up her hands.

"I figure they can stay with me right after the baby's born. Besides, you'll have your hands full with the little guy," she explained.

"You're the best," Clara said.

"Let's get going," Rose called out to everyone.

As they stood in line for security checks, they hugged and dried each other's tears. Rose watched until the last person cleared.

"Love you," she mouthed to Clara.

Chapter 28

Forgiving Times

Swinging out of the airport, Rose enjoyed the quiet, peaceful drive home. William had gone by the church and she wasn't on call at the hospital for the next three days. She intended to relax and treat herself to a long, therapeutic massage as soon as she could. She blasted the sounds of The Gospel Way and sang along as she drove home. As soon as she turned the corner, she immediately noticed the black Range Rover in her drive. It was Gwen's new truck.

The drive from their homes was an hour and half away now. "Before she traveled that far, she would have warned me she was coming, unless something was wrong," Rose thought.

She whirled the car into the garage. Rushing in, she found Gwen bending over in the refrigerator already munching on a piece of the sandwich she'd made.

"You want me to make you one? This steak is delicious," Gwen said, looking up.

"No thanks, I'm not hungry. What in the world are you doing here?" Rose asked, dropping her purse and keys on the counter. "Where are the kids? Is everything okay?" she asked, kissing Gwen on the cheek.

"I didn't bring them and nothing is wrong, so get that look off your face."

"I'm not used to you coming this far and not letting me know first. It freaked me out when I saw your car."

"I thought when you gave me the spare key and the code to the alarm, it was an open invitation to come whenever I wanted," Gwen said smiling.

"Just call and let me know so you won't scare the dickens out of me like this."

"Okay worrywart, I promise." They chatted as Gwen devoured the last of her sandwich.

"Rose, I do have something I need to talk with you about, but I wanted to do it in person," she finally said.

"Gwen, you are scaring me. Is everybody alright?"

"They are fine. Calm down," she said. "Rick knows I'm spending the night with you and that I'll see them all in the morning."

Rose took another deep breath. "Okay, what is it?"

Gwen shook her head not knowing where to begin. "It started after the twin's concert at Madison Square Garden...which by the way was completely amazing."

Rose smiled.

"William was ecstatic when he saw us walk in. While you were in the ladies room, he introduced Rick and me to all of Clara's new folks. They were extremely nice and I actually found myself enjoying being a part of it all. There's just one problem. I don't think Clara will ever allow me to be a part of the family. She will never forgive me for what I did to her. It was a horrible thing and if she finds out, she will walk right out of my life— again. I know rejection from her at this point would permanently destroy whatever relationship we could ever think of having. So, when I saw her that night, I felt it was best to walk away."

"What did you do, Gwen?" Rose asked. She almost didn't want to know.

She started out slowly, "Remember the day I left you in the hotel—the day after mother died. I went back to the hospital to take care of her paperwork. When I did, I also went upstairs to thank the nurse that took care of her. It was weird. When I got there, I ran into one of Clara's old roommates. A lady named Marty."

"You met Marty?" Rose asked. "She and her family were at the concert too."

"Yes, and when I saw her, she told me Clara was in ICU on the same floor. Needless to say, I was in shock. I didn't want to believe she was there until I walked into the room and saw her for myself. It was actually Clara lying there! She was very sick and…she…was in the room… right next to mother."

Rose slumped down in her seat. "No, Gwen!"

"Yes, and it gets worse. As Clara slept, I noticed how thin and helpless she looked. I didn't wake her to tell her mother had just passed away—not because she was too sick to hear the news. It was because I didn't want her to know. In fact, I walked away hoping she would die."

Rose gasped, placing her hand over her mouth. She stared hard at someone she thought she knew so well. "Who had Gwen become?" she thought. "How could you do something like that?" she asked, sinking further into her seat.

"When you told me how Clara reacted after she found out mother died, I knew I couldn't tell you or her, what I had done. It was after the concert and the long ride home that I had time to rethink things. I realized she may have been able to come to the funeral if I had told her."

"If we delayed the funeral a few more days until she got better, perhaps she would have been able to tell mother good-bye," Rose said, as the tears began to fall.

"I'm sorry, Rose. I shouldn't have done that. She didn't deserve to be treated that way. She doesn't have to know what I did, does she?"

Rose pressed past her emotions and spoke from her heart. "Clara has been a wonderful sister to William and me," she said, drying her eyes. "One day she'll be a wonderful aunt to my children. We have a very close relationship and I don't know if I can keep something like that from her forever. I wouldn't do that to you either."

"Can you forgive me for what I've done, Rose?"

"Of course I can. In fact, I've already done that. It's Clara I'm worried about."

"You're not going to tell her any time soon are you?" Gwen asked.

"No, I'm not. I will leave that up to you."

***

Three months had passed since the twin's concert. Clara was quite uncomfortable now—her due date was tomorrow. With a sudden burst of energy, she went outside to work on her garden project. She turned when she heard the car's tires crunch the gravel drive. Holding her back, she watched the tall, thin lady climb out of the Town car.

She would recognize that face anywhere. Gwen looked exactly like their mother.

As she walked towards her, Clara removed her garden gloves, dropping them to the ground...her heart racing.

Both sisters stood quietly facing each other.

Emotions, fueled by thoughts of uncertainty took them both by storm.

Clara wanted to grab Gwen and never let her go, but was afraid to. She wanted to burst into tears, but fought hard to keep them at bay, afraid they would frighten her away. She wanted to run inside the house from it all, yet she dared not. Had Gwen, the middle child she'd grown up with, come to confront her after all these years? Nothing about her face said she wanted to. Still, she didn't know what to do or say.

So, she stood there.

Clara had all but given up reconciling with her sister. No matter how much she wanted to, the hurt seemed to prove too much for Gwen to overcome. Even at that, she prayed each night for God to bring them back together. She wanted one last chance to tell her how sorry she was. She vowed if she was ever given that opportunity, she would pour out all that was in her heart—that she did love her very much and needed her desperately in her life. It wouldn't be hard to tell Gwen, the one she fought so hard with that. In fact, her heart was screaming it right now. Everything she had prayed for was standing before her and yet, she could not move.

"It's been a long time," Clara finally whispered.

"It has been a very long time," Gwen said.

In a moment's time their world's changed. Gwen reached out her arms and Clara fell into them.

They both wept—their tears proving to be the only words necessary.

Gwen held on tightly almost afraid to let her go. Was she dreaming or was she holding, comforting her adversary from years past.

"I'm sorry about the intrusion," Gwen, said, straining from all the emotion rumbling inside. "Rose told me you were home these days."

Clara looked up at her sister. "I've waited a long time for this moment. I had given up," she said.

"I know and I'm sorry for any part I played in that," Gwen whispered.

"Can we start all over?" Clara asked.

"I would be truly grateful if we did," Gwen said.

Grimacing, Clara reached around and rubbed her back. She had been having pain in that area ever since early this morning.

"Are you okay?" Gwen asked, reaching for her hand.

"I'm fine. I suppose it's the excitement of seeing you that has Little Alan all worked up."

"Rose told me you were waiting on your new arrival any day now," Gwen said.

"I spoke with her yesterday. Did she know you were coming?" Clara asked.

"Gwen nodded. We had a very long talk—the kind that kept us up all night. It helped open my eyes to a lot of things, Clara. William and Rose prayed for me and you know what… it actually felt good. I believe it's the reason I am here today," she chuckled.

Clara smiled. "Well, how are Rick and the kids?"

"They are all fine. In fact, Lizzy is at Disney World with your twins right now."

"Are you kidding me! Rose has all three girls with her!"

"Yes, she does and I hear Disney World will probably never be the same."

They both laughed, still somewhat unsure of what to say or do.

"You have a beautiful home," Gwen said.

"Hey, why don't we go inside? You can take her bags inside, please," Clara said to the driver.

"No, Clara, I can't intrude like this on such short notice. The paparazzi and all that comes with it is too much to ask."

"Nonsense. I wouldn't have it any other way. You're staying here with me. Please, I haven't laid eyes on you in a very long time. We have too much to catch up on."

Clara faced her sister determined not to miss the opportunity God had just given her. "For years we've had this crazy tension between us. We never really acted like sisters and for that I am truly sorry. I said some hurtful things Gwen, and if I could, I would take it all back." She looked deep into her eyes. "I now understand I was dealing with some serious hurt and anger issues. I just wish I had gotten it together before mother passed away. She deserved that." She took in two deep breaths and rubbed the pain in her back.

They slowly walked the path to her home.

Once inside Gwen knew it was time to tell Clara what she had done. It was what drove her there today. Yet, the worry tore through her mind as she hoped it wouldn't destroy what had already begun to mend.

"There's something I need to talk to you about, Clara," Gwen said.

The sudden change in Gwen's demeanor caused her pause.

"We said and did some pretty hateful things to each other and for that I'm truly sorry as well," Gwen said. "Despite all of that, there's one thing I did, that may be…." She pushed out the next words. "Unforgivable. I really regret having done what I did to you."

Clara sat as the bulging contraction squeezed down hard upon her.

Gwen pressed on. "When I came to your city, I discovered that you were in the hospital quite ill. Mother was also very sick and in fact she was in the same hospital where you were. When I came to see mother, your room, she paused, "Was right next door to hers in the ICU."

A mixture of shock, sadness, and disbelief formed around Clara's eyes. The grief she had finally pushed aside came marching its way back in.

"I saw you lying in room five, but I didn't want you to know mother had died, Clara. So, I left you there. I didn't even tell Rose I had found you." She looked into her teary eyes. "You deserved to have been there to say your goodbyes…to put closure to the end of our mother's life, but I denied you that opportunity."

Gwen hung her head and cried. "How could you ever forgive me for what I did? I don't even know how to forgive myself. That was the cruelest thing anyone could have ever done to their own sister. There are rules to fighting and this goes way beyond them. I know forgiveness can be a difficult thing. If you can't find it in your heart to do that, I will understand," she cried.

They both sat silently as Clara turned her head away. She rubbed her hand against her back and pulled in quick short spurts of air.

"Please say something," Gwen finally said.

"I wanted to see my mother so badly," Clara finally blurted out. "I had so much to tell her, but it was too late. Don't let that happen to us." Clara pushed through the tears. "Let me tell you a story," she said, adjusting to a more comfortable position. "My husband's first wife was driving home after she picked up their daughter from day care. On the way, a man who had too much to drink, crossed the line and hit them head-on. His wife was killed instantly and three days later his daughter passed away. The driver was sent to prison because of what he did.

Phillip ministers in that jail frequently and ran into the same man that killed his family. He prayed for him and today that man is saved. Each Christmas we receive a card with a thank you note from the man and his wife. Phillip was able to help restore a man responsible for the death of his wife and child back to his family as a sober, loving husband and father. The only reason he could do any of that is because...he was able to forgive. The Bible has taught me a great deal about that subject. I realize how much I have been forgiven. The way I used to act towards you and mother. The way I treated Rose... the way I looked down on people... God forgave me. So, I have learned to forgive others and I can't tell you the peace and freedom I now have. While I am hurt by what you did, I still fully understand why you did it."

She wiped Gwen's tears away. "It's okay," she said, hugging her. "You are my sister and I will never let anything else ever separate us again. Ever."

Gwen looked lovingly at her. "Wow, all that Rose said was true. There is definitely something to what she and William have been trying to tell me. I believe it's time I start listening," she said.

"I believe it's time too," Clara said.

"Yes, they have my undivided attention now," Gwen said.

"No-o-o-o, the baby. It's time. My water just broke and I am in some serious pain."

"Oh my goodness," Gwen yelled for her driver. "Quick, grab her bag," she said, handing it to him.

***

Two hours later, baby Alan Christian Brown was born.

***

Two years later a family photo was taken.

While the twins and Lizzy were now inseparable, Clara, Gwen, and Rose also stood side by side, smiling widely as each of them held their own sons.

This time, the tears in their eyes.... were tears of joy.

About the Author

A native Memphian, author Rhonda Washington Nelson is a graduate of the University of Tennessee at Knoxville, where she obtained a Bachelor's Degree in Nursing. She continued her education at the University of Memphis and received a Master's Degree in Public Administration.

Professionally, Rhonda has been a Joint Commission Surveyor and Chief Nursing Officer of several hospitals. She is an active member of Temple of Deliverance Church of God in Christ. In the community Rhonda has served in many capacities and on various boards including, Girls Incorporated of Memphis, Memphis City Beautiful Commissioner and the Advisory Board for Nurse Executives. She is a graduating member of Leadership Memphis and a member of the Alpha Kappa Alpha Sorority.

Being called to do the work of the ministry, she is a licensed Evangelist and has made several mission trips to Nigeria, Africa.

Despite her numerous accomplishments, her primary goal and focus in life is based on the scripture given in Matthew 6:33.... "but seek ye first the kingdom of God and His righteousness, and all these things shall be added unto you."